A CONSPIRACY OF KINGS
THE SEQUEL TO THE LADY OF MERCIA'S DAUGHTER

M J PORTER

MJ PUBLISHING

CONTENTS

❀ Created with Vellum

This one is for my breakfast buddy, CS.
Thank you for your unending and continuous support.

BRITAIN IN THE 10ᵀᴴ CENTURY

N
W   E
S

ORKNEYS

CAIT

SCOTTISH
WESTERN
ISLANDS

FORTRIU

*Atlantic
Ocean*

KINGDOM
OF THE
SCOTS

DAL
RIATA

ATHOLL

ST ANDREWS

*North
Sea*

KINGDOM OF
STRATHCLYDE

BAMBURGH

Tyne CHESTER
LE STREET

EAMONT

KINGDOM OF
YORK

YORK

*Irish
Sea*

Ribble

DUBLIN

IRELAND

Mersey

Dee

GWYNEDD

POWYS

Severn

Trent

TAMWORTH

Welland

EAST
ANGLIA

OFFA'S
DYKE

HEREFORD

Wye

DEHEUBARTH

GWENT

MERCIA

WESSEX

Thames

KING'S
WORTHY

KINGSTON
UPON THAMES

WINCHESTER

KENT

EXETER

Tamar

English Channel

0   50   100   MILES

PART I

CHAPTER 1

TAMWORTH, THE KINGDOM OF MERCIA, 918

W e feast that night. There are smiles and tears on everyone's faces as Tamworth's great hall is swept clear of the men and women from Wessex. My armed guard ensures no one hurts them as the Mercians pull tables and benches to fill the vast space left behind. My servants, taken only somewhat by surprise as they were expecting a feast one way or another after the witan, rush to ensure everyone has a drink, if not food.

Cousin Ecgwynn hurries to me as I watch the activity, questions on her lips and I throw my arms around her, unheeding her sumptuous gown while I wear the clothes of a warrior. Usually, she would protest. But not today.

'Enough of that,' Cousin Ecgwynn complains, batting my embrace away, and not delicately. She holds my arms away from her, glaring at me.

I can see the flicker of rage in her blue eyes and the tightness of her stance.

'You let me believe you were dead! I've been mourning for you, as I would a sister, and coming so soon after the death of Lady Æthelflæd….' Her normally serene face floods with tears as her words trail off. I thrust my arms around her again, holding her tighter, hoping to make her understand, using my strength gained on the training field to overpower hers. I absorb her scent, the familiarity of home, the reminder of all that my uncle and Archbishop Plegmund tried to take from me.

'I'm sorry, dear Ecgwynn. It was.' I pause, unsure what to say, speaking into her ear as I continue to hold her tight. 'Well, in all honesty, it was all we could think of to ensure that Uncle Edward's treachery was exposed.'

I don't call King Edward of Wessex her father. That would be too cruel. I think that, like me, Lady Ecgwynn could happily forget that a man was even involved in her conception and birth. Certainly, he's done little enough for her since he became the king of Wessex when she was no more than a child and banished her to Mercia alongside Cousin Athelstan.

But Cousin Ecgwynn's not finished yet. Once more, she pulls her way clear of my embrace, determined to argue with me.

'But my brother knew and still didn't tell me. That's too cruel,' her angry voice is gaining force. I know there's nothing to do but try and explain. I could make excuses all night long, but she's almost my sister, and she deserves the truth.

'He knew. But only because he came to me and saw that I still lived after the attack in the north. Admittedly, cousin Athelstan could have told you that I wasn't dead, but then, how would you have greeted King Edward when he came to Mercia to stake his claim for it? He couldn't know that I yet lived.'

'I'm not a woman to have her head turned by the arrival of a man whose only call on her affection is to claim to be her father. I wouldn't have put your scheme in peril!' Her voice is shrill with outrage, all tears forgotten, as she chastises me, her words coming almost too fast to decipher.

To the side, cousin Athelstan hovers, and I know why. He's not scared of facing any man on the battlefield, but his sister? Well, he'd sooner not see her angry, and certainly, he's content for me to be the one to soothe her.

I realise then that we erred when we made our plans.

'No, I know you're not. Apologies, cousin Ecgwynn. It wasn't done because of a lack of trust. It was just better if as few as possible knew the truth.' I can see that being so brutally honest at least pleases her, even if her forehead remains lined with anger and her lips purse tightly.

I hold my arms out once more. This time she steps into them willingly, a faint wrinkle on her nose because I smell of horse and sweat. I feel her shoulders sag, and her body trembles as though she's going to cry. But she steps away from my embrace mere moments later, a watery smile on her face.

'If only everyone I ever loved who died could come back to life, as you have. It would make my heart ache less.' I nod. Abruptly, my thoughts focus on my mother, and despite my warrior's prowess, my grief is fresh. I'd gladly step into my mother's arms and cry away all my sorrows and disappointments at my uncle's actions.

'What would your mother think?' Lady Ecgwynn asks, her thoughts following mine as she loops her arm through mine to walk amongst the people toasting my good health and the future of Mercia. Their voices range from soft to the roar of a battle cry. I chuckle at the exuberance, aware that cousin Athelstan stays close. He and cousin Ecgwynn will need to make peace with each other at some point. But not yet.

'I hardly know what my mother would think or do. She and Edward were never close; at least, I don't think they were. But, I believe she understood his ambitions well, all the same.'

'Your mother was an excellent judge of character,' cousin Ecgwynn confirms. 'Although she did trust Archbishop Plegmund, the poisonous snake.'

My voice ripples with laughter as I picture Plegmund's face too easily as the head of a snake.

'I hope the archbishop has only just changed his allegiance to King Edward. I wouldn't like to think that he's been slowly undermining my mother throughout her years of rule. 'But,' I stop, my thoughts suddenly cloudy, 'I suppose it is possible. He is, after all, the Archbishop of Canterbury.'

'Yes, but Kent has only just come into King Edward's possession through his third marriage to Lady Eadgifu. Let us hope that's the reason for Archbishop Plegmund's betrayal.' I nod but resolve to consider the matter at a later date. For now, I wish to celebrate and not worry that my court is actually filled with men and women who mean me harm. I've had enough of that. The thought of what my mother would have said to my uncle brings a smirk to my face.

My mother would not have spoken to her brother after his actions. She'd have refused to acknowledge his relationship to her or even his position as the king of Wessex.

I hope uncle Edward knows that.

Not that I have time to dwell on such thoughts. Men and women call to me, raising their tankards to toast my safe return. I have no choice but to join in. And then there's dancing, and more raucous dancing, the beating drums seeming to thrum in time with my heartbeat. The floor grows sticky with spilt ale and wine, sweat and probably other substances that I don't wish to think about.

The hunting hounds, keen to join in at the beginning of the feast, slink to the side of the hearth, then to the dais, desperate to avoid being stepped on. When the food's ready, most people are too drunk to appreciate the care and skill that's gone into preparing it. The hounds gorge on all the meat that's carelessly dropped on the floor.

I laugh, as I haven't since my mother died. Or perhaps, I've never laughed quite as much before.

I'm passed from one partner to another, all of them blurring into the same haze of smiling lips, sweaty palms and breathlessness. In the morning, I know I'll struggle to remember who I danced with, but it doesn't matter. I won't be the only person in such a state.

Men and women sleep where they fall and then wake and continue as though nothing has happened. My female warriors win plaudits from all who are alert enough to understand their essential role in my survival. They stand guard around me, taking it in turns to protect the Lady of Mercia, a constant menace amongst so much joviality. It's a reminder that we have tonight to smile and laugh but that tomorrow Mercia might well be threatened once more.

Tamworth feels like home that night, and in the half-grey light of early morning, when I'm busy restocking the flailing fire, or at least, that's what I'm attempting to do, Ealdorman Æthelfrith's son seeks me out. Lord Athelstan looks as though he's drunk little, and the smile on his face as he lifts his drinking horn to toast the future is strained. He notices my scrutiny.

'I've torn my leg wound,' he whispers, 'don't tell my father. Just about doing everything hurts, and drinking seems to make it worse, not better.'

'You should have the healer look at it,' I urge him, pleased when my words aren't slurred. He shrugs.

'The bastard is too pissed to stand, let alone sew me back together.' With a tilt of his head, Lord Athelstan indicates where my healer is slumped over a table. His head rests on his arms. He snores as though the world depends on it. A puddle of drool has formed on the table.

I laugh a little. I've never seen the old man in such a state. I'm not the only one to have let down their guard.

'I could look at it for you,' I offer, but he chuckles softly.

'I think I might need slightly steadier hands.' So speaking, he stands and takes the smaller logs from my hands. I've been trying to wedge them onto the hearth, but even I know I'm doing a poor job of it. The fire is in danger of going out altogether.

'Well, I did drink quite a bit earlier, much earlier. It might even have been yesterday,' I add hastily. Lord Athelstan smirks at my words before hissing in pain as he overreaches himself placing a log.

'Here, I could at least bandage it for you,' I suggest. His smile is more forced this time.

'I think I could allow you to do that for me,' he grunts. I realise he's in a great deal of pain. As he slumps beside me, I reclaim the wood from his hands. The fire is still far from blazing, but I'm unsure what to do.

Instead, I catch the eye of one of the servants in my hall. She's been watching me try to rebuild the fire with almost as much trepidation as Athelstan.

I explain what I need, indicating that the fire is all hers to tend.

She dips a deep courtesy. I ignore the soft sigh of relief that escapes from her mouth. Perhaps I need to accept that I'm not good at everything.

While the girl bustles about, efficient and clearly very sober, I lean back against the side of the hearth. I seek some warmth from it while the servant is off fulfilling the other tasks I've given her. Last night I was advised to change out of my warrior's clothes and don a dress. Having worn nothing but my warrior's clothes for the previous month, I'm cold in my skirts and wish I had something clean to wear. I shiver a little, and Lord Athelstan notices.

He shambles to his feet, his injured leg held straight out in front of him, and reaches for small pieces of kindling before sliding back to his seat.

'You need to start small,' he advises me, feeding the strips of tree bark and discarded shavings from whatever woodwork has been done to the almost extinct fire. 'Only when it catches do you add some of the larger logs.' I knew this, I did, really, but in my haste to rebuild the fire, I confess I started with the more massive logs and forgot about the smaller ones.

I watch his hands as he works. He knows what he's doing, and that surprises me. He's a noble lord's son, just as I'm a noble lord's daughter. Why would he know how to rebuild a fire quite so well? But then, the servant brings me some clean cloth and a bowl of warm water, and I turn to administer to his injury. I imagine that we all have skills that don't quite fit with our positions in life. Perhaps it's part of a warrior's training that I've overlooked.

Even in the dull light, I can see the gleam of fresh blood on his clothing. As the fire springs to life, I wonder how we'll manage the awkwardness of me tending his wound. Luckily, my servant seems to have thought of the problem. She quickly takes control, handing him a larger piece of linen so that he can slip his leg coverings down, with a loud groan of pain. He reseats himself in a way that preserves both of our sensibilities.

I can clearly see where his wound had been healing against the paleness of his skin. For some reason, only half of it has adequately sealed itself, and from the end of the original injury, fresh hot blood slips, gleaming dully red in the muted light.

'Oh. This doesn't look too good,' I mutter. Lord Athelstan winces as I place the warm water over the cut, cleaning it carefully. The skin is puckered and sore. I half wish he was the one who'd drunk too much last night. It might make this easier for him to endure.

'I'll bandage it for you, but you'll need it sewed back together.'

My servant watches my movements, having satisfied herself about the state of the hearth fire. She grimaces as I talk.

'I can do it, my lady,' she offers, rushing around us both. Although I consider arguing with her, I think it would be better to have the wound correctly tended. I offer Lord Athelstan a smile of regret and relinquish my place to her.

She works quickly and cleanly. I wonder what she did before coming into my service. I resolve to speak to Eoforhild about her. She'd be worth training and having as a member of our group of warriors with such skills. Certainly, the muscles that bunch on her arms show that she's a woman of strength.

While the servant works, I try to distract Lord Athelstan by discussing anything that comes to mind. The first subject I think of is one that's always made me smile and which I can foresee causing no end of problems in the future.

'Isn't it confusing that you share my cousin's name?'

Lord Athelstan flinches and then tries to smile as the servant administers to him.

'Sometimes, yes. But neither of us can help the names our parents decided upon. I would change mine, but that, I fear, would cause even more confusion.'

I mull over his words, considering whether he's right or wrong. My father was Lord Æthelred of Mercia, before him, there was a King Æthelred. I'm aware that parents choose the names of their children to reflect both family names and to honour kings and queens. I've never realised just how difficult that makes life. I don't know why my mother decided upon my name. I suppose I should have asked before she died. I appreciate that it's unusual.

As Lord Athelstan grunts in pain, I try to think of something else
to talk about. What I eventually settle on is mostly a repeat of the
comments that my men and women have said to me throughout the
long night. Some of the discussions have been downright outrageous,
others filled with admiration for what I've accomplished, but it's one
phrase that's stuck in my mind, and which I share with him now.

'I've been asked at least ten times if I've made a marriage alliance
with Lord Rǫgnvaldr. To begin with, I thought it was a shocking
thought. Why would I need to marry the man to gain his support? But
as the night's worn on, I've realised that even here, in a kingdom that's
been ruled by a woman for seven years, men would feel better if they
took their commands from a man.'

I can't deny that there's an element of hurt in those words. I've
fought and bled for Mercia, and still, even though they don't want my
uncle to rule them, it seems they'd prefer a man to govern them.

'Would you consider marrying him?' Lord Athelstan asks with a
hiss. I chuckle. I can't help it, and instantly I regret it because his face
flickers with hurt at my reaction.

'Apologies, Lord Athelstan. I couldn't marry Lord Rǫgnvaldr. He's
my ally, nothing more. He's a good warrior. He fought for me when I
needed it. But he waged war for himself as well. He needed me to help
him gain York. I needed him to keep Mercia. He'll rule there, and I'll
rule here, alone and without the aid or support of my uncle.
Genuinely, I couldn't imagine being married to …. Well, to a Viking
raider.'

I think I might have taken the edge from my initial reaction, but
Lord Athelstan still looks thoughtful. For a wild moment, I wonder if
he thinks of me as I do of him, but I dismiss the idea. He's merely the
son of my ally, nothing more.

'There are some here who think it would be a good match,' he
prods. I shake my head vehemently.

'They think it a good idea now, but if I were to marry Lord Rǫgnvaldr, grandson of Ivarr Ragnarsson, I'd open myself up to all sorts of
recriminations. Many would view my marriage to a Viking raider
with distaste. The Five Boroughs would accept it, Nottingham and

Derby, especially. But to the west, and perhaps even to the northwest, any thought of union with a Viking raider would lose me allies, not gain them.'

'Then you won't consider marriage at all?' Lord Athelstan delves, a gasp of agony making his word carry a heavy sharpness. The servant girl douses his wound with more hot water to ensure it's thoroughly clean.

'I would consider marriage,' I chortle, amazed to be having this conversation with him. 'But not to a Viking raider, and not to a man from Wessex either.'

'You limit yourself,' Lord Athelstan simpers, sweat beading his face as the servant cleans his cut.

'It's difficult not to be limited when Mercia has so many enemies.' Those words force me to consider the truth of what I've said.

I have Mercia back, firmly under my control. I have a new ally to the north, even if he's yet to make significant inroads into ruling York. But I have many enemies, my uncle and cousin foremost amongst them all. I would add the two archbishops to the list as well, Archbishop Plegmund because I publicly humiliated him, and Archbishop Lodeward because he wasn't victorious against me and must now be ruled by Lord Rognvaldr. I would be idiotic to think retribution isn't on their minds.'

'And they're the enemies that I know I have. I'm sure there must be many others who would sooner I hadn't lived through the attack.'

Lord Athelstan follows my train of thought.

'King Edward won't take kindly to being demeaned like that.'

'I don't take kindly to having people think I'm dead when I yet live. Or of those people plotting my death.'

'That's fair enough,' he retorts. 'But King Edward won't change his intentions just because he's lost on this occasion.'

'I don't expect him to,' I sigh heavily. I've finally warmed up in the heat from the resurgent fire, but a headache is starting to pound. I need to sleep.

'I know he'll try whatever he can to undermine me. Only this time, he'll have to do something that doesn't involve killing me.'

I stand abruptly, wobbling unsteadily on my feet.

'Apologies, Lord Athelstan, I must sleep and then I'll be able to think more clearly.'

His face fills with understanding as he to hobbles to his feet, his wound now cleaned, stitched and bandaged, the servant hastily tidying away her supplies.

'We'll speak again soon,' Lord Athelstan promises as he bows to me. As I walk away to my bed or rather sway, I think I might enjoy that.

CHAPTER 2

No matter the traumas I've experienced since becoming the Lady of Mercia, the battles and betrayals, the actual role of governing Mercia hasn't changed at all. Within just one day of my re-acclimation as Lady of Mercia, I'm embroiled in affairs of state. I'm dealing with matters of taxation, the maintenance of the burhs, and ordering more warriors sent to guard the borders with Wessex. Not to mention handling questions about coinage and which member of the Five Boroughs I should approach next to reintegrate into Mercia. Derby and Nottingham are reconciled to Mercia, but Lincoln yet stands aloof.

I know my uncle has returned to Wessex, escorted by a large contingent of my household warriors. Already there are murmurings of discontent. The tariffs with Wessex are immediately raised almost as soon as my uncle crosses the River Thames. Where once we traded freely with Wessex, there are suddenly restrictions. They anger the traders but equally convince them that they're better off being ruled by the Lady of Mercia than the King of Wessex. They immediately turn their attentions elsewhere, to a busy York, resurgent under Lord Rǫgnvaldr. Traders are always keen to find somewhere new to ply their business.

Within two weeks of my return, I'm forced to preside over a problematic witan held in Tamworth's great hall.

I would have thought that cousin Athelstan would have been content now that his father's been dealt such a blow. However, he seems even more distressed than usual. His temper is already frayed as he and Ealdorman Æthelfrith openly clash about future steps.

'We should attack Wessex,' is cousin Athelstan's outrageous suggestion. Even I find my mouth dropping open with shock at such an audacious move, but Ealdorman Æthelfrith is far from struck dumb.

'That's a ridiculous suggestion,' he roars. Now I'm surprised by the vitriol of the ealdorman's reply as much as by cousin Athelstan's initial suggestion.

'Wessex is weak. King Edward is weak. Mercia can reclaim its position as the most prominent of the kingdoms.'

'King Edward is only weak in Mercia,' Ealdorman Æthelfrith tries to reason, fighting for some calmness in his response. I can see he breathes too heavily. I'm unsure why this suggestion upsets him as much as it does.

'In Wessex, everyone would lay down their life for King Edward, after all, he is his father's son.'

'No one in Wessex knows how to fight,' cousin Athelstan counters, he's also struggling for calmness.

'Don't be a fool, Ætheling Athelstan. Don't see what you hope to see. I know you want your father to fail in his power grab, but he has already. Wessex is strong, and he's strong. If Mercia were to invade Wessex, it would lose. The warriors of Wessex will fight to protect her.'

I find it offensive to hear the older man speak as he does, but he has far more experience than any of us. I try and temper my initial fury.

'We should build defences on the banks of the River Thames instead, think about reclaiming London for Mercia.' Ealdorman Æthelfrith's suggestion is less incendiary than cousin Athelstan's and perhaps much easier to accomplish because of that.

I consider both suggestions carefully. Absentmindedly, I twirl the signet ring I wear, the ring of the Mercian ruler. It's a constant reminder of my responsibilities and my mother, who first had it made from silver. It's a weighty piece with the two-headed eagle emblem depicted as an engraving.

They're both right in their ways. Mercia needs to devise a plan that will capitalise on her current gains. I've already received messengers from the Welsh kingdoms. Also, from Constantin of the Scots and the independent kingdom of Bamburgh, who want to ally with Mercia now that we've shown Wessex isn't the strongest kingdom within my grandfather's dream of 'England'.

I admire cousin Athelstan's plan. I'd very much enjoy ensuring that Mercia grows as powerful as she can be, returning her to the status she enjoyed under the kings Penda and Offa. But neither do I wish to stretch myself too far.

I've still only held Mercia for a handful of months. I want to ensure I firmly hold what I have before making any irreversible decisions.

'Both ideas hold merit,' I mollify, and two pairs of angry eyes glance my way. I meet their gazes firmly. They must realise that I rule here, not them and that the decision is mine.

'I want to ensure that Mercia makes a grand statement going forward. Mercia is finally back in control of its destiny. We must ensure her strong borders. We must be sure of her allies. We should send emissaries to the Welsh kingdoms, to Lord Rǫgnvaldr, and to the Northern lords, Constantin and Ealdred of Bamburgh. See what they have to offer Mercia. Then I'll decide what the future holds.' I speak firmly, asserting my right to rule and make such decisions.

This seems to satisfy both of them. I turn to find my cousin watching me. Cousin Ecgwynn is wrapped tightly against the cold. She has a unique insight that I value. Now she smiles at me and begins to speak in no more than a murmur.

'I hear worrying rumours of Lady Ælfwynn's intentions. I know them to be false, but I've heard them from more than one source, and that makes me think that Mercia's enemies have no intention whatsoever of biding their time.'

Her words jolted me from the careful consideration of the future to the here and now.

'What do you hear?' I demand. She flinches at my anger.

'I hear that you're married to Lord Rǫgnvaldr. That you carry his child. That you'll unite Mercia with York and allow him to rule in your joint name.'

I gasp in shock to hear those words from Lady Ecgwynn. I'd thought the marriage rumours strange when I'd spoken of them with Lord Athelstan. I'd not expected them to gain much traction.

'Whom do you hear this from?' I demand. She winces at the coldness of my tone, which is icier than the temperature of the hall.

'I hear it from all who would speak to me. From traders, from reeves, from men and women in the fields, but more than anything, I hear it from Wessex. My father has changed tactics. No longer will he allow Lord Rǫgnvaldr to kill you, but rather, he'll lose you your power by having him marry you.'

'But there's no marriage. Everyone who fought with me knows that. There was no time to even talk about marriage, let alone consummate one.' I laugh hysterically as I conclude my sentence. What must these people think of me?

Lady Ecgwynn's eyes are pained as she continues to speak.

'There are many too keen to believe the lies, my lady.' For a brief moment, I wonder if she's one of them, but then I dismiss the idea. Lady Ecgwynn and I are closer than sisters. She wouldn't take joy in anything that harmed me. She has no love for her father and no desire to rule. She's always been content to be my ally and, more importantly, my friend.

'And there are some who would pay others to lie.' Her tone's filled with a warning, telling me I shouldn't ask the next question, but we all know I'm going to.

'Who is being paid to lie?' I growl, my voice has dropped so low that it barely registers above the snap of the fire at our back.

'If I knew that, my lady, I'd share the information with you. All I know is that there's supposed to be at least one witness.' She casts her eyes down, and I glance at her hands, which she rubs together with worry. They look pale and weak; the fingernails gnawed almost to the quick. This stressful situation is not good for my cousin. Not at all.

'Will people believe the lie?' I ask, hungrily looking around at the rest of my gathered allies. I want them to say no.

Ealdorman Æthelfrith meets my gaze; his eyes are filled with remorse.

'The people of Western Mercia will not accept that their Lady has married a Viking raider. They'll rebel.' I wonder if he speaks for himself as well, but I quickly turn to meet cousin Athelstan's eyes.

'The people from the North West, from Chester, Runcorn and Eddisbury, will take the news very badly. They'd rather expel Viking raiders than live alongside them.'

Finally, I turn to Ealdorman Æthelfrith's son, Lord Athelstan, trying to ignore the welter of hurt in his eyes. It's as though all of these people believe I really am married, despite my conversation with him beside the hearth on the night my uncle was removed from Mercia.

'And Nottingham?' I swallow thickly. He's spent the most amount of time there; he'll know their true feelings.

He takes his time in answering. I try to ignore the chill of his words.

'Nottingham and Derby, and even Lincoln, should it ally with Mercia, will little care whom you wed.' At the end of that sentence, I hear the unsaid words, 'but I do', and I try to ignore them.

'He means to divide my country then?' I hazard. The eyes of those who meet mine all show varying signs of agreement. 'He means to divide the loyalty of my followers with his lies, that somehow I've married a man I haven't, a man who half my people despise for being a Viking raider. They were content when Lord Rǫgnvaldr was just my ally and had kept me alive, but now, really? They'd rather consent to King Edward ruling them than a Viking raider?'

I'm talking out loud, giving voice to my thoughts, but no one tries to stop me or offer fake assurances.

It seems that I've fought to keep my kingdom safe, but in this war of words, there's little I'll be able to do to stop my uncle.

But that's not the end of the rumours. Others quickly surface. The first is that King Edward plans significant retribution against me. The second is that cousin Ælfweard has vowed to send assassins into Mercia. Thirdly, I hear that Constantin of the Scots has become an ally of King Edward and that together they'll attack Lord Rǫgnvaldr and myself. I also hear that Lord Rǫgnvaldr has already forgotten our alliance and plans to invade Mercia. It's hard to give any credit to these rumours.

My continued existence has upset more than just King Edward's plans to rule Mercia. It seems that the basis of his grabbing reach into any kingdom other than Wessex has faltered. I know, with mounting dread, that when vengeance comes from my uncle, it'll be swift and deadly.

For all that, being back in control of Mercia is all I've ever wanted. I could only wish that my mother were here to see me. I hope she'd be proud of me. I take the time to make plans for her tomb. She wanted to be buried at Gloucester and was, but now's the time to order stone-masons to begin work on making it as regal as befits her. She should lie in state, especially during her long years of death. It'll give people a focus to mourn her and will act as a reminder that she was my mother while I rule.

If any forget, I resolve to arrange for a celebration of her life, and in doing so, people will recall why they want me to govern them. The legacy of my mother's life is both a difficulty and an advantage. I must only act as she would have done, but equally, what she would have done can guide me when I'm faced with decisions that I find challenging to make.

I miss my mother. Even now, a whisper in the great hall, a comment made by anyone from a servant to a noblewoman who shares her voice, makes me believe my mother is with me.

Damn my bastard uncle. He couldn't even give me time to grieve before he tried to take my kingdom. Each day I hate him more while learning to pity him.

I know I should be frightened of him and wary of what he'll do next, but I find him beneath my contempt.

He tried to kill me, and he failed. Will he try again? It's impossible to know. What I do know is that the Mercians will suspect his involvement if I should suddenly die. In those circumstances, I believe they'll turn to cousin Athelstan, not King Edward.

King Edward's failure is complete. I resolve to enjoy the triumph.

CHAPTER 3

A nd the most visible sign of my enjoyment is in the work I commission for Gloucester.

Not that my mother and father hadn't already ensured St Oswald's Priory was well endowed before their deaths. But there's more I can do.

As the weather begins to turn visibly and the days draw shorter and shorter, I make the short journey to Gloucester along the Foss Way. My female warriors, Ealdorman Æthelfrith and his sons accompany me. Cousin Athelstan remains in Tamworth, although I know he would sooner come. Someone must stay behind, and although Lady Ecgwynn is keen to do the honours, cousin Athelstan still feels weighed down by his father's betrayal.

He's happy and sad whenever I speak to him, but most of the time, I detect melancholy in his words and actions, even when a smile pulls his lips upwards.

Cousin Athelstan can't forgive himself, and that saddens me.

Gloucester is no more than a day's hard riding from Tamworth, but while the weather might not be the best, I determine to travel at a more leisurely pace. I want the men and women of Mercia to see me and to know that I yet live. I don't know how far my uncle's scheme percolated through to the general population of Mercia. Still, I'm determined to show myself as very much alive.

The fields are mostly bare, with the harvest long since collected, and yet the trackways remain busy. Many people are about tasks that need to be completed before the winter days become too short, making it impossible to accomplish anything.

When my cavalcade, complete with the eagle banners of Mercia, comes into view, the gentle wind bringing life to the banners, cheering voices greet me. A few even seek an audience with me to assist in matters that bedevil them and which need a voice of authority to solve. I do my best. This isn't a formal court or witan, but there's still the potential to summon witnesses or arrange to have them meet me at Gloucester or in Tamworth.

Mercia is a patchwork before me. Some fields are brown and expectant, waiting for better weather. Others are dormant, devoid of all signs of life, left fallow for the ground to recover. And in others, those animals selected to survive the winter watch our passage with disinterest, chewing the grasses available to them. There'll not be many more days before they're taken inside to endure the biting winds and bitter chill of full winter.

I smile to see my kingdom as it should be.

There should be peace and tranquillity, with the promise of warmth and food throughout the winter, with the hope of resurgence that comes with warmer weather.

As I ride, my mind is busy with plans and thoughts and how I can improve my fellow Mercians' lives in the coming years.

It wasn't so long ago that fear would have kept animals locked up tightly in barns and people as well. Pride swells within me to see all that my mother accomplished while realising all that's left for me to do.

Ealdorman Æthelfrith is full of conversation beside me. He's keen to talk about the changes he's seen during his lifetime. I settle to listen to him. His rich voice rumbles contentedly along, and even with his few words, he conjures images before me of burning buildings and ransacked fields. I think we both sit a little straighter and appreciate just what has been accomplished in Mercia since the death of my grandfather.

'We'll stay in Worcester tonight?' he queries. I nod. The grey of the coming night is already starting to filter across the trackway, making it difficult to see the holes that mar the road after a busy year.

'Yes, we will. And then tomorrow, we'll travel to Gloucester. I'm keen to hear news of the Welsh kingdoms.'

He nods, almost whistling below his breath, and I grin.

Although I would never say it to him, Ealdorman Æthelfrith is a comfort to me. I no longer have parents or an uncle I can rely on, but I do have a well-respected ealdorman. And, of course, his son.

After our early morning conversation, I've found myself seeking out Lord Athelstan more and more often. He makes me laugh and drives the worries of rule from my head for the time we're together.

Our being together elicits no outraged comments from anyone within Mercia. I suppose they have a good point. If my mother's line is to continue to rule in Mercia, then the next generation of our family needs to be born. That means I need a husband, and one suitable for all of Mercia as well as myself.

Ealdorman Æthelfrith's son seems to be that person, although I've kept those thoughts to myself. I don't wish to be too hasty in forming any attachment to the handsome man. Yes, I confess, he's somewhat younger than I am. Still, when we're together, talking and laughing or even discussing politics, I don't notice.

I'm well aware that if I don't marry and have children, it'll just give King Edward and his host of children an open opportunity to take Mercia from its ruling family in the future.

But it's an intensely personal choice, and not one I wish to make too hastily. Even at my age. Most women with as many winters to their name as I have would have children already, perhaps many. I need to wait a little bit longer yet. I have much to do before I can genuinely consider marriage and children, and no one has mentioned it to me.

Well. I reconsider. No one has mentioned it to me unless in connection with the rampant rumour that I've contracted a marriage alliance with Lord Rǫgnvaldr of York as part of our decision to fight together. Which I haven't. And never would, as I told Lord Athelstan.

As Worcester comes into view, I reminisce. I once spent many years living in Worcester. My mother and father built a residence on land inside the earthwork defences purchased from Bishop Wærferth nearly three decades ago. As a child, I always felt safe inside Worcester. Its twin layer of protection, the tumbled-down remains of the Roman wall, and the far newer burh walls, built by my mother and father, made me believe that the Viking raiders would never attack Worcester. And if they did, they'd never breach the walls.

For that reason, I take my time, even though it's dark, to inspect the burh walls with the help of a collection of brands held by my escort.

I have memories of the wall being built when I was no more than a very small child. My mother allowed me to watch the men and women at work as they laboured to create an earth rampart to such a level that it allowed me to roll down it with some speed. My shrieks of delight were a welcome counterpart to the noisy construction work, and I remember seeing smiles on dirty faces when I was allowed to indulge in such play.

In front of that earth rampart, a wall was then built using rubble from the ruined Roman buildings, and it put an end to my games. Those men and women sweated and sometimes bled to make the settlement of Worcester so well protected. The sound of wooden uprights being struck fast in the ground greeted me each time I woke for the length of one long summer.

The bishop and my parents rewarded those who built the burh walls with land inside the settlement, and small estates outside the protection of the walls, to farm when it was safe to do so. It was a promise that they would banish all Viking raiders from the kingdom. Now, as I view the area, I can see it's in a good state of repair. Bishop Wilferth has proved to be assiduous in his duties to Worcester and his diocese, considering his short tenure so far.

Eventually, satisfied that all remains as my mother would have wanted it, I make my way through the carefully guarded gate and into the trading area, rife with the smells of food and industry. Worcester is carefully divided, and as of yet, the industrial area hasn't mingled with that of the monastery grounds and the vast graveyard.

The graveyard eloquently speaks for the long-standing churches inside the settlement. In time, I imagine Worcester will need to expand beyond its walls if it wishes to grow. Either that, or it'll need to disinter the dead.

The monastery where Bishop Wilferth spends much of his time is more ancient than the burh walls but not as old as the Roman ones. I consider, in the flickering brands, that it might require some repair. But for now, I keep the thought to myself. The purpose of my journey is to ensure the Priory of St Oswald's in Gloucester is richly endowed. Only after that's accomplished will I think of other religious establishments.

And, I consider Bishop Wilferth has, at his command, all the riches that Bishop Wærferth once amalgamated when he was so powerful under my parents' joint rule. I can't see how the bishopric lacks the required funds to undertake the repairs.

Bishop Wilferth greets me in the courtyard before the monastery church, the scent of the nearby river rife. He's huddled against the cold weather, a rich cloak around his shoulders, the wind turning more and more bitter the longer I tarry outside.

The bishop bows his head as I dismount from my horse. I notice where his hair's beginning to thin on the back of his head, but I keep the thought to myself. After all, it's his wise eyes that are the most arresting of his features.

'Lady Ælfwynn,' his voice rumbles like thunder, dying away and then bursting back to life once more, even in the space of those two words. He has great skill when he preaches. He's learned to use his voice as a weapon. I admire that.

'Bishop Wilferth, your greeting is most welcome, but it's a cool night.' He nods as though in agreement and turns to lead me inside the monastery. Behind me, I leave a mass of men and women dismounting from their horses. Eoforhild is quickly at my side, her face flushed with the exertions of being outdoors in the cold wind.

The monastery isn't as austere as others I've visited. Quickly, I'm seated before a blazing hearth, my cloak discarded, and my feet tingling as warmth floods back into them.

Bishop Wilferth joins me, as does Ealdorman Æthelfrith. Food has been prepared for those I travel with, and I turn to Bishop Wilferth.

'I hope you've enough left in the stores for the coming winter?' It's not truly a complaint but rather a compliment that it seems there's so much to spare.

'A good harvest,' he confirms, a twinkle in his eye, sipping from a full goblet of wine, savouring the taste. He's pleased with the excess and has every right to be.

'Tell me of the borders,' I enquire. He nods once more as though expecting my question.

'The grandsons of Rhodri Mawr concern themselves with in-fighting and with barely a thought for Mercia or even Wessex. I'm content that peace with them will continue. Not indefinitely, of course, but for some time yet.'

This pleases me as I sip warm wine, delighting in the rich spices that drive the ache of cold from my throat.

'And what do you hear of events in Wessex?'

We might only have ridden for a day and a short day at that, but Worcester is still closer to Wessex than Tamworth.

Bishop Wilferth's mouth curdles at the question.

'King Edward continues to rule as before. It seems he's done no damage to his reputation in Wessex. However, I do hear that Lord Ælfweard is incensed with his father's refusal to grant him a position in Wessex in the wake of the loss of Mercia.'

'Cousin Ælfweard is a fool and not capable of ruling.'

'That might be the case, but King Edward has kept a firm command over the oldest son from his second marriage until now. It might be that Lord Ælfweard can undermine his father's rule should he gain enough allies.'

The thought is an intriguing one and also a new one for me. My emotions have been so focused on hating my uncle that I've failed to

deduce that there's a potential situation that I could exploit. If only I
didn't detest my cousin as much as I do my uncle.

'Do you think it to be something worth exploring?'

'It's too early to say. Lord Ælfweard might well just be sprouting a
great deal of hot air. But King Edward must be aware that his sons
could be a greater liability than he once thought. Lords Ælfweard and
Edwin are keen to rule. They see Athelstan in Mercia, and I believe
they're jealous of his freedoms.'

I grunt softly. Cousin Athelstan doesn't see Mercia as his freedom,
but I take the point that others might well do so.

'Keep me informed of all that you hear,' I ask, and then our conversation moves to matters that concern Worcester and Bishop Wilferth.
Unsurprisingly, they're not the same concerns I have about my uncle
but rather focused on Worcester itself.

The weather turns bitter during the night, and as we mount up,
our breath plumes, and I consider that my decision to visit Gloucester
at this time of year might not have been a good one. Still, I desire to
see my mother's place of burial, and so I ride on, even though there's
some grumbling from my escort. There's no hint of snow in the air
yet, but it will come sooner than I might like.

We follow the River Severn all the way to Gloucester. The river is
busy with small crafts journeying up and down the busy waterway. I
consider stopping to visit the ancient royal site of Kingsholm, just
outside Gloucester itself, once important to my father, but I dismiss it.
My business today is with the priory. There'll be other opportunities
to visit Kingsholm in the future.

Gloucester, like Worcester, is a burh settlement but one where the
burh walls are based entirely on the ancient Roman ones which once
entirely enclosed it. Most ancient Roman buildings have been quar-
ried for use elsewhere, and the newer buildings are an assortment of
repurposed stone, as well as the more usual wattle and daub.

The River Severn runs, as in Worcester, to the west of the settlement, a wooden bridge spanning its expanse for those who wish to
cross it on their way to Hereford or the Welsh kingdoms.

Gloucester is governed by a stocky portreeve, who greets us even though we arrive on horseback and not on one of the many ships I can see moored along the banks. I've always preferred to ride than travel by boat.

Portreeve Ealdred bows so deeply before me that I fear he may never rise without help from those who accompany him. I met Ealdred at my mother's funeral, and he seemed a kind man. I can't say the same now, as his face is lined with worry. But, he understands I've come to visit St Oswald's Priory. As he escorts my small party, he wisely holds his tongue. All the same, I appreciate then that I'll not leave Gloucester without giving due time to whatever troubles him.

St Oswald's Priory is close to a sizeable hall, home, at the moment, to Portreeve Ealdred. The building, made from repurposed Roman stone, is open to the river on one side but guarded on the remaining three by a wooden enclosure that's recently been repaired. I can clearly see where the brightness of new wood shimmers against the older, more wizened wood. I eye those repairs keenly.

As much as I hope Mercia will know peace in the future, I also appreciate that the art of survival is in being prepared for all eventualities.

When I was in Gloucester for my mother's funeral, I focused on other matters. I remind myself to compliment Ealdred for his attention to such issues.

Only then, I'm before the priory, and all thoughts of defence flee from my mind.

I slide to the ground, absentmindedly handing the reins of my horse to Erna. She hastens to take charge of my mount while I walk toward the priory building.

My mother and father were particularly pleased to place the holy relics of St Oswald in the heartland of Mercia. I've always found the act a strange one. After all, a Mercian king murdered St Oswald of the Northumbrian kingdom nearly three hundred years ago. Why, then, would the rulers of Mercia wish to venerate his relics?

I remember asking my mother the question at the time, and her answer has still never satisfied me.

'The Viking raiders destroyed so many of Mercia's relics that it was necessary to find another. King Oswald was renowned for his piety.'

'But he clearly wasn't very good with a sword,' I'd commented sourly. When I was younger, I'd revered all who'd won great victories in battle. Before my own experiences of war, I'd been swept up in the heroic nature of it all. My familiarity with battle has tempered that admiration with the truth. I now know what it means to fight and feel the blood of a foe engraved on my skin. I might admire warriors more because I understand the hard truths of taking lives and fighting for your survival.

'Perhaps not, but he was a good Christian king, and the Viking raiders desecrated his shrine.'

'But Penda was a Mercian king.' I'd stressed that fact, wondering why it wasn't Penda's bones that had been recovered.

'King Penda was a pagan,' my mother had replied, her eyes alight with the distinction.

'So, it's more that King Oswald was a Christian and Penda a pagan than anything else?'

'It wouldn't be right to revere a pagan, not when our enemy is pagan. The churchmen tell us that we'll only win victory because of God's intervention.'

The answer hadn't really satisfied me then and certainly didn't now, but I could be respectful of my mother's wishes. After all, it's not as if I could argue with her about it now.

When my mother and father first conceived of the new priory, it had been to have a much larger building to show their piety than the one I view now, but space hadn't allowed for it in the clustered settlement. Gloucester, being old and filled with other churches and cemeteries, hadn't easily given up space for the new building work, even if ordered by the lord and lady of Mercia.

Above my head, the curving arches of stonework hold up the weight of the roof that covers the plain rectangular building, but still, I duck my head, making my way inside the priory itself.

The monks haven't come to greet me. I'm pleased with the chance to spend some time alone.

My eyes flicker to the expanse of gold, silver and priceless cloth that festoons the interior. Although the crypt calls to me, I take the time to admire the wall paintings and embroidered hangings first, commissioned by my parents. The interior shimmers, even without the need for candles and light.

I slip from the church itself with a soft sigh, keen to make my way to the stone steps leading into the depths of the building, the east porticus where my mother and father eternally rest.

The priest is waiting for me in the lea of the wooden doorway, far smaller than the main door, huddled into a thick cloak and stamping his feet together to keep them warm.

When he senses my arrival, the priest glances at me. I remember that he's both old and blind. His fingers seek out the keys that jangle on a considerable chain at his waist, and I wait patiently. Some might think it strange to leave a blind man on guard duty, but Priest Beornstan was once a warrior. His reputation, more than his skills, keeps the crypt safe from interference from anyone keen to disturb the dead.

It's well known that the burial of my mother and father is finely endowed. For now, the respect my mother was held within serves to help Priest Beornstan. Some come here to pray and seek miracles. Few are allowed within the area where the coffins actually lie. And fewer actually want to be there, not when St Oswald's relics are easily accessed from above.

I murmur my thanks to Priest Beornstan, and then I'm inside the crypt. The space is far more extensive than the name implies. There are candles to light the way. I assume they'd been lit when my arrival was known. I can't imagine it always makes sense to have a fire burning down here. It would be a waste of precious resources.

This is the royal crypt for the rulers of Mercia. It's similar to the ancient one at Repton, only without the taint of the Viking raider occupation. My parents built St Oswald's Priory in fear they'd never win back Repton and wouldn't be able to be buried there. I imagine I'll join them here one day, to lie beside them.

The smell of incense hangs heavily in the air, and above my head, I notice the arches that hold up the roof of the crypt. The stone has been daubed so that it shimmers white and despite it all, I think this isn't a bad place to be laid to rest.

Surprisingly, the air is free from the river's stench. Although I pull my cloak tighter, I don't feel cold. Not until I face the two coffins, my father's and my mother's, and the sacred space where the relics of St Oswald are kept when they're not being used, do I actually shiver.

I recall that conversation with my mother when I questioned her about St Oswald, and I also think about what I know about him.

That he was deemed a saint seems obvious, but whereas cousin Athelstan would be enthralled to know the story of the miracles ascribed to St Oswald's body after his death, I'm far more interested in what he actually did during his life. After all, what control does he have over his mortal remains? It's what he achieved that fascinates me, and really, I'm not sure that was quite as much as others might try and make me believe.

He became king in the wake of the death of a man killed by King Penda and his allies. In turn, King Penda killed him. I'd sooner have my mother's legacy against the Viking raiders than Saint Oswald's, even if my mother never becomes a saint. I'd sooner have King Penda's reputation, pagan or not. He was a man I think I'd have liked.

Lovingly, I caress the stone coffin my mother lies beneath. The stone has been left blank until now, but I would have some symbolism added to it. That's why I've made the journey. I know that cousin Athelstan agrees with my desire to make the coffin more magnificent. He loved my mother as though she was his mother as well.

I bow my head and clear my mind of all but the most pressing problems. And then I begin to speak. My mother has always been a good listener. Even in death, I find comfort in sharing with her the events that have befallen me in recent times. I appreciate that I'll get no answer, but just saying the words aloud is soothing. I'd never do this elsewhere.

I'd never admit my real thoughts to anyone.

When I reach the end of the story, I listen to the echo of my voice die away, and a sad smile touches my lips. I'd not expected any sort of response from my mother. I'm not disappointed, but all the same, this is a place of miracles. I'd be lying if I didn't confess that I'd been expecting something to happen.

When a stray tear lands on the stone beside my hand, I'm honest enough to admit that I miss my mother. Despite my attempts to appear strong, I feel quite weak and, sometimes, incredibly scared.

It appears I made this journey for more reasons than I thought.

I allow more tears to fall, to feel sorry for myself, to rant at what's happened since she died and what might well happen in the future.

In the absence of anyone else, I appreciate what my mother was to me.

For everyone else, she was the Lady of Mercia and a woman of profound strength and resolve. But to me, she was my mother. And I miss her.

In the depths of my sorrow, I make some promises to myself about the future. When I emerge, much, much later, the sky above my head is far darker than even in the crypt, but I feel refreshed and restored.

Saint Oswald has done nothing for me or for Mercia but my mother. Well, as always, she's made me stand taller and take greater pride in my accomplishments, and for me, that will be the miracle of St Oswald's Priory.

CHAPTER 4

That evening I speak with Portreeve Ealdred as we eat. Outside, the sky's crystalline, the air almost too cold to breathe. In his hall, the hearth burns fiercely, while food and drink are plentiful. The building is in an excellent state of repair, and only when the door opens and closes does the night air infiltrate inside.

It seems that there's been a good harvest in Gloucester as well as Worcester. That pleases me.

'The traders are unhappy with the Wessex tolls, but of course,' and here Portreeve Ealdred chuckles his vast belly wobbling. 'They've found a way around most of them.'

'Tell me,' I demand, and he nods, fingering his full lips in thought.

'The Wessex boundary, whether it truly is or not, has always been the road that runs from London along the River Thames. It's there that the Wessex reeves wait to pounce on all who wish to trade in Wessex itself. So, the traders of Gloucester have been travelling by way of the Severn and coming ashore deep inside Wessex. There's been a fine trade in men and women learning to speak with the Wessex drawl.' Portreeve Ealdred laughs joyfully as he speaks, and I copy him.

There's little to tell a man of Wessex from a man of Mercia. There is the accent and, more often than not, the physique. No one in Mercia grows soft with age, but instead, everyone is lean and fit, ready to face any enemy that they must. The same can't be said for the people of Wessex. Even the king has grown soft, and I doubt that cousin Ælfweard could hack down a wheat field, let alone an army of Viking raiders.

'As long as there are no problems, I'm content for the people of Gloucester to trade as they can. Certainly, the people of the Five Boroughs are keen to trade with York.'

'Hum.' Only now does the flicker in Portreeve Ealdred's eyes concerns me.

'Excuse the presumption, my lady, but there are rumours that you mean to marry the new lord of York.'

I sigh, the sound so soft it's almost a caress.

'Gloucester isn't alone in thinking as much. But I've made no marriage alliance. I know I should marry, but in due time and when I've settled on a suitable candidate. I'll not sell myself to anyone, not while I have a kingdom to rule and make no mistake, it is mine to rule, not any husband I might take.'

The surprised look in Portreeve Ealdred's eyes tells me more than he probably realises. His words worry me. I've heard this throughout Mercia. How can one rumour be so virulent? Well, of course, it's not the first rumour to have caused me problems, but whereas King Edward announced I was dead when I yet lived, this insistence that I'm married, or plan to marry Lord Rognvaldr, could do me far more significant damage.

While the people of the Five Boroughs were pleased to know that a Viking raider aided me in my battle to the north, they'll not welcome having a Viking raider lord control them. Aside from my personal preference, there's a genuine need for me not to be ruled by a man with the same heritage as those Mercia has been fighting for so many years.

I meet the eyes of Ealdorman Æthelfrith, my thoughts turning to his son. I fancy I could marry him, but I should like to know him

better first. Ealdorman Æthelfrith's eyebrow arches at my look, and
for a moment, I worry that he can read my thoughts.

With a great deal of effort, I focus on Portreeve Ealdred.

'Tell me of the Welsh kingdoms?' I demand, hoping to distract
myself as well as others.

'There's little to say. Hywel and Clydog share their father's
kingdom equitably enough, and Idwal is contained to the north.
They're wary of Lord Rǫgnvaldr and events in Dublin. And they're
increasingly concerned with King Edward's intentions. They were
your mother's allies, never his.'

It pleases me to hear this, but it seems that Portreeve Ealdred isn't
to be distracted from his primary concern.

'But it's the marriage that concerns most people,' he speaks with no
hint of apology, and inside I seethe while trying not to show it.

Marriage is a personal choice, not a political one. Or so I think.
But of course, my mother married for political gain, and so has my
uncle, on three different occasions, the first might have been for love.
Possibly, Uncle Edward was once a kinder man. I doubt it, but I don't
dismiss the possibility out of hand.

The rest of the meal passes pleasantly enough, but I'm relieved
when I can retire for the night. In the morning, I speak with the
stonemason about my mother's coffin and the engravings I would like
it to have and leave as soon as possible.

As we journey back to Worcester, my thoughts are consumed with
anger. How is it possible that I can survive an attempt on my life but
risk losing everything because of a marriage I haven't even proposed,
let alone consented to undertake?

'It would just be easier to make a marriage on your terms. As your
mother, it need not be for love but for the good of Mercia.'

I've not invited Ealdorman Æthelfrith to speak to me. Still, he's
brought his horse alongside mine, and it's impossible to ignore him.

'It's not your concern.' I try and close down the unwelcome
conversation before it can begin.

'It is if it affects Mercia.'

Furiously, I rein in my horse, turning to face Ealdorman Æthelfrith. I'm surprised to see a smirk on his lined face, as though this response delights him.

I gaze at his amusement in shock, and it merely stokes my anger.

'It's not your damn concern, and I'll not be forced to make a marriage just to stop a rumour.'

'So, you'll fight and risk your life, but you won't risk marrying? That makes no sense to me. None at all.'

'It's a private matter.' And now the ealdorman shakes his head sadly.

'It's as far from being a private matter as it can be.'

I feel my face flush.

'I…. I've never considered marrying. My mother didn't rush me, and there's no need to make a hasty decision now.'

'Not even to save your kingdom?'

I feel my face blush ever brighter. I'm a warrior. Matters of the heart have never concerned me. In all honesty, I've never looked at a man and thought of him as someone I'd allow to touch me, let alone share my bed with them. Well, not until recently, and now I find myself having this conversation with the very man whose son it might apply to.

'I would do anything for Mercia. You know that,' I say staunchly. 'Tell me then, whom should I marry?'

'I think we both know the answer to that,' Ealdorman Æthelfrith states, but it's not without some understanding in his voice.

I want to argue again, and deny it even more. But instead, I give it the thought it deserves. I feel foolish and ridiculous. Ealdorman Æthelfrith's son and I have made no formal declarations of interest in each other. We just like spending time together. Does he even think of me the same way I'm beginning to think of him?

'Would he, would he even consider it?' The words are wrenched from deep inside, and as soon I've muttered them, I wish I could take them back.

'I don't think I'm the right person to be speaking to about it. But I can't imagine the answer would be a no. My son isn't blind to the problems within Mercia. It would be a political match, or perhaps not.

Either way, my son would be a suitable husband for you. You need not be close. The marriage could be similar to your mother and father's.'

I grimace at that. I'm not sure that Ealdorman Æthelfrith truly understands my motivations and needs, but all the same, I appreciate his advice. It's not meant unkindly. Or at least, I don't think it is.

'Then I'll give it due consideration,' I sigh as I speak, my thoughts on the cold marriage my mother enjoyed with my father. I don't like to think I was the product of such a clinical coupling, even though no one can deny it. There was never any real affection between them. I know my father resented my mother for always holding more sway with the Mercians than he did. But of course, my mother was half Mercian and was entirely royally born. Unlike Lord Æthelred.

All the same, I wouldn't wish my children to feel the way I do.

When we ride into Tamworth the following day, I find myself seeking out Lord Æthelfrith's son, disappointed when I don't see him immediately. Instead, cousin Athelstan greets me, and the look on his face fills me with foreboding.

'What has happened now?' I ask, dismounting from my horse and striding to where he waits for me in the courtyard, pacing from side to side. The night is drawing in, and the temperature has dropped even lower. I want nothing more than to warm myself before the hearth, but I sense that my cousin wishes to speak to me alone.

'My father has sent a messenger. My sister and I are to return to Wessex immediately.' I gape in surprise. Of all the things I might have worried about, this wasn't one of them.

'And you intend to go?' I surmise, feeling my frustration building once more.

'No, we will not go,' Cousin Athelstan complains, coming to an abrupt stop in front of me, his eyes as wild with fury as mine.

'Our place is in Mercia, not in Wessex. We'll not go to Wessex and have Ælfweard mock me or my father's new wife look at me with disdain. She's younger than either of us.'

'Then why are we discussing this outside?'

'Because my father seeks to undermine you, either by taking me from your side or by ensuring everyone distrusts you because of this foolish marriage suggestion.'

'But everyone knows about the marriage.' I'm trying to work out why cousin Athelstan is so incensed beyond the obvious.

'Yes, but they don't know about my father's latest demands.'

'You think if it becomes common knowledge, then it'll cause me greater problems?'

'I believe people will interpret it in one of two ways, either my father is meddling in Mercia if I do go, or I'm working at my father's behest if I stay. Neither option aids you.'

'No, they don't. I agree. But Ealdorman Æthelfrith and I might have a solution to the marriage problem.'

My cousin exhales loudly, his keen eyes meeting mine as he comes to an abrupt stop before me.

'You'll marry someone else? Someone suitable for Mercia? I would have suggested it, but I didn't wish to offend.' Now I sigh.

'I might marry,' I shrug, dismayed to realise that even cousin Athelstan has decided it would be the best option. My cousin has never given me bad advice.

'You should have married many years ago,' Cousin Athelstan confirms. 'As should my sister. My aunt was as guilty as everyone else in failing to see the necessity.'

I don't like to hear any criticism of my mother, but I know that cousin Athelstan wouldn't speak the words lightly.

'If you had children and a husband, then my father wouldn't be able to remove you because the family line would be secure.'

'And you would marry in the same situation?' Cousin Athelstan has the good grace to look uncomfortable at my question.

'I wouldn't wish to inflict the sort of life I've led on to my children.' His eyes blaze as he speaks, and I almost regret my hastily snapped question. Cousin Athelstan has been the victim of his father's political ambitions for nearly all of his life.

His answer tempers my frustration. Instead, I tilt my head to one side, considering the busy work of the men and women in the stables. They must bring each horse in, one by one, remove their riding equipment, and brush the animals down before leading them to a stable to eat and rest. It's soothing work, but not when the weather is so cold.

'And do you think that Ealdorman Æthelfrith's son would take me for a wife?'

My cousin's eyes widen in surprise as I make the admission.

'Lord Ælfstan?'

'What's the matter with Lord Ælfstan?' I demand, for some perverse reason deciding not to correct his assumption.

'No, no, nothing, sorry, you just surprised me.' I chuckle then, determined to enjoy myself. I don't want to be the only one made uncomfortable by the thought of marriage.

A silence falls between us as cousin Athelstan opens and closes his mouth as though about to say something, only to think better of it.

I wait, the silence building between us, enjoying the awkwardness of forcing my cousin to think of something to say about something that will never happen.

Cousin Athelstan and Lord Ælfstan are great friends, but Ælfstan isn't the easiest of people to get along with. Other than when in conversation with my cousin, Ælfstan likes to be right. He likes to be the centre of attention. He's somewhat dismissive of me, as he was my mother, although never to the point of being outrightly offensive.

'I,' still cousin Athelstan struggles. His eyes look behind me as though seeking some sort of inspiration. Then he runs his hand through his blond hair, shakes his head, and meets my eye.

'I'd have expected you to choose someone more like yourself than Lord Ælfstan.' It's a diplomatic statement. My cousin has learnt his craft well at my mother's side.

I grin, rubbing my hands up and down my arms, trying to entice some warmth back into my body.

'I meant bloody Lord Athelstan, not Ælfstan,' I smirk, grinning even wider when my cousin's tight face relaxes, his relief clear to see.

He chuckles then, appreciating the uncomfortable situation of his own making.

'I think that you can be a little cruel sometimes, but equally, I shouldn't have made the assumption. I'll be more circumspect in the future.' It's an apology, and I appreciate it without asking for more.

'Then you would approve?'

'I would. Have you spoken to him of this?' Now cousin Athelstan's forehead furrows in concentration, and I shake my head.

'No, but I will. It'll be excruciating.' The thought of having to profess any feelings of affection for Lord Athelstan, out loud almost has me reconsidering my options. Perhaps it would just be better actually to marry Lord Rǫgnvaldr. At least everyone expects it. But I shake my head, dismayed that I should be so terrified of a simple conversation,

I can face my death, look death in the eyes, and kill men and women easily, but this, well, this is not my particular skill.

Once more, cousin Athelstan chuckles at me.

'I wish you luck,' he bows his head as though to walk away from me, but I reach out and grab his arm.

'You'll speak to him for me?' I might have been looking for Lord Athelstan, but now a new possibility presents itself to me.

Now it's cousin Athelstan's mouth that falls open in surprise. I allow a slow gasp of mirth to escape me. I can see why he's been enjoying the moment so much.

'I. Well. I. What would you have me say?'

'Apart from my uncle, the king of Wessex, and my other uncle, who only does what the king tells him, you're my sole male relative. It should be you who speaks to the potential groom.'

'I. I.' He still seems unsure of what to say.

'What would you have me say to him? You say you've already spoken to Ealdorman Æthelfrith. He can speak to his son about it.'

'Someone must negotiate for me. Ensure everything is as it should be. You know that. You should already have offered,' I tinge my voice with a hint of annoyance, and cousin Athelstan isn't immune to it.

'Ah, Ælf, really? I'd sooner not. He's my friend, and you're my cousin, and I think of you as a sister.'

'It's for the good of Mercia,' I retort. I leave unsaid that it'll also be easier for me if I don't have to hold the awkward conversation with a man for whom I might well have feelings. I don't want to see his face if the offer disappoints him. I don't want to know if our conversations have meant nothing to him.

'Fine, I'll speak to him. But I'm only doing it because you're making me. I don't understand why you can't do it. You spend as much time with him as I do. If not more.'

'I.' Now I falter. 'I.' I try again, and cousin Athelstan is watching me intently, his tight lips slowly relaxing as he appreciates just how embarrassed I am.

'I'll do it,' he reaffirms, squeezing my hand, compassion on his face. 'I'll do it. If I were ever to marry, I'd have you do the same for me,' he complains before striding from my presence. I know he'll be speaking with Lord Athelstan immediately, and my heart stutters in my chest, my breathing ragged.

CHAPTER 5

I laugh at myself, but the sound that emerges from my mouth sounds archaic, an echo from the grave. I'm suddenly so damn nervous.

What if Lord Athelstan says no? What if our camaraderie has only been that and not what I took it to be? Angrily, I make my way to the training ground. I might only have just returned from my journey to Gloucester, but I don't need to rest. I need exactly the opposite.

Striding through the palace, I make my way to the training ground. It's nearly fully dark, but even so, I hear the crash of iron on iron and the grunt of people exercising. The long winter nights are torture for men and women used to the activity of the summer. Three brands burn brightly, trying to push back the darkness of night. In the flickering shadows, I make out about ten people, all of them taking advantage of the smallest tongues of daylight to exercise.

Some of my women are here, and so too, I notice is the very man I've sent my cousin to seek out. I sigh forcefully, reaching for a heavy sword, the blade and edge purposefully blunt so that no one can accidentally draw blood from the blade. Only bruises.

I swing the heavy sword from side to side, testing the weight, aware that behind me, Mildryth hasn't let me out of her sight. Then I drop the weapon on my feet, windmilling my arms around to get some feeling back into them. It's been cold while I rode back to Tamworth. I don't wish to injure myself in training.

'Come, we'll spar,' I state, turning to Mildryth, noticing that she squints into the darkness, a look of unhappiness on her face.

'It's too dark. We'll injure each other.' Her complaint is entirely reasonable. Even as she speaks, three of the warriors begin to make their way inside.

'We'll use blunt weapons. Now come. I need to work the ache of diplomacy from my body.'

Mildryth shakes her head, the long braid that runs down her back swaying from side to side, but she makes no further complaint, merely complying with my request. She would have realised my intention as soon as I stepped foot on the training ground. My demand that she trains with me won't have been a great surprise.

'Only until the sun has fully set,' Mildryth sighs, testing the weight of another blade, the cart animal already harnessed to take the equipment inside for the night. The ever-patient groom waits. It's not unusual for him to have to wait to complete his task. Indeed, the animal is chomping noisily from a feedbag, and I nod at the foresight. Why should the animal suffer just because my warriors and I are so contrary?

Mildryth takes her position before me. Following my action, she windmills her arms, looking resigned. Her face clears once the sword is in her hands.

Why I chose a sword, I'm unsure. I know how skilled she can be with them. I should have taken a war axe, or a seax, or even a shield, but no, just a sword.

We size each other up, the gap between us about four strides. The spluttering flames cast her face into shadow, only the tip of her weapon truly visible where it catches the light from the brands.

I make the first move, rushing forward, the sword across my body as though I'll swipe across her body downwards. Mildryth easily meets the blow with her sword, the sound aggressively loud against the crackle of the flaming wood. I grunt as her blade counters mine, the familiar throb of the resistance felt in my shoulders.

I grin. This is far easier than matters of the heart.

We step apart when the tension becomes too high for both of us. This time, it's Mildryth who sizes up the best move as I feel the thud of my heart and the flicker of life beneath my skin. Fighting is my talent. It's what makes me feel alive.

Mildryth's action is conventional, her sword flicking high as though to graze my cheek or neck. Again, I counter it just as quickly as she did mine. I step backwards and immediately into another attacking position, my sword slashing low.

Mildryth grimaces as she realises I'm not about to give up with a few routine movements. Still, she grips her sword more loosely, the challenge accepted.

And so, we spar. The two blades flash quickly before us, the clash of iron against iron consuming my thoughts. My body loosens under the familiar movements, my mind clearing its worries as it becomes obsessed with evading the reach of Mildryth's blade.

I almost laugh aloud with delight.

This is what it truly means to feel alive.

'My lady,' the voice that calls to me is filled with respect and a hint of impatience. I step back from the battle with Mildryth, abruptly aware that the sun hasn't only entirely set but that the darkness seems impenetrable. We're but a point of light on a field of darkness.

It's the groom who calls me. There's no one else on the training ground. Two of the three fires have been extinguished so that only Mildryth and I, breathe pluming before us remain alongside the groom and the horse. Even the horse looks impatiently at me, kicking at the ground, straining against the harness.

The night has turned even colder. I can see where a frost already sprinkles the worn ground.

'Apologies,' I feel contrite but also alive. My face is flushed, sweat pooling uncomfortably down my back, and one glance at Mildryth offers a reflection of just what I must look like.

'Apologies,' I offer again, walking to the cart and laying my sword amongst the other ones, carefully wrapping it in a piece of treated linen as I do so.

The groom takes his place at the head of the horse. When Mildryth places her sword beside mine, she meets my eyes with a grin on her gleaming face.

'Go, we'll extinguish the flames,' Mildryth calls to the man, and without even attempting to argue with us, he, the horse and the cart begin to make their way back inside the settlement. The horse moves at a considerable speed, the thought of a warm stable no doubt enticing the animal.

'Grumpy sod,' Mildryth complains, striding to the fire burning in the barrel lined with iron. She makes short work of pouring water over the eager flames, the sizzle of wet flames a counterpart to our panting.

I shiver.

'Where did everyone go?' I ask, wondering if cousin Athelstan has seen my exertions or if Ealdorman Æthelfrith's son has. How long have I been sparring?

'They've gone inside. Come, so should we.'

Hastily, we make our way toward the beckoning lights of the palace, my stomach growling angrily at being denied food for so long.

'You fought well,' Mildryth acknowledges. 'You would have got me with the attack to my belly if you hadn't lost your balance.'

'And you would have sliced my neck if you hadn't been holding the sword wrong.'

She grunts at the words.

'I did that on purpose,' she proclaims, but I'm shaking my head.

'No, you didn't. It was a knee-jerk reaction because you thought I was aiming for your arm.'

'Perhaps,' Mildryth acknowledges, and then we're back inside the palace complex. I blink rapidly, the sudden brightness of the brands lighting the pathways, a counterpart to the gloom of the training ground.

'Urgh. I need to bathe,' I complain, making my way inside, Mildryth trailing me.

'You can bathe as well if you want to,' I offer, and she nods.

'When I'm relieved, I will,' she confirms, following me to my chamber, and standing helpfully out of the way while my two servants prepare my bath and fresh clothes for me.

She's silent, and so am I, as my skin begins to cool from our labours. I welcome the heat of the bath when I sink into it. I wrinkle my nose at the stench of a few days on the road, followed by our sparring. Only when I'm clean and dressed again do my thoughts return to what might have happened in my absence.

Perhaps my cousin has spoken to Lord Athelstan, or maybe not. I almost fear entering the main hall, but I know I must. With the virulent rumours circulating, I must be both seen and seen not to be married already.

By the time I'm seated in the great hall, there are few people left to witness my arrival. I shrug at my feeling of self-importance. Most people have already sought their beds, but my rumbling stomach means I still need to eat and relax.

Mildryth leaves me, and in her place, Eoforhild escorts me as I take a seat close to the hearth. Those who travelled with me to Gloucester aren't in the hall, and neither is cousin Athelstan. I allow my flicker of worry to dissipate.

'My lady.' Ealdorman Æthelfrith's son stands before me, a knowing smile on his face.

'My lord Athelstan,' the words escape me with a hint of panic. I cough, trying to clear my suddenly too-tight throat, as he reaches for the jug of wine and splashes some of the fluid into a waiting goblet. As he hands it to me, I admire his hands.

As I take the goblet, my hand brushes his and my face flushes.

Feeling foolish, I try and recover, sipping deeply from the goblet. Only I try and swallow too much, and suddenly, I'm gasping, suffocating, fighting for air, as I choke on my stupidity.

A sharp thwack on my back, and Eoforhild inspects me with concern as I finally suck in a hungry breath and try to regain my composure.

Lord Athelstan is watching me with anxiety on his face, and behind him, I just catch sight of my cousin. Cousin Athelstan is actually laughing at me, and if I thought I could stand without falling over my own feet, I'd be demanding an explanation from him. Instead, all I get when I can breathe and have wiped the tears from my eyes is a small nod of his head.

It seems it's done. I would be thankful, but I still feel too foolish.

I sip more delicately when I'm recovered, savouring the warmth of the wine and taking the time to find the composure that's deserted me.

'My lady,' Lord Athelstan's voice is smooth as he bows before me again. I indicate he should sit beside me. Eoforhild has thankfully retreated out of earshot, her shining eyes reflecting her amusement at my embarrassment.

I focus on Lord Athelstan, trying to find something in his face that offers an assurance that this isn't about to be the most awkward conversation I've ever had. I find nothing, and suddenly doubt my interpretation of cousin Athelstan's nodding head.

'You should eat,' Lord Athelstan turns to beckon a waiting servant closer.

'Food, for my lady, but none for me.' The servant bobs and hurries about the task. I watch her, preferring to look anywhere but at Lord Athelstan, reminding myself that I meant to speak with Eoforhild about the girl.

What was I thinking? I can't marry this man. I can't even look at him. Not at the moment.

'Lady Ælfwynn,' his voice is abruptly rich with understanding. Such a sudden change makes me lift my head to meet his eyes. They shimmer in the light from the hearth. I feel all my arguments against this match drain away. When it's just the two of us, it's much more relaxed.

But it seems my mortification isn't yet at an end.

'I've been speaking with your cousin and my father. I hope it was with your agreement?' I nod, words beyond me. When have I ever failed to find my tongue before?

He nods, showing no surprise at my sudden muteness.

'It wasn't an easy conversation,' Lord Athelstan confirms, his gaze flickering from his fingers, scrunched up on the table before him, to the fire. I can't take my eyes off his face. What will he say? Did cousin Athelstan's nod merely mean that the conversation was concluded? I've taken it for an acceptance of what I want to happen, but maybe Lord Athelstan has other ideas.

I nod. I want to say, 'I imagine not,' but my tongue is stuck to the roof of my mouth, my heart hammering so loudly in my chest that I consider whether it's audible to Lord Athelstan as well.

'I know we've spoken a great deal since you became the Lady of Mercia. I'm aware that you need to marry someone other than Lord Rognvaldr. I...' His voice trails away. I imagine his mind has been as busy with implications as mine has been. I'd hoped that he might feel some affection for me, but now I'm not sure.

Perhaps, after all, I should have chosen a husband as my mother did; coldly, without thought for happiness, merely for the need to have children and leave an heir.

'I,' his hands abruptly reach out for my hands, gripping them tightly between his. Peripherally, I'm aware that the servant is waiting to place my food on the table but that she's uncertain of what to do. She's been edging closer and closer, her gaze flickering between us. I wish I could tell her to go away, to leave us to this moment, but in a show of resolve, she steps smartly forward, places the sizzling platter of meat on the table to the side of our clasped hands and smartly moves away.

I'm sure she'd run if she could.

Lord Athelstan sighs at the intrusion, but his hold on my hands doesn't falter. I'm pleased he holds my hands inside his. My hands are clammy.

'I,' he begins again, his voice straining for control.

'I.'

He sighs and goes to take his hands away from mine, only I grab them, and hold them in place, despite knowing they're uncomfortably slick.

'I didn't think this would be so hard,' Lord Athelstan confesses, making no attempt to move his hands.

'I would marry you. I hope you know that. Despite the problems it'll cause, and even though you'll rule Mercia, and I won't. But first, I would know if you marry me to solve the problem of Lord Rǫgnvaldr, or because you want to. There, I've said it.' He leans back on his chair, his arms outstretched as mine tightens over his.

Lord Athelstan puffs out his chest, no doubt relieved to have voiced his concerns.

'I could ask the same of you,' I state, a little hurt that he'd question my motivations.

'I think you know better than that,' Lord Athelstan counters, his eyes on mine.

'Then I think you know better than that as well,' I counter.

He bites his lip in thought, the skin there showing white against the flush on his face. This isn't quite the conversation I thought I'd be having with him. Why I think, couldn't my cousin have handled the proposition better? He should have ensured that Lord Athelstan knew all this anyway. Although. Well, it might have been hard for my cousin because I didn't precisely state it would be a romantic attachment.

'I do,' Lord Athelstan surprises me by saying. 'But allow a man a moment of indecision. I would hear you say it. If only once.'

'Then I would hear you say it, as well,' I dispute.

This conversation is going nowhere fast. Only then, Lord Athelstan disentangles his hands from mine. I know a flicker of worry. He stands, and I fear he'll leave, but instead, he places his hands on the tabletop and leans forward on them.

The brush of his lips on mine is soft. It seems he demands nothing more from me. I inhale the smell of him, the hint of hay from the stables, the muskiness of a man who should probably also have bathed before this conversation took place.

His lips linger, and I respond, my neck craned upwards.

When he pulls away from me, his skin is flushed, and there's a wicked glint in his eyes.

'I would rather show you,' Lord Athelstan promises, reclaiming his seat, his eyes holding mine.

I can feel the blood rushing through my body, and I can see where his pulse flutters on his neck, just where a stray piece of his long hair curls down its length.

'And I would rather show you,' I respond, my voice soft but firm.

His laughter's unexpected.

'We'll get nowhere unless we learn to speak plainly to each other.'

I nod, swallow and open my mouth to speak, only for Lord Athelstan to beat me to it.

'I would marry you, Lady Ælfwynn, because I fear I love you, and I'd not let another hold you in their arms without wishing to tear them from your side. I would marry you because I wish to spend my time with you and, if we're blessed, to have children together. I'll not marry you to help you rule Mercia. Mercia is yours, and if we marry, you must command me, as you do all other men and women who make Mercia their home. That's my restriction, and you must agree to it and ensure all men know the same.'

'I'd not have you in my shadow as your mother once was. You have the right to rule, and you'll do so.' I can't deny that his words have more than stunned me.

For a moment, I think of taking them as an insult, but I realise then that my choice is the best possible one. Lord Athelstan is a man I've grown to care genuinely for and admire for his attention to the interests of Mercia, but he's also intelligent. No other noble in Mercia would take kindly to any man trying to rule in my name. Indeed, if that were the case, the attempts to put King Edward to one side would have been for nothing.

I nod.

'I'd hear you say it aloud,' Lord Athelstan demands.

'Then I would marry you because I care for you and because you'll support me in ruling Mercia and will, hopefully, be the father of my children. But you'll not rule Mercia. I'll command you as I do all Mercians.'

Lord Athelstan smiles then and stands once more. I think he'll kiss me as he did before, but instead, he takes to one knee, a mischievous glint in his eyes.

'Then, Lady Ælfwynn, would you marry me?'

Even now, there's an edge to his question. I breathe deeply, assuring myself that I'm doing the right thing.

'I will,' I confirm, and his smile lights the room.

It's done. I'll have a husband. And damn Lord Rǫgnvaldr and my uncle. I'll have a husband I care for and one who doesn't want me so that he can rule my kingdom.

CHAPTER 6

But of course, nothing is accomplished quite that easy. It never is.

Lord Athelstan might have made an agreement, and we might both be pleased with it. But there is, as Ealdorman Æthelfrith and Cousin Athelstan delight in telling me, more than just two people in the marriage.

Blood-month or Blotmonað has passed by the time the announcement can be made, and the wedding planned.

For all I never thought I wished to marry, I find the delay to be intolerable. More than once, I bite my tongue so hard I taste blood, as I'm forced to endure tedious meetings.

Personally, and of course, I share the opinion with no one else, I'm convinced that the extended delay is merely because the weather has closed in around us. The threat of snow is never far away, and the men and women who've chosen to reside in Tamworth for the dark time of the year, want something to occupy their bored minds.

Why else, I decide, would there be such dreary arguments about the smallest of matters. Lord Athelstan and I have our agreement. We'll not waver from the decision that we'll marry. Lord Athelstan will be my husband, not my lord to command me, and Mercia. I see no reason to have the stipulation written in law.

'It's because I'm a woman,' I rant to Eoforhild, when frustrated by yet another meeting, I stalk outside. Despite the hard ground and crisp frost, I proceed to demand we train with seax and shield.

We're not alone on the training field, but we may as well be.

Another duo duel with each other, but they're much closer to the palace complex, and I know they're only outside because cousin Athelstan has ordered it. They'd sooner be playing *tafl* within the great hall, but an argument yesterday grew too rowdy and bloody. Cousin Athelstan, outraged by the altercation, has sentenced them both to train, each and every morning, for two weeks. No matter the weather.

'It's because you're the Lady of Mercia,' Eoforhild responds with equanimity. We've had this discussion on any number of occasions in the last three weeks.

'I know who I am,' I huff, my shield before my body as Eoforhild tries to get close enough to make her 'kill.'

'Then you shouldn't have expected it to be easy.'

'But I'm the Lady of Mercia,' I complain. 'I command them. No one else.'

'It doesn't work like that,' her voice is muffled as I attack her shield and she holds it before her body and head.

'Well, it bloody should be,' I argue, shoving my shield against hers, and trying to find a space between her shoulder and shield to angle my seax.

'There's no need to rush,' Eoforhild tries to distract me with those words. As she abruptly dashes toward me, my grip loosens on my shield. Her arm's extended and her shield held to the left.

'Bugger,' I complain, throwing my shield to the hard ground as I feel her blade against my sleeve. I wish I could stamp my feet and shout my frustrations, but of course, someone would notice and then everyone would be whispering about it.

Eoforhild laughs, and while her breath steams before her, chest heaving, I consider, for a split moment, charging her and thrusting her to the floor.

'Don't even think about it,' Eoforhild gasps, realising my intent, almost before I do, eyes flashing dangerously.

She's wearing all of her warrior's gear, complete with the silver Mercian eagles that glint on her shoulders. They're my symbol, the symbol of Mercia and I'd far sooner wear them than the Wessex wyvern, and yet they mock me.

This should be my kingdom to order. But in a matter as close to me as my marriage, I'm thwarted. I should be married already. I shiver at the thought. I don't know if it's with dread or desire.

I never thought to hunger after the touch of a man. But perhaps I do.

'Your cousin will have the matter concluded soon. I'm sure.'

Cousin Athelstan. He's become strangely reluctant about the marriage in recent weeks, and so too have others. I imagine I know why. But it's disappointing.

Lord Rǫgnvaldr is the problem.

His rumours are insidious, but they also seem to mask some truth. He wishes to be my husband, and although I don't know how he learned of my intentions toward Lord Athelstan, the border with York has been far from calm. Indeed, Ealdorman Æthelfrith has ridden to the borderlands to determine just how much damage has been done.

There are whispers that Lord Rǫgnvaldr prepares an attack on Derby and a delegation, led by Reeve Sigehelm arrived at Tamworth only two days ago.

I've spent my valuable time discussing the problem with him. I'm not sure I've accomplished what I wanted to, and when I've finished with my training, I must endure yet another meeting with him.

'The matter will be concluded when all the interested parties have rung from me the concessions that they want.'

'Well, that as well.' Eoforhild agrees. She's waiting; hand on hip, for me to decide my next move.

I don't want to call an end to our training, neither do I feel the usual satisfaction that such physical activity gives me. In fact, Eoforhild has beaten me four times so far. Unusually, my skills seem to have deserted me, or rather, my mind can't find the purity of resolve it usually does.

'Bugger it,' I complain again, slumping to my knees, unheeding of the cold that seeps through my trousers as I twist my seax between my thumb and fingers.

I could wish the blade was sharp enough to draw blood and rouse my skills, but I know it isn't.

Eoforhild remains standing, her expression pensive.

'Your mother never found it easy,' she conveys, as though imparting a great secret. 'She was as frustrated as you are for much of the time. Lord Æthelred's death was a blessing for her.'

'So you're suggesting that all will be better if my husband-to-be were dead already?' Eoforhild's face bleaches of colour at the interpretation I've given to her words.

'No, that wasn't what I was suggesting,' her counter loud and vocal.

'Well, it sounded like it was to me.'

'What I was trying to say, is that your Lady Mother rarely had it her own way all the time, either. Her rule was more often than not through compromise than through exerting her will.'

'She had the reputation to make the nobility do as she wanted them to do. I'm not so blessed,' my lips sour as I speak. I'm not used to feeling dejected, but I do.

'Lord Rǫgnvaldr is all spit and bile. He won't attack Derby, and even if he does, Derby has a solid burh wall around it now. He'll lose many warriors, and Derby won't fall.'

'That's not the point, though, is it? I never agreed to a marriage with him. In fact, I made it bloody clear that it would never happen. Now, I'm being forced to marry hastily to stop the rumours. Yet, in doing so, I'm threatening the stability of Mercia, just as much as I threaten it while the whispers remain current. I can't win, either way and fuck it, it's annoying.' I end on a screech of frustration, my cry echoing in the cold air.

I can feel Eoforhild watching me, but I refuse to meet her gaze. I know she'll want to say something to drag me from my dejection, but right now, there's nothing to do but wait, and of all things, it's that which frustrates me the most.

Why should I be patient? Why should so many other people manipulate me when I'm the ruler of Mercia?

Surely I should be able to resolve this problem now that I've found the solution. But apparently, I can't.

The silence grows around us. I don't know what I want her to say, but the silence is as vexing as the waiting, and no doubt she knows it.

'Fuck it,' I mutter, climbing to my feet with resignation when the quiet lengthens to uncomfortable. 'Let's fight.'

'My Lady,' she half-bows. It's all the respect I'm going to get until I take her down, for the first time.

With my seax and shield back in my hands, I concentrate on more than my frustration. This time, when I make the first attack, I feel Eoforhild's stance gives a little.

Good, I think to myself, I haven't lost all of my skill as well as my control.

Not that Eoforhild makes it easy for me to restore my self-belief. By the time I've forced her to counter my attack five times, and she's fought her way beyond me only once, sweat runs freely from my hairline and into my eyes. I feel more alert, and more settled, and damn it, she knows it.

'Better?' the taunt is there just to make sure I won't lash out again.

'Perhaps,' I counter, unprepared to allow her to revel in her achievements.

'You won't be able to do that when you're with child,' she counters, her voice sour. I round on her, the comment unlooked for and unwanted.

'Why do you say that?' I demand to know.

'You're giving all this up,' and she indicates our weapons with her outstretched hand, 'just to stop some idiots from spreading tales about you. I wouldn't do it,' she complains. I bite back my initial retort, allowing her to continue.

'Go to York, defeat Lord Rǫgnvaldr. He's only a man. We could take York from him. Secure the walls around the place. Keep it as part of Mercia, and there'll be no need to marry. You could live your life without the duties of being a wife.'

Her words so closely resemble how I used to think, that they force a ripple of laughter.

'Who would I leave Mercia too then?'

Of all the things I could have said, this stops her straight away.

'Whoever wants it?'

'But it was my mother's.'

'She can't have cared for it that much. She never arranged a marriage for you, a good marriage. She never even advised you to marry and have children.'

'My mother nearly died birthing me. I doubt it was her highest priority.' I hear the outrage in my voice, and I try to consider whether Eoforhild's words might be correct.

'Did she intend for her brother to claim Mercia after her death then?'

'I doubt it, but whatever else you can say about her, she was a dutiful daughter to her father. Everyone says King Alfred's aim was to unite Wessex and Mercia.'

'No,' and here, I lower my voice. 'That's only what people say. My mother had no intention of doing that. She married my father for an entirely different reason. She believed in an independent Mercia, not a Mercia ruled by Wessex.'

'So why didn't she make you marry and why would you now?' The heat of the question surprises me.

'Why shouldn't I marry?'

'Why should you? Others can do such a simple task as breed. Few can fight as you do.'

'Perhaps, but no one can fight as I can, and give birth to the next generation of rulers of Mercia.'

Eoforhild grunts unhappily as I speak and falls quiet.

'I don't marry to get away from all this,' I eventually say, lifting my arms to indicate the training ground.

'Then you'll still need your warriors?' she queries. All of a sudden, I understand the fear behind the questions.

'I'll always need people to guard me, fight with me, and keep me safe. I'll always need you, and Ymma, Lioba, Firamodor, Leofgyth and Erna. Never fear. Anyway,' I bite. 'Why would I have to give up my warriors when I marry? My husband wouldn't expect me to, and he won't be giving up his warriors. It's a ludicrous worry,' I conclude, a sliver of irritation in my voice.

'You bloody fool,' I finish, and she has the good grace to look reticent.

What else we might have been about to discuss is lost by the arrival of Lord Athelstan, looking altogether too pleased with himself.

'Tomorrow the announcement will be made, and a feast will celebrate our intended union, which will take place in the new year.'

'Thank fuck for that,' I mutter, taking in his self-satisfied smirk that quickly falls from his face at my less than timorous words.

'What?' I demand to know, my eyebrows high, challenge ripe in my voice.

'Nothing, my lady. I'm just pleased it satisfies you.'

'So you should be,' I state, aware I'm sweaty and dishevelled, my hair coming loose from its tight braids. With a wink to Eoforhild, I hand my weapons to her and link my arm through Lord Athelstan, where he wears his court robes. He grimaces at my stench, and I laugh.

'You don't expect me to give up my fighting, do you?' I demand to know, riled by Eoforhild's words, despite my denial of them.

'Far from it, my lady. I think I made clear what I expected.'

'Excellent. Then let's ensure that everyone else knows that as well. I'll not have any more damn complaints about my leadership and rule.'

He inclines his head, eyes flickering to Eoforhild. She glares at him, and I hear a soft sigh escape his mouth at her fierce gaze.

'Everyone makes assumptions before they know the actual truth.' His voice is rough with frustration, and I realise that he's being subjected to just as many complaints as I am.

'Perhaps, we can prove everyone wrong. Together,' I announce. He grins at my words, while Eoforhild has the good grace to look reprimanded.

'Come,' Lord Athelstan states. 'They want to tell you in person, and I think you might need to change clothes before they believe you're the Lady of Mercia.'

I chuckle at his words.

Lord Athelstan will never forget who I am.

CHAPTER 7

'M y Lady,' the voice is rough and filled with dread. I turn to face the person who speaks, while my mind tries to wrench itself away from the tedious details of the feast ordered to celebrate my forthcoming marriage. Lady Ecgwynn is gracious as she assists me, but even she lifts an eyebrow at my aggravated tone. Perhaps she knows that I've been hoping for such an interruption.

'What is it?' I demand to know, imagining all sorts of scenarios. I take in the sight of the man admitted into my hall, Eoforhild at his side.

Has my uncle chosen to invade Mercia on this most auspicious of occasions? Have the Welsh finally decided to rebel against Mercia? Have Viking raiders been sighted on one of the many rivers?

'Derby, my lady. Lord Rǫgnvaldr leads the attack, in person.'

'Damn,' I complain, already starting to remove the crown settled on my hair only moments ago.

'Damn, damn, damn,' I continue to complain, looking down at the dress I wear in place of my usual trews and tunic. I need to change. I don't miss Eoforhild's hint of amusement at my obvious distress.

'Tell me everything,' I instruct, looking around, but already I can see that Lady Ecgwynn is issuing instructions to the women who serve me in my bedchamber. She's resigned to what will happen next. Lady Ecgwynn already knows that they'll be no feasting tonight.

'I saw the men when I travelled to Derby. The settlement doesn't burn, but the force encamped around the burh walls is large. The tents stretched off far into the distance north.'

'Why did no one tell me of this sooner?' I don't expect an answer, as I rush to my chamber. The man doesn't follow, but Eoforhild does. She must know the story because she continues to speak.

'My lady, I don't believe anyone from Derby can escape to inform us.'

'It's bloody winter,' I fume, hastening back to my hall, my eyes taking in the sight of the greenery festooning the ceiling and walls, the winter flowers and warm spices that infuse the air, on what should have been the night of my marriage announcement feast, but which now won't be.

'Get me Ealdorman Æthelfrith and Lord Athelstan. Get them quickly.' A servant scurries away to find those I need, while Eoforhild stands ready for my instructions, muttering under her breath.

'Rǫgnvaldr. The damn bastard.'

I nod, my expression tight.

'My mother always warned me against allying with the Viking raiders. She was right to do so.'

'I'll ensure your warriors are ready,' Eoforhild bows her head as she strides toward the door, flinging it open without waiting for the door wardens, and only just avoiding the hurrying figures I've had summoned.

'What's happened?' It's cousin Athelstan who speaks, although Ealdorman Æthelfrith's mouth is also open, the question dying on his lips.

'Derby's under attack.' I find no need to honey my words.

I turn then, aware I know little else.

'You. Come here. Tell me, what's your name?' The man who came to warn me turns his face upward, and I realise he's little more than a boy, almost blue with cold.

'Get him some clothes,' I demand before he can answer my question.

His mouth trembles and I wish I'd thought to feed him as soon as he entered the hall.

'Warm wine, food, feed the man.'

He nods gratefully, suddenly the centre of everyone's attention.

'Sigurd, my lady. Sigurd, son of Ivarr, the skald.'

'He sent you?'

'My lady, he did. He said you should know straight away that Derby's under attack, that he estimates there are five hundred enemy encamped, that they've brought many baggage carts. They block all of the gates into Derby.'

'And where's Ivarr?' I'm trying to remember who Ivarr is, and whether I've actually ever met him.

'He's hurt his leg, and can't ride as fast as I can. He's coming to Tamworth, only more slowly.'

'What are your commands?' If Ealdorman Æthelfrith is dismayed by the abrupt change to the evening's arrangements, he doesn't show it, even though he wears his ceremonial tunic.

'We'll ride out, access the situation, and then drive Lord Rǫgnvaldr back to York. Hopefully, we might get the chance to kill him along the way. We'll break Derby free from the menace. Damn,' I complain. 'Derby has only just accepted the rule of Mercia. I won't lose her now. My uncle will infer that it's my weakness as a ruler that allows Derby to fall back under the clutches of one of the Viking raiders.'

Ealdorman Æthelfrith eyes me steadily as two of his sons rush into the hall, my future husband one of them.

'It doesn't matter what King Edward of Wessex believes. It's the Mercians who matter. They'll not blame you for what's happening in Derby.'

I sigh with annoyance, but Ealdorman Æthelfrith's words steady me.

'It'll soon be dark, but I think we must ride all the same.'

I become aware of something touching my left hand and turn, my right hand flashing to my seax, only to realise that one of my women is fiddling with my hand. I look down, the flash of the ceremonial jewellery catches my eye. I dredge a smile from somewhere and hold my hand steady as she unclasps the bracelets and then forces the rings from my fingers.

She bows and darts from my side.

I should have thanked her, but she's gone too quickly.

I can't imagine, for the women who see to my needs, that I'm an easy mistress. Certainly, they try hard not to chastise me for my rough skin and bruises earned on the battlefield.

'I agree. It's a well-worn path, and the moon's bright tonight. And, Lord Rǫgnvaldr won't be expecting you. A dawn attack would bring this outrage to a quick and tidy end.'

I nod my agreement. I thought I'd be spending the night doing something else entirely. But this is just as appealing. I should like to grind Lord Rǫgnvaldr's bones into the dirt.

'Who'll remain in Tamworth?' It's cousin Athelstan who asks. I'm not sure, from his tone, whether he wishes to take the dubious honour or not.

'Lord Ælfstan can hold Tamworth, and have the command of the reserve force, although let's hope it won't be needed. But someone will also need to go south and west, ensure that Wessex and Wales haven't arranged a concerted attack against us. I don't trust my uncle not to have organised something on such a grand scale.'

More and more people join us as we stand and make our arrangements in the hall. I truly want my husband-to-be to ride north with me, but they esteem him on the borderlands with the Welsh, and that makes his presence there vital. Ealdorman Æthelfrith's family is long-lived in the area.

'I'll go west,' Lord Athelstan's firm voice brokers no argument, and I feel grateful he's decided for me.

His father nods, as though he expected the same. Ealdorman Æthelfrith will want to come with me, but he's so well respected in Mercia, and so well known that he'll have to go south for me.

There's a pause, as though he waits for me to speak, but then he nods his head.

'Ætheling Athelstan, you'll have the honour of ensuring your cousin remains safe, and of fighting at her back. I'll go south. I know my fighting days are behind me, but my warriors are more sprightly than I am. I trust that's acceptable?' The ealdorman's fierce eyes meet mine.

'Yes. Then we all know what must be done. Let's hope that in a week's time, we can continue our feasting and celebrating. Know that I trust all of you with my life, and more importantly, with maintaining Mercian independence. Now, let's prepare.'

'My lady,' the acceptances are roughly spoken. I might not always have been the one issuing the commands, but we've all been at this game for long enough. We're not fooled enough to think no one will die, or that we'll all be here next week. That said, I also know the strength of each of my allies. If this attack is just from Lord Rǫgnvaldr, there's no real need to fear.

If it involves Wessex and the Welsh, then our chances are narrower, but all the same, I think we'll prevail.

With that, everyone turns to leave, all apart from Lord Athelstan. He, too, is dressed in his ceremonial clothes, and I notice that the deep blue of his tunic suits him before I focus on his voice.

'My lady,' his voice is filled with warmth as he takes my hand. I look into his eyes, seeing a turmoil of emotions, all too difficult to voice.

I smile at him.

'This, my lord, is what you can expect when you're my husband.'

He grins at my sharp tone and then leans forward to kiss me gently, his breath a whisper against my skin.

'Be careful, my lady and my love.'

Without further words, Lord Athelstan strides from my presence. I watch him walk away with a pulse of desire, and also respect. He's not burdened me with any promises to stay alive, and I've returned the favour. I hope I'll see him again.

Lady Ecgwynn remains at my side, and she smirks at me, perhaps noticing that my skin flushes from his kiss.

With no more time to think, I follow my future husband outside. It's another cold night, and my breath plumes in front of me.

In front of the stables, men and horses mill about. There's a haze of exhaled air and smoking brands. I shudder. It's no night to ride to battle, but at least none of us will need to worry about being too hot.

Erna waits with my horse in front of the melee. She's hopping from foot to foot, no doubt to keep some warmth in them.

She grins at me, as Firamodor walks around the rest of the animals, checking equipment, and slapping the animals affectionately while admonishing my warriors when she discovers a problem.

Cousin Athelstan stamps to my side.

'There's no true need for you to go,' he says under his breath. He should know better than to argue with me, but it's just become our way of doing things.

'I'll be needed. I need to show myself to Lord Rǫgnvaldr. I'll not have him say that I made my cousin fight this battle for me.'

Cousin Athelstan grunts softly and then grips the tops of my shoulders with his hands.

'Then know that we'll beat him, and keep Derby safe. Then we'll ensure your kingdom isn't threatened again.' I know he means well, but I lack his conviction.

'I'll believe it when I experience it,' I mutter, before grinning. 'We'll fight together this time, as we've done in the past.'

'We will.'

When he's gone, I think my last-moment conversations are done with, only for Lady Ecgwynn to materialise from the fog; her cloak flung around her shoulders, her wrinkled nose a sign that despite the cold, all these animals in such a small space still stink.

'My lady, I pledge my support to you and assure you, this time, I'll not believe any rumours of your death until I see your cold, dead body for myself.' Her voice is part contrition and part defiance, a wobble in her voice revealing the depth of her emotions. I wrap my arms around her, feeling her body shiver beneath me.

'All will be well. I'm not going to let any Viking raider bastard kill me. Now, keep Tamworth safe, and work with Lord Ælfstan. You never know, we could celebrate a double wedding.'

'Urgh,' Lady Ecgwynn's cry is filled with distaste. 'I could never be with such a cold man.'

'He's not so bad,' I argue as she vehemently shakes her head.

'You only say that because you love his brother. No, Lord Ælfstan is too similar to my brother. Both of them are primed only for honour and duty.'

'I'm sure you could work on him, make him a little less severe.' I tease her, and she knows it.

'Of course, I could,' she complains, her head tilted upwards, arrogance evident in every line of her body. 'But I don't want to. No. Marriage doesn't appeal. Not with those I've seen as examples, and not just your mother's to your father.'

'Then, keep Tamworth safe for me and try not to argue too much with Lord Ælfstan.' This comment is more to her liking, and she kisses me on both cheeks and then turns away decisively.

'You know I don't like to watch everyone riding to battle,' she cries over her shoulder, and I nod, even though she can't see me. It's always been the same with Lady Ecgwynn.

CHAPTER 8

As I feared, the night is bitterly cold. I'm not alone in hunkering as low as possible into the saddle of my horse, pulling my cloak as tight as it will sit around my neck.

Bloody Viking raiders. Icy cold seems to run in their veins. Certainly, the weather is poor for battle.

I've heard many tales of the lands to the far north from where the Viking raiders originated. I've listened to the stories of the deep snow and ice that never seems to clear, other than from under the heat of the near-constant summer sun. It doesn't surprise me that people who live in such frozen conditions find Mercia so much more appealing.

Cousin Athelstan brings his horse to my side, his face all but hidden beneath his cloak.

'Bloody bastards,' his muffled words almost bring a smile to my face, but my cheeks feel frozen in place. I'd give almost anything to be sat beside the fire, absorbing the heat and thinking only of marriage.

But I know my responsibilities.

'Soddin' bastards,' I agree, tasting the ice that's forming along the trackway we follow to Derby.

There are scouts ahead of us, and every so often, a voice can be heard from out of the gloom assuring everyone that the way forward is clear.

Other than that, there's little to mar the silence of night other than the steady plodding of the horses' hooves and the occasional jingle of the harness. The smoking brands that are held aloft by every other rider cause pools of light to form over the silent landscape. The fields are bare of all life, and those animals lucky enough to be selected to live through the winter, are kept safe in the winter lodgings prepared for them.

We could almost be alone in the world.

'Thank you for allowing me to come with you,' cousin Athelstan's words surprise me, and I think he realises when a prolonged silence falls between us. I'm busy opening and closing my mouth, trying to decide how to respond to such a statement.

'Why wouldn't I?' I eventually manage.

Now it's cousin Athelstan's turn to stay silent too long. I hold my tongue, refusing to break the peace even when it stretches for so long. When he eventually speaks, I jump a little in shock.

'Well, it is my father and my brother who tried to take Mercia from you.'

'But you didn't,' I state. I'm both surprised and unsurprised that cousin Athelstan finally voices the worries that have concerned him since his father tried to bring about my death. Cousin Athelstan is too honourable not to worry about what happened, but I know it was nothing to do with him.

'But others might not see it that way.'

'Then they're fools. You and your sister have always been loyal to Mercia. My mother knew that, and so do I. Whatever your father does is nothing to do with you. While he acknowledges you as his son, that's all he does, and only when he wants something.'

'All the same. I wished you to know that I appreciate you allowing me to ride with you. It'll stop the rumours, I hope.'

'Well, just make sure you live through whatever attack we might face,' I order, dismayed to hear the unease in cousin Athelstan's voice. I don't like his doubts, even if I doubt myself.

It's not like him.

Silence falls between us, and I allow it. There's a comfort to having an ally beside me as the cold slowly drains the life from my fingers and toes. I only hope that Lord Rǫgnvaldr and his force don't come upon us right now. I can't imagine that any of us would be able to hold a weapon, despite the thick gloves we wear.

As wintry as it is, as the horses make their way along the many streams that block our way, a haze of fog envelopes us, making it even more challenging to see. If it weren't for the glow from the brands, dampened by the mist and made into flames no more substantial than those found on a candle, I'm sure many would become lost.

But, emerging from a band of fog, a voice from one of the scouts reaches my ears, although there's really no need for the cry.

In front of us, I can see the sky lit against the darkness of the night.

'Fire,' the words wrench from my throat. I didn't expect Lord Rǫgnvaldr to fire the settlement. I hadn't actually considered that he would. I've always thought it stupid to burn the very resource that the battle is over. I'm disappointed in him once more.

The scouts rush in from all sides, and I face cousin Athelstan, pulling back my hood so that all can recognise me in the light of the lamps.

'Fifty men to the western gate.'

'Fifty men to the northern gate.'

'The fires are burning on the outside.' The final statement causes my forehead to wrinkle in consternation as I listen to my scouts.

'So, it's not Derby itself that burns?' I call to the last scout before he can ride out again. His face shows his surprise at my question.

'No, my lady. Derby's wall is secure, and the gates as well. The fires are in front of the eastern gate.'

I hear my warriors reaching for weapons, the sound of iron being drawn echoing in the early grey light of a new day.

'How many warriors to the eastern gate?'

'I couldn't say, my lady. The flames make it impossible to see.'

'Take another scout with you, see if you can get closer, but don't risk yourselves unnecessarily.'

The scout turns to ride away, and I feel cousin Athelstan's gaze on me.

'Why would they set fire to the ground outside of Derby?'

'They want me to think Derby's under attack and rush in. No doubt there are more warriors waiting to trap us between the flames and the gate while they advance on us.'

Understanding washes over cousin Athelstan's face.

'Bloody bastards,' he complains, but already his thoughts have gone where mine have.

'I'll take twenty men,' cousin Athelstan states, and I nod and then grunt an agreement, realising that he might not see the action.

'I'll ride into the trap once we know it is a trap, and I'll trust you to come and rescue me.'

'I doubt you'll need rescuing, but I'll stay in the shadows. Do you think they know how large our force is?'

'It's impossible to tell. I thought we'd be safe from observation because of the dark and the cold, but allowing so many brands to be lit has probably given away our strength. Sigurd said there were five hundred men. We don't have that many, but our force will still be superior, provided Lord Rǫgnvaldr believes his trick fools us.'

Cousin Athelstan turns his horse to face back the way we've just come before he reaches out to clasp my arm.

'Stay alive,' he cautions me, his voice rich with the command, for all he speaks quietly.

'And you,' I repeat the instruction, and for a glimmer of a moment, we gaze into each other's eyes. I hope he sees the resolve I want him to see. Certainly, I'm sure he'll rescue me, should it come to that.

As he rides away, like cousin Ecgwynn earlier, I refuse to watch.

There've been too many battles for either of us to know that the survival of anyone we care for is guaranteed. I would never want the final glance of my cousin to be of his back, riding away, to carry out my express commands.

I know that I've fought for my birthright, but there are some aspects of it that I find almost too hard to carry out. And yet, I must.

For I'm the Lady of Mercia, and cousin Athelstan is my oathsworn warrior.

He'd not thank me for worrying about ordering him to his death.

I only wish I didn't.

Eoforhild takes his place. In the shadows, I can see her brow's furrowed, hands busy on harness and seax.

'Bloody bastard,' I laugh softly, the sound surprising Eoforhild, whose eyes flick toward me.

'It's what cousin Athelstan said,' I explain, reaching down to ensure my stirrups are the length I like, adjusting them a little when I stand upright and realise one leg is lower down than the other.

How these things happen when I'm riding, I have no idea.

'They mean to trick us,' Eoforhild's voice is ripe with scorn. She believes in a fair fight. I agree with her.

'He does, yes. Damn fool. Doesn't he realise we've witnessed every Viking raider trick there is or been told about them by our parents?'

'I thought him a more honourable man than this.' Contempt ripples in Eoforhild's voice.

'I think we all did. But, it won't be the first time that men have kept their loyalty for only as long as it takes them to think of a new betrayal.'

'I'll lead the warriors into the attack. You should give me your byrnie and stay safe with the relieving force.'

The words are spoken by rote. Just as cousin Athelstan asked me to remain in Derby, Eoforhild knows I'll never agree to her suggestion. Neither do I offer her a reply. She knows better.

'Then we should get closer,' Eoforhild states. 'At least act as though we suspect Derby to be on fire.'

'I suppose so,' I'm squinting against the gloom, trying to decide whether the scout was correct in his interpretation of what's happening. Not that I don't trust him, far from it, it's just that I know the darkness can be deceptive.

'Only thirty warriors to the southern gate,' still my scouts ride in, give their information, and then turn and race out again. There's some distance to go on the road, and while I should really rush headlong to the eastern gate, as though concerned Derby burns, I don't want to. Not yet.

'We'll go with the light,' I eventually announce. I think that Lord Rǫgnvaldr will believe I suspect a trap if I don't show some rudimentary caution.

'My lady,' Eoforhild gives no hint in her voice to show whether she agrees with my decision or not, just rides smartly away to issue the commands to those who'll ride with me.

My force isn't as large as Lord Rǫgnvaldr's, not if the scouts are correct, but it's not the numbers that worry me. It's whether Lord Rǫgnvaldr acts alone or not.

Do I suspect my uncle of being involved in this? I'd be lying to myself if I said I didn't. But would he honestly rather have an alliance with one of the despised Viking raiders than seek to mend the rift between us?

I wish I knew, especially as unease shudders down my back, almost as audible as the thick ice that's formed on the trackway during the elongated darkness of a winter's night.

Is this a ploy, a plot, or just the actions of a man desperate to bring about something he knows will never get my agreement?

'A hundred men,' my scout's returned to me from the eastern gate. His eyes are haunted.

'A hundred, are you sure?'

'As sure as we can be. They're hiding wherever they can, using the shape of the land to mask them. The main camp, as far as we can tell, is to the north, as you'd expect, but it's lightly guarded.'

This doesn't make the five hundred warriors that Sigurd told me were here. Did his father miscount, or is Lord Rǫgnvaldr concealing his men somewhere else?

I rein in my horse and turn to survey the landscape, wishing the cover of night would lift so I could see more.

Ahead, the hint of dawn is steadily growing, while behind me, the land remains cast in darkness. It could mask anything. Certainly, I can't see my cousin, and I know some of the warriors he took with him had brands.

In my mind, I consider the layout of the land as I remember it. Derby is below us, in a natural dip, the river running through it, the recently completed walls topping the earthen bank, the enormous wooden gates heavy and awkward to move.

I feel as though I'm missing something.

Why would Lord Rǫgnvaldr lay such a trap? It's both more compli- cated than I might expect while also being far too simple.

Perhaps I'm looking for betrayal in the wrong places. Maybe it's not my uncle who aids Lord Rǫgnvaldr, but the people of Derby?

As much as I hate to admit it, this revelation settles my unease.

If we ride to the aid of Derby, will they simply attack us? Is Derby, despite all I thought to the contrary, willing to be ruled by the self- proclaimed king of York?

I wish I'd kept cousin Athelstan by my side. I'd seek for his advice.

'What is it?' Eoforhild rides back to me, the impatience evident in how she holds her reins and directs the horse, even without the acerbic tone she uses.

'It's a trap,' the words taste leaden in my mouth.

'Yes, we know that already.'

'No. It's more than we thought. I've been betrayed by someone inside Derby as well.'

'What?' her response is whip sharp. I feel it straighten my back, unaware it had even slumped.

'The fires, they mean to trap us, and then some force or other, perhaps the Derby fyrd members, or even some of Lord Rǫgnvaldr's men, will attack from behind. We're supposed to think that the flames are the enemy and that if we get beyond them, we'll have the safety of the wall and earthworks at our back, but we won't.'

'How do you know this?' Eoforhild's confusion almost brings a smile to my tight lips.

'It's obvious, unfortunately.'

'Then what will we do?'

'We've little choice. We have to ride into the trap, but I need more than cousin Athelstan to be held in reserve. Halve this force. We'll take only the smallest number to be convincing. That messenger who came to Tamworth might have given us more warning than Lord Rǫgnvaldr planned, but our enemy knows we're here and have moved quickly to put their deceit into action. This is meticulously calculated much better than the half-arsed way it appears.'

'That'll leave us with only thirty Mercians, and the messenger says there are five hundred warriors. The scout reports a hundred of them were outside the eastern gates.' It's not fear that makes Eoforhild speak, but bewilderment. Why she's thinking, would I leave myself so exposed?

'Yes, there are,' I don't offer an explanation. 'But we have no choice. I want you to focus on finding Lord Rǫgnvaldr. I want him to personally answer for this. And I'd not have his life taken from him too cheaply.'

'But I must fight at your side.'

'No, you mustn't. I want you to find Lord Rǫgnvaldr, and Firamodor will have the command of the remaining force. They'll ride to my assistance only when cousin Athelstan makes his intentions known.'

Again, I wish that I'd kept cousin Athelstan at my side. I don't want him to panic and attack too soon. I need to give Eoforhild time to find Lord Rǫgnvaldr.

'My lady,' the scout from the western gate's returned. I'm surprised enough time has elapsed to enable him to ride around Derby and return, but it has. His message confirms my suspicions.

'My lady, the western gate lies unprotected by Lord Rǫgnvaldr's warriors.'

'Ah, there we have it,' I nod, satisfied with my reasoning. 'They've gained admittance to Derby. It's they who'll attack us from the eastern gate. Now, you need to go back that way,' I point along the trackway we've just ridden. 'Find Lord Athelstan, tell him that Derby's betrayed. Order him only to ride to relieve my force when all appears lost. Inform him I'll have fewer warriors than he believes.'

'My lady?' The messenger bows his head despite his question and encourages the horse away from Derby. I appreciate that he doesn't dispute my instructions. I interpret that as a sign that he believes my reasoning to be sound. I hope it is.

'Are you sure about this?' Eoforhild, of course, doubts me, and I nod. It wouldn't be right if everyone just followed my instructions without thought.

'Yes. Now go. Find Lord Rǫgnvaldr for me, and if you can't, then chase him as far from Derby as it's possible to get.'

Without arguing, Eoforhild calls Mildryth and Ymma to her side, and I listen to them ride out of hearing distance.

CHAPTER 9

F iramodor quickly replaces Eoforhild. As I issue my instructions, her face remains impassive. She'll not question me.

In no time at all, everyone is aware of what's happening, and the force has been divided. I reach down and whisper to my horse.

'Now's the time for action,' I confirm. She startles at my tone of voice before calming. It's always the way. She senses what's about to come as surely as I do.

'Ride on,' I order, the sun just beginning to stain the horizon with the reds of a cold winter's day. I'm not in the front row of warriors. Instead, my loyal Mercians ride ahead of me. These men protected my mother before her death. They're fearless warriors, schooled in the art of defeating Viking raiders. I wouldn't say that they live only to fight because they also love to drink and fornicate, but they're the men who quell others and excite fear in almost everyone.

They'll enjoy this, even if some of their comrades fall in the attack. Then they'll mourn them, drowning their sorrows in gallons and gallons of ale, mead and lousy wine. They'll shout toasts to the dead, and when they can take no more, they'll slump into sleep, only to wake, empty their bladders and begin all over again.

I've witnessed the ritual too many times. It'll never change. The people conducting it will, but the tradition is set. I approve of it.

Firamodor grins recklessly at me from her place at my side. Her horse is as frisky as ever, scenting the smoke but keen all the same. Lioba rides to my left. She's more dour but probably more determined. It's in silence that she finds the strength to kill and to live to see another battle.

We ride three deep, the noise of hooves over the brittle road loud to ears grown used to little more than the thrum of deepest night and their own breath. While I'd hoped to arrive before Lord Rǫgnvaldr knew of our approach, the depth of the silence assures me that men are alert to our passage. Perhaps they almost hold their breath to avoid being detected.

If I hadn't realised what was planned, I know I'd be riding into a trap that could bring about my death. Or worse.

But, to convince Lord Rǫgnvaldr that his perfidiousness hasn't been discovered, I must act in the way I imagine he'd think I would.

With a flash of remorse, I give the command.

'Charge,' the word echoes through the sharp coldness. As though the animals were waiting to hear it, I feel my horse's legs bunch and then fly forward, the actions mirrored by the other animals.

We'd not normally fight from the saddles, but today might be one of those rare occasions.

As though waiting for my action, the sun abruptly bursts open across the horizon, like an egg broken before it can be cracked. Yellows and oranges burn with the deeper red of winter, and we can see both more and less than when night still reigned supreme.

Trusting my mount, I tighten my hold on the saddle, not on the reins, and as she thunders forward, hazard a glance around me. I'm hoping to find where Lord Rǫgnvaldr's men are hiding, but the horse moves too quickly. There's a blur of white, a glimmer of bare earth, the winter stealing the heat from the land and the air while the plants struggle to maintain a tenuous link on the soil.

My enemy has chosen their places of concealment well. I'm frustrated and awed.

I've no chance to look further before the warriors at the front of the pack are playing their part in the subterfuge.

'Derby doesn't burn,' the words are repeated as loudly as they can be shouted. Our orderly procession comes to an abrupt stop, horses turning at their riders' commands, hands, already close to seaxes, hovering ever closer as the ruse is discovered.

'The gates are opening,' another shouts into the confusion. All eyes look toward Derby and to where the gates are visible through the guttering flames.

'It's the enemy,' the voice is frantic, almost hoarse. I'm pleased I've placed my helm to cover my cheeks; otherwise, Lord Rǫgnvaldr's men might see my wry smirk of surprise at how well my warriors can lie.

'It's a trap,' Firamodor is the one to shout the warning, and our small force seems to descend into panic, although instructions have been given as to who goes where. It appears we don't know what's happening. The truth couldn't be more different.

Only then do the enemy finally emerge from their hiding places.

They're fully armed, not just byrnies, but mail coats as well. The men that Lord Rǫgnvaldr commands are skilled warriors. Or, at the least, they dress as though they are.

In the glow of a new dawn, men rush at the horses with weapons raised, reflecting the yellow light of the flames that still burn, along with the rising sun.

'Dismount,' Firamodor yells the command as heavy feet fall to the hard earth, the movement jarring toes and legs numbed by the low temperature and the length of time in the saddle.

I do the same, turning my mount and reaching for my shield simultaneously. With a slap to her rump, my mount heads back the way we've come, the majority of the other horses following suit. Only one or two head off in stray directions as their riders shout curses after them. We'll not fight from the saddles, after all. Not today.

'Shield wall,' I bellow the order. To ward off the enemy from the front and the rear, we must make a tight circle, one shield overlapping another. There'll be no one to fill any gaps that form when the assault begins.

The sound of one shield slapping into place against another reminds me of thunder. I even find myself glancing upwards, just testing the sky to see if black clouds have formed, presaging a storm. But of course, they haven't. It's the wrong season for thunder. It's the wrong season for fighting as well.

With my shield before my eyes, I can see little of Lord Rǫgnvaldr and his men. I hope Eoforhild has found Lord Rǫgnvaldr, but there might not have been time. I look forward to punishing him for his treason, either on the slaughter field or when he's bound and on his knees before me.

He might think he's the lord of York, but after this outrage, he won't be. I might even claim it in my name and for Mercia, as Eoforhild suggested.

The first strike comes from the rear of the small circle. Thirty men and women, standing close enough together that shields can overlap, don't take up a tremendous amount of space.

'Hold,' the order shouted by one of my mother's warriors, his voice firm.

I hear my heavy breath. The anticipation of what will happen next is almost too much for me, and then it happens.

Whatever's been flung against the shield wall, it's heavy enough to make even my hand vibrate with the force, and I'm far from the impact site.

I grit my teeth, the necessary thirst for battle abruptly stealing my reasoned calm of earlier.

'Hold.' My voice ripples through the air. I feel those to either side of me, Firamodor and Lioba, ensure the grip is secure on their shields, their stance firm and their weapon of choice held just tightly enough in their hand to be effective. No one ever won a battle by clutching a blade to him or her like it was a child. Better to hold loosely, better to risk losing it, than have it rip your hand apart.

More and more thuds are felt on the shield wall. The shouts of my enemy are finally loud enough to penetrate beyond my heavy breath.

I strain, hoping to hear Lord Rǫgnvaldr's voice, but it's not him issuing the command.

'*Angreb.*' I've fought enough Viking raiders to know what that means.

'Steady now,' I mutter, ensuring my shoulder is close to my shield should I need more than just my hand and arm to keep it upright.

Almost as one sound, each enemy selects and attacks a single shield. It's timed to perfection. If I hadn't known there were thirty-one weapons all moving simultaneously, I could have been mistaken for thinking there was only one.

My arm absorbs the impact, preparing for what must come next.

I imagine if I had the vantage point, as the people of Derby do, that all they would see was the thin rim of a shield wall made by my warriors. That thin rim is surrounded by a horde of Viking raiders, all desperate to be the ones to cleave a path through it.

I hope, although I can't see, that the greatest concentration of that enemy is in front of my shield.

I stamp down, hard, on the blade that tries to work its way beneath my feet, perhaps slice upwards, thinking I'm a man and will do anything to protect my cock.

The ground's solid beneath me, the blade almost fracturing under the twin onslaught of ice and the fire that guides my actions.

More and more points and blades attempt to work themselves below, or even above, the shield.

I force them aside with my seax, stabbing across, or down, or even up. My feet are busy beneath me as I try to evade the blades that seek there.

To either side of me, I'm aware that my warriors replicate my actions. We're heavily outnumbered. The thirty men from the western gate have joined those who hid amongst the clumps of decaying growths, taking a route through the centre of Derby, and so eighty warriors attack our thirty.

And we must hold. For now.

Cousin Athelstan won't come to my aid. Not yet.

He knows that first, the Viking raiders must exhaust themselves trying to penetrate the shield wall.

My greatest fear is that the Viking raiders will have horses to drive against the shields.

No one will be able to stand against the weight of such an animal.

I hope our mounts have made their way to safety.

I pray that Lord Rǫgnvaldr hasn't even considered that we might abandon the animals before the battle.

'*Angreb.*' The word's angrier now, laced with a hint of derision. They thought this would be easier than it's proving to be.

'*Angreb.*' With each cry, the enemy redoubles their efforts. My shield hand begins to tremble, my teeth gritted against the agony of holding such a heavy piece of equipment in place for so long.

I might have complained that I was frozen solid before, but now sweat flows freely, dripping down my back, along the rim of my helm, and even turning my hands slick inside my thick leather fighting gloves.

I feel a lack of tension in the shield wall.

'Stand,' I shout. 'Stand and hold,' I bellow when that doesn't seem to have the desired effect.

A few of us could fall from the shield wall, and it should remain, provided those to either side are quick enough to sense the danger.

'Stand,' I holler, unable to look around and see if my plan has come to nothing.

'*Tæve,*' again, I recognise the Norse. It seems my cries have given away my position.

'Bastard,' I repay the kindness, wishing I could lower my shield and face my enemy eye to eye. But it's still not time.

The shield wall hardens, and I know whatever's happened has been dealt with. I pray one of my warriors hasn't been killed.

I've not yet drawn blood, but the frustrated strokes of my enemy, assure me that the time's nearly come.

It's not really a battle until my blade glints with the lifeblood of another.

My feet continuously move, my eyes alert to all dangers, the ragged blade of a sword or seax, trying to decide where my face might be.

I watch it curiously. It thinks I'm taller than I am and overextends. When too much of the arm's exposed, a slither of pale flesh showing above the leather gloves and below the trailing edge of the metal coat, I stab downwards with my blade. I watch the blood well with gratification. The blade thuds to the floor, the arm retracting too slowly. I force blood from the white flesh again, and while the wound's far from mortal, it gives me satisfaction all the same.

A bellow of rage echoes through the air. I think they shout 'tæve' once more. I smirk, making sure I'm not allowing such delight to give another enemy the opening to cut me.

I wish I knew how many had been injured and how much longer our shield wall needed to stand. But it's impossible to tell.

Something substantial hits the far side of my shield. I grimace. Whoever's replaced the bleeding warrior, if indeed they've been replaced, uses much heavier weapons. My arm screams with agony. I bite my lip, determined to distract myself from the effort.

This was my plan. I can't be the reason it fails.

I can't be the reason that Mercia falls, and not to my traitorous uncle, but to a bloody Viking raider, who may or may not, have been acting alone.

Realising just how stark the choices are, floods me afresh with the desire to succeed.

'Hold,' I reinforce. 'Hold, for Mercia,' the cry's taken up by Firamodor and then by the rest of our small group. I grin with savage delight as the chant of 'Mercia' booms louder than the feeble attack.

We'll stand, and we'll wait, and in the meantime, Lord Rǫgnvaldr's men will waste their strength and skill on a shield wall that'll never buckle.

My seax is busy in my hand, my eyes open so wide I feel as though I can see everything without having to move my head from side to side.

The blows on my shield grow intermittently stronger and then weaker, as though they try to fool me into dropping my guard, thinking my enemy floundering. But this isn't our task. Not today.

The blade grows thick with blood, and still, I'm uninjured.

But that's not the same for everyone.

Firamodor groans instead of chants, and I glance at her.

Her eyes meet mine.

'I'm hit, but I'll stand,' the words are a roar of rage and anger combined.

'I know you will,' I reply, noting the paleness of her lips. She's wounded, perhaps mortally, but I know better than to comment or even try and force her to rest.

She'll fight, and if she dies doing so, that's how it must be.

'It won't be long,' I growl, suddenly aware that my shield arm shakes with the effort. 'It won't be long,' I repeat, realising that the fighting is becoming dirty and reactionary.

My shield wall no longer stands proud but instead more by dint of sheer bloody determination than any great skill.

'Come on, cousin Athelstan,' I mutter, wishing I could summon him with just a thought and that I hadn't been so firm with my instructions. He could have arrived by now. I wouldn't have been angry with him for defying my command.

'For Mercia,' I try and entice my warriors to greater efforts. But we've been standing proud long enough that the ground beneath us has thawed, the hard edges of ice melting under the onslaught of feet and hot breath, and of course, the blood that's been shed.

This time the cry's more ragged, but it's still there. And still, we labour and fight for our kingdom.

And then, finally, when my shield arm's throbbing, my seax hand almost numb, the blade threatening to slide through unresponsive fingers, I hear the sound of others joining the battle.

I hope it's cousin Athelstan.

I hear something else too, and I giggle, the sound unbecoming on a battlefield, but the intensity of my relief allows it.

Derby might well have fallen under the sway of Lord Rǫgnvaldr, but the men and women who must defend the burh walls have come to our aid. Or so I surmise.

The whoosh of arrows rings through the air, thudding, not into my warriors' shields, but rather picking off the attackers behind me.

To the front, I hear the snarl of a voice I've never been more pleased to hear.

Cousin Athelstan has come, as I told him to, and no matter that Lord Rǫgnvaldr's men outnumbered my warriors, they're now just as trapped as they thought to make us.

The archers from Derby, as few in number as they are, pick off the Viking raiders behind me. To the front, cousin Athelstan and Eoforhild battle the warriors who thought they need do nothing than batter at our resolve to win.

Once more, strength flows through me. I'm stabbing and slicing whatever limbs or weapons make their way beyond my shield wall, or that of Firamodor's. Her actions are slower now. I protect her as much as I do myself. I'm mindful that, to her right, another of my warriors does the same.

He's a wiry man, built for speed, not strength. Now he uses his swiftness to stab and slash far more quickly than I could.

When he catches my eye, in a brief lull, his eyes shine forth from his helm with delight. He was born to kill Viking raiders.

The cry for Mercia still resounds, but it's sporadic until taken up by the force that comes to relieve us.

The rain of arrows falters. Only then do I dare to look anywhere but in front of me or at Firamodor. The shield wall is intact, but only just. If I squint, I can see the people of Derby on their burh walls. Above the gate, a small crowd of them cheers, their fists raised high. I hope they do so because we've won.

I look down, grimacing at the sight of so much churned blood. The tip of the grasses that have stayed frozen seem to gleam like rubies and not the pure diamonds typically left after such cold weather.

And then the cry comes.

'Trække sig tilbage,' I know what that means.

'Don't let them get away,' I roar. I want as many of them at my mercy as possible.

The shield wall abruptly disintegrates, with every man and woman determined to fight for themselves. They want to track down an enemy so that they can lay claim to one final kill.

I survey the landscape, not at all surprised to find the grinning face of Eoforhild hovering in front of me. The man, who must have been attacking me, slowly slides from the end of her blade, bright blood gushing from a deep wound, his mouth opening in surprise.

'Didn't see me coming,' she chortles, her lips flushed with triumph, which quickly clear as she catches sight of Firamodor.

'What the fuck happened to you?' Her voice is almost too loud, even above the hubbub of horses and people running and fighting, shrill with concern.

'Care for her,' I command, determined to have a kill to my name before the battle's finished.

'My lady,' but Eoforhild's words are lost below the sound of my feet moving quickly over the churned quagmire. I've caught sight of something that pleases me. I'm determined to reach the arrogant bastard before he makes his escape.

Lord Rǫgnvaldr did fight with his men, after all. Now, they rush for safety while he watches on, his lips, the only part of his face apart from his eyes that's visible below his helm, twisted with distaste.

He stands alone. His sword points downwards so that the tip drags on the hard ground, his clothes stained with Mercian blood. He's dressed as a warrior, his beard tied with yet more trinkets, perhaps from the kills he's made, and his nose as crooked as the last time I saw him.

Damn the bastard.

He oozes confidence even as he watches his men lose the battle.

'Lord Rǫgnvaldr,' I call his name, but the sound's weak, my exertions threatening to prevent me from achieving my wishes. He doesn't even look my way.

I pause, watching him. The urge to strike him down, here and now, is too strong to counter.

I can't deny how much I despise him and all the problems he's caused me. I thought he was my ally, but he wasn't.

As so often has been the case during my life, allies are only allies when it's convenient. He gained York with my assistance, even if all I did was help him kill the force led by Archbishop Lodeward. It was enough. Evidently, it isn't anymore.

I breathe deeply, trying to banish the ache in my back and the shaking of my thigh muscles.

This battle has been long, and still, I want Lord Rǫgnvaldr's death on my hands.

He remains. Does he wait for me? Or does he have some other surprise?

'Lord Rǫgnvaldr,' my voice finally finds some strength. He turns to gaze at me with the sound.

'Lady Ælfwynn,' I'm unsure of the tone he uses. It's certainly not that of a defeated man who faces his greatest opponent.

'I told you, I'm no 'lord.'' Lord Rǫgnvaldr smiles as he speaks, perhaps replaying the conversation in his head from when we first met. I would wipe that smile from his face.

'You told me you were no lord, that's true, but you were a king of Dublin, and so I'll name you 'lord' regardless of your wish.' My voice is filled with ice. 'Why don't you run?' I demand to know. It's my primary concern, far and above what he should be called.

'I don't run from the field of battle.'

'Not even when you've lost?' I taunt. His smile spreads into a grin as I face him, only ten paces between us. It would take nothing to rush across that small gap and slice my blade through the lips that mock me.

'Good, it'll make it easier for me to kill you,' I reach for my sword with my left hand. My grip's weak, but I persist, a seax in one hand and a sword in the other. I'll take Lord Rǫgnvaldr's life and enjoy doing so.

His laughter ripples loudly through the crisp air. I narrow my eyes at him.

It seems Lord Rǫgnvaldr thinks I'm incapable of killing him. That disappoints me.

'You'll not fight me?' I force as much resolve into my words as I can.

'Oh, I will. But not today. It looks like you might fall if I breathed on you the wrong way.'

'Looks can be deceptive,' I growl, infuriated by his mocking tone. Damn the bastard. I grip my seax tighter, opening and closing my fingers to assure myself that the grip can still be controlled.

There are still just ten paces between us.

Lord Rǫgnvaldr observes me, the ghost of a smile on his lips. It seems he's finally realised I'm serious in my demand for a battle between the two of us.

'You've won the battle. It'll all have been for nothing, though, if I kill you now.' The words are both compliment and contemptuous.

'You're very sure that you can do that. I beg to disagree.'

'That's because you're not standing where I am.' He raises his chin as though there's something behind me that I should see, but I don't move my eyes from his face. Behind me is the field of slaughter. My warriors move around it carefully, ensuring the dead are dead. They look for friends amongst the fallen and enemies among the breathing. They'll also be watching events play out between Lord Rǫgnvaldr and me. No harm will befall me.

Lord Rǫgnvaldr's full of tricks and deceit.

'Oh, very well,' he huffs, lifting his blade from where it rested on the ground, turning it upright so that the edge glints in the weak winter sunlight.

I notice then that there's no blood on that edge. Either he's found the time to clean the blade already, or he's made no kills.

Perhaps he's keen to blood it finally.

Lord Rǫgnvaldr walks towards me, his blade high and his other hand empty of a shield or a seax.

I follow his actions. One step, then two, and then three. We're close enough now that I detect his stench. Has he been sleeping in a pile of manure? It certainly smells as though he has.

He pauses, but I don't, taking another step and then another. We're close enough now that I can see where his pulse quickens on his neck, above the line of his byrnie.

Lord Rǫgnvaldr's almost within my reach. I can feel the battle calmness descending on me.

I grit my teeth, ready for him to make the final move, while I hold my sword ready to counter whatever move he makes. I've seen him fight. I know he's a clever opponent. Still, I'm sure I can better him, no matter what he does.

Time seems to stretch, and still, he does nothing. Instead, I hear the thud of horse's hooves over the ground, and relief seems to flicker in Lord Rǫgnvaldr's hard eyes.

But I'm done with waiting. With two quick steps, my blade is where his throat was, only a blink ago, but Lord Rǫgnvaldr's no longer there.

With my blade still high, I turn, startled. Where's he gone? The shimmer of the sun hitting my weapon dazzles me. By the time I find Lord Rǫgnvaldr, he's mounted on a fine black stallion, the animal throwing up tuffs of grasses as it dashes away from the field of slaughter.

I scream. The sound wrenched from my throat as though I keen for the dead.

How dare he flee this fight!

Only then my eye settles on my blade, and I feel all the frustration drain away.

There's a slash of blood there, Lord Rǫgnvaldr's blood.

He might have ridden away from this fight, but I scored first blood, and in time, I hope to finish the task I've begun.

CHAPTER 10

Cousin Athelstan finds me still standing at the spot where I hoped to kill Lord Rǫgnvaldr.

'Cousin?' the question in his voice is understandable. I've lost track of the length of time I've been motionless, looking without truly seeing.

'Yes?'

'There are traitors in Derby. Reeve Sigehelm has uncovered the plot against you.'

'Already?' I gasp, surprised and dismayed in equal measure. Recalled to the here and now, I'm suddenly aware of just how bloody cold I've become. The sweat of my exertions has dried, and now I shiver. Quickly, cousin Athelstan flings a cloak to me. I wrap it around my shoulders, trying to ignore the thick stench of horse and take the time to truly look at my cousin. He seems unhurt, although some blood mars his clothing.

'They did little to mask their treason because they were so sure of success.'

'Damn fools,' I complain, bending to wipe my bloodied blade on a straggling piece of weed. I don't feel the need to keep the reminder that I struck first blood. I'd sooner save my blade from rust.

'Take me to them,' I command, and cousin Athelstan moves to dismount.

'I'll walk, no need for that. Tell me. How many were killed?' Whether cousin Athelstan approves of me walking while he rides, I don't much care. He has no choice but to follow when I begin to make my way back to the field of slaughter.

'Less than half, I think. They all had mounts. They'll be back at the Humber River in no time at all.'

'Then we were successful, but Lord Rǫgnvaldr will live to fight another day.'

'He will, but perhaps he'll be warier now.'

I snort loudly.

'You fought well?' I ask him.

'Yes, but you and your warriors did all the work,' he grumbles. 'I waited as long as I could. It appeared your defence would collapse at any moment.'

'I was almost begging for you to arrive,' I confess, walking around a dead body, staring at the upturned face, trying to decide if I knew the man or not.

'Then I timed it perfectly?'

'As always,' I chuckle softly. 'I'd have preferred to capture Lord Rǫgnvaldr,' I confess ruefully.

'I'm sure there'll be more opportunities to do so,' Cousin Athelstan's comment doesn't fill me with the hope he thinks it will.

'You believe he'll attack again?' I turn to face him, stopping so abruptly that his horse has moved beyond me before an answer's forthcoming.

'No, but I don't believe he'll stop trying to worm a toe-hole into Mercia either. No doubt he believes himself capable of leading the second Great Heathen Army. The Viking raiders are always keen to emulate their forefathers.'

I growl then, the sound low in my chest, noticing from the corner of my eye that Firamodor is being tended to on a cart.

'Will she live?' I demand of Lioba who supervises her, even though she's covered in enough blood, I think she must have been wounded as well.

'Of course, she will. She's a stubborn goat.' I'd laugh at the roughness of the response, but I'm not a fool. I can see the great red stain that mars Firamodor's byrnie, and her skin flashes painfully white where it shows.

'Bloody hell,' I complain, stepping to get a closer glance, but a huge swathe of linen wraps her chest.

'How bad is it?'

'I've seen worse,' is the less than helpful response.

'Can she travel? If she can, take her back to Tamworth. Lady Ecgwynn will nurse her.'

'Yes, my lady,' throughout the exchange, Firamodor hasn't stirred but now she does, a low moan from her tight lips.

'Stop bloody fussing,' she mutters, only for her eyes to shut again.

I sigh. I knew her injury was terrible when she stood beside me in the shield wall. I didn't realise it was this bad.

'Take her, and take Leofgyth with you. Where's Eoforhild?'

Abruptly, I realise I've not yet seen her.

'She, Mildryth and Ymma are still chasing the enemy. I'm sure they'll return in good time.'

'They're not alone,' cousin Athelstan hastens to reassure me before I can complain about their recklessness. 'Fifteen of your warriors went chasing after the Viking raiders.'

'Very well,' I relent from my bubbling complaints. 'Take me to the traitors.'

I've managed to avoid most of the bodies, but closer to the gates, I see a small collection of more with arrows protruding from their backs, showing me clearly how they met their deaths.

Damn fools.

Reeve Sigehelm stands just inside the open gateway. Above his head, those who protect Derby watch attentively, gazing into the far distance and occasionally dropping that gaze to see what's happening below them. There are about twenty perched on the wooden gangway, with weapons limp in their arms. I search for the archers amongst them. I'm keen to thank them for their assistance.

'You have traitors?' I should greet Reeve Sigehelm more calmly, but exhaustion makes my temper fray.

'My lady.' Reeve Sigehelm hasn't forgotten his courtesy as he bows deeply. I curb my irritation, aware that I'm once more the object of a great deal of scrutiny. 'They opened the western gates, allowed thirty Viking raiders inside Derby and then opened the eastern gates again to let them escape.'

'Where were your guards?' I demand, as he indicates I should follow him to the small building that serves as a prison.

'They were the guards,' Reeve Sigehelm's voice is filled with horror, but I stop and turn to stare at him, searching for something in his face. He looks to be the same man I met only a few weeks ago, but is he? Something seems a little off. I banish the thought and try to focus on what can be proved, blaming my exhaustion for my suspicions.

'Here,' a huddle of misery appears before my eyes. If I thought the battlefield was bad, this somehow seems worse.

'You had them beaten?' I demand to know. Reeve Sigehelm shakes his head in denial as I examine the group of five men and a child. He really can't be termed anything but a child.

'No, the Viking raiders did it. It seems that young Ælfhere thought to try and stop them. They didn't take too kindly to that, and it all descended into a riot. Or so they say.'

I look at young Ælfhere. He's gazing at me with something like devotion, and immediately I decide I like him. His lip's bleeding, his nose blackened, and where his eyes should be, I detect only green and purple. For all that, I can sense no deceit in him.

'They made a mess of him,' I confirm, eyeing the other five men with interest.

I should like to say that I know them, but I don't. I don't think I've ever seen any of them before.

'Why?' I ask, only for a sullen silence to greet my words. Not even

Ælfhere looks as though he'll answer, and my good impression of him begins to fade.

'The boy's mute,' Reeve Sigehelm informs me.

'And the other men? Can't they speak?'

'The wounds weren't all visible,' he states, and now I make more sense of the scene.

'They've all been beaten. One of them says he can't hear anything, as to the other four, they seem beyond the comprehension of anything.'

'But these men opened the gates for the Viking raiders, you're sure of it?' Again, I'm suspicious that these wretches would have the wherewithal to take such actions.

'So it seems. They were caught by the eastern gate this morning just before the sun rose. They must have been waiting for much of the night.'

Something about the story doesn't ring true, but I nod, determined for now to ignore my worries. When it's less public, I'll ensure that a more thorough investigation is conducted as to what really happened in Derby in the last few days.

'They'll travel to Tamworth with me. I would sooner know more before I have them tried for treason.'

'My lady,' Reeve Sigehelm bows again, but my doubts have been pricked. I think he waits too long to stand, perhaps trying to cover his true feelings. What, I think, does Reeve Sigehelm know but not wish to tell me?

I'll find out. But not today.

'Are the gates secured now?' I stride from the fetid room, blinking in the sudden brightness of the short winter's day.

'My lady, only the most loyal now guard it.'

'And how do you know they're the most loyal?'

The question seems to confuse Reeve Sigehelm, for his eyebrows disappear into his hairline, his mouth opening and closing as though unsure how to respond.

'I'll check,' cousin Athelstan calls from astride his horse.

'Take four warriors with you,' I instruct him. There could still be enemy warriors lurking in the streets, hiding and just waiting for the chance to attack for a second time.

'And check the southern and northern gates as well. We can't leave Derby until the people feel secure and protected.'

At this Reeve Sigehelm looks about to argue, but I quell him with a hiss and stride to meet those who still stand and watch what's happening.

I tap my hand against my thigh. I'd like to ask all of these people questions about what's happened, but it's impractical. I don't have the time to ask every single person if they've heard rumours of attacks. No doubt they'll all be desperate to think of a response and tell me inconsequential matters.

I consider what my mother would have done and realise she'd have taken the time to offer reassurances. I resolve to do the same now that the crisis has seemingly passed.

But as I step toward a mother, her child clinging to her, they step back. I grimace. I'm wearing the blood of my enemy. It's not the correct attire.

'People of Derby. I'll take some refreshments and change and then address you all. But know that I'll not tolerate treachery. Derby is now safe. Lord Rǫgnvaldr hoped to capture me, not you. I'll not let that happen.' This short speech receives far more acclaim than it deserves as I meet the eyes of the small child, the hint of a smile on the cold face.

'Go about your business. It's a miserable day. I'm sure you'd sooner be sitting before a warm hearth than watching me. My warriors and I will remain and guard you this day.'

Whether the words are reassuring or not, one, and then two more, and finally, all of the crowd break up and begin to make their way back to their homes or businesses. Despite my cloak, I shiver. The cold has penetrated so deeply I think I might never be warm.

Reeve Sigehelm steps to my side.

'My home is available to you, my lady.'

'I'll be along shortly. I must speak with the injured and ensure the dead are cared for. Have the gate closed behind me. We should take no chances.'

'Very well, my lady. I'll have food prepared for your warriors, and I'll make certain the priory is available to tend to your dead.'

I nod and then with a final glance at the interior of Derby, move beyond the gates.

As soon as I'm once more exposed and walking amongst the dead and wounded, I feel a weight lift from my shoulders.

Something within Derby isn't right, but how I'll find out the truth is beyond me for the time being.

There's only so much I can absorb in one day.

LATER THAT DAY, with my wounded on the way back to Tamworth under heavy guard, cousin Athelstan and I sit before a wide hearth, fragments of a discarded meal before us. I feel my eyes growing heavy, but I fight my fatigue.

I remain uneasy, and cousin Athelstan keeps trying to catch my eye. I'm wondering if he feels it as well.

Reeve Sigehelm is expansive as he discusses events in Derby in recent weeks. He seems keen to please, but I'd sooner he left me alone to my darker thoughts and the company of cousin Athelstan.

Eoforhild hasn't yet returned, and neither have the other warriors. I appreciate that on the short winter day, it might be impossible to make it back to Derby safely, not with the sky cluttered with fore-boding clouds. Her continued absence adds to my tension.

'I've looked in on the traitors,' cousin Athelstan speaks when a harassed-looking clerk calls Reeve Sigehelm away on business. 'They don't look capable of doing anything like this. They won't even meet my gaze.'

'I agree, but there's no one to speak in their defence. Not here. And, it can't be denied that the Viking raiders entered Derby with someone's aid.'

'No, it can't, but the gate wardens are alert to the danger of the Viking raiders. All of the gates were tightly barred.'

'Yes, they are now. Perhaps Reeve Sigehelm isn't quite so in control as he seems. I'd sooner have someone with more authority here. Perhaps more warriors who report directly to me as well.'

'Next year, you should make Lincoln accept you as their ruler.' Cousin Athelstan makes it sound easy. I'm unsure I possess the diplomatic skills that my mother utilised to bring Derby under her control after decades of being ruled by Viking raiders. Cousin Athelstan senses my hesitation.

'Stop comparing yourself to her. You're a warrior, and she was, but not with a blade. Remember that. She had her tongue and men who would fight when commanded. And, of course, she had the advantage of already being married when her husband died. You don't have that. That's why Lord Rǫgnvaldr's rumours have been so malignant. Look how easy it is to combat him with your blade in comparison.'

I consider his words, trying to decide whether they're right or wrong or whether he just speaks to cheer me up.

I shrug a shoulder.

'My mother had many advantages to me, but also disadvantages.' Cousin Athelstan waits as though I'll say more, but instead, I smirk and meet his eyes. 'My father being her disadvantage.' Amusement flickers in cousin Athelstan's eyes, and then he turns serious again.

'Your mother left you a legacy that's almost impossible to live up to, and more, a task unfinished.'

'I think we'll just contend with one problem at a time,' I caution him. I dream of bringing all of the Five Boroughs back under the control of the Mercian ruler, but it'll take time. For now, I'm content to have four of them. Lincoln feels as though it's more likely to look to York than Mercia for leadership.

What I need to do is to ensure that I have the time to invest in Lincoln to reunite it with Mercia. It would be a crushing blow if Lincoln no longer maintained its independence from York. That means I need to return to Tamworth and marry Lord Athelstan.

'Two days,' I say to Cousin Athelstan. 'We'll return to Tamworth then.'

He nods and turns aside, his thoughts a mystery to me.

Does he wish that he ruled Mercia in my stead? Is that what he's always dreamed of, and now he feels that my responses are too slow? I shake my head.

I shouldn't second-guess myself. My mother wouldn't have done so. She was always calm, even in the most significant moments of crisis. I resolve to do the same, but I can't help wishing that Lord Rǫgnvaldr hadn't escaped. I'm sure he'll cause me more problems in the future.

PART II

CHAPTER 11

DECEMBER 918

There's no warning. Looking back, in the years that follow, I realise my foolishness. Lulled into a false sense of accomplishment after deflecting the attack on Derby, I should have known better. I should have been wise to the fact that I was right to suspect I had more than one enemy.

Rough hands on my arms and across my body are the first inclination I have that I've been betrayed. By who is what will plague me, although I'll have my hunches from the first touch.

'What the fuck?' I'm struggling against the attempts to bind me. I can feel the coarse rope around my ankles as I kick and twist. Either the candles have been extinguished, or my eyes have been covered. It's too dark to see anything.

'Help,' I screech, the word cut off by a piece of linen stuffed inside my mouth. I curve my tongue around it, prepared to spit it out, only to find it attached to a longer piece of linen tied around my head. I wriggle. I twist. I kick. I'd ball my hands and thump whoever attacks me, but my hands have been tied too tightly behind me.

All I have are my feet, and I can feel frantic hands trying to contain them as I kick out.

What's going on?

With my feet tied, my arms behind my back, blinded by the darkness, and a gag in my mouth, my enemy must think me contained. Abruptly, there are no hands on me as I sit, marooned in the centre of my bed. But I have one last trick I can try.

I know tears stream from my eyes. My heart's beating too fast. The gag fouls my breath, so I have to concentrate on breathing through my nose.

How could this happen? Who are these men?

I know they're men as I can hear them speaking.

'What now?' the voice is rough and tinged with a Wessex accent. I could scream. This has to be the work of my uncle.

'We take her. As agreed.' This voice is smoother. Do I detect one of my uncle's ealdormen here, in Mercia? There bloody better not be.

'Rather you than me,' the first voice says. I detect wariness there. Good. They need to fear me.

'Do your job, you bloody fool. You'll be well rewarded.'

The weight of another body on my bed, and I grimace, knowing this is my final moment.

Why I think, have none of my warriors raced to my rescue? Where is everyone? Where are my door wardens? My servants? Where's the man I plan to marry the next day? Where the fuck is everyone?

I allow the man and his stink close to me, almost shuffling closer to him to gain traction. I'll only have one chance at this. I need to make it work.

The grip on my tied hands is tight. I moan with pain. Arms and hands weren't made to go in such a position.

Crude laughter reaches my ears. I can't wait for him to feel my wrath.

I'm pulled to the side of my bed, my feet dropped to the floor, with my legs tied too tightly together. I might have to jump when I manage an escape.

'Not such a fighter now, are you?' This is my chance, and I take it. I launch my head at where I hope the man's head is. The crunch as my forehead collides with his is sickening. But I'm already trying to bolt as I feel his grip slip, shocked, no doubt, by the fact he either has a bleeding nose or broken teeth, hopefully both. It'll make it easy to track him down when I'm free and seeking revenge for this outrage.

I can't tell how tall he is.

He grunts.

'Contain her,' the other man mutters unhappily. I try to avoid the reaching hands, stagger to my feet, and shuffle forward using the tiny steps my bound feet allow me to where I hope the door is. If I can just make it into my hall, someone will see me and leap to my defence.

I'm not used to needing the help of anyone, but I imagine this is how it's done.

'Stop her,' the other man's voice grows impatient. 'It's just a bloody nose. It'll heal. You've taken worse.' I wish it were the condescending man's nose that I'd broken. It'd give me much greater satisfaction.

Before I've moved no more than a foot toward the longed-for door, I feel abrasive hands pinching my hands together again behind my back. I cry out, the linen rag muting my voice. Rage and pain bring a fresh burst of tears. I've never felt so helpless before, and I don't bloody like it.

'Come here, you little bitch.' The rough man's voice is laced with anger and stuffiness caused by his broken nose. This gives me some small comfort, but it doesn't last long.

The man must bend at the waist before me because the next thing I know, I've been hefted onto his shoulder. The stench of his clothes almost gags me afresh, my chest compacted against his shoulder. My feet leave the floor as he begins to walk through the door I'd been hoping to reach. I'm frustrated by how close I'd been.

'It's about time.' Again, it's the more polished voice that speaks. I lash out, hoping to catch a kick to his mouth, but for my pain, all I do is kick the wall, numbing my toes and sending stabs of pain up my lower legs.

'Keep still, you damn bitch.'

When I break free from my confinement, whenever that may be, I'll kill this man for daring to touch me and more for calling me a damn bitch.

The creak of a door alerts me to the fact that we're in the main hall. Now I expect to hear a crescendo of outrage from my women warriors and my nobility. I don't anticipate complete silence. Where is everyone?

I wriggle and moan, earning myself nothing but a wallop to the back. It forces the air from my body while tears stream down my face, my nose constricting. If they're not careful, I'll be bloody dead. Is this what they intend? Surely my uncle wouldn't countenance the murder of his niece?

But the thought chills me. I don't know my uncle, not at all. Perhaps he would think nothing of murdering his niece in cold blood now that his allies have failed to bring it about.

A strange thudding noise reaches my ears. I've no idea what it is until I hear a soft groan. It seems there was someone in my hall prepared to come to my rescue, but my captor knocked him or her unconscious.

I wish I knew who it was. But I hazard a guess all the same. Some would rather die than see this happen to me.

Another door opens, and the cold winter air envelopes my body, covered only by the trews and tunic I prefer to sleep in. My face stays too hot in the confines of the sack that covers it. It's been a bitterly cold winter. Tonight is no different. Ice has formed over the top of any surface holding water, and icicles dip down from the roof, their points a mockery of the iron of deadly blades. If I could just get my hands on one of them, I'm sure it'd be possible to cause some damage to my enemy. But they stay out of reach, and I cannot break free.

I smell the horses. I hear impatient stamping. I brace myself for what must come next. The air leaves my body once more as I'm slung over a saddle, and ropes are quickly tied to keep me secure.

I'm sure that if they mean to steal me away to Wessex in such a position, I'll be dead long before we get there. The gag is making it all but impossible to breathe. My tongue feels both dry and too big for my mouth.

If I try and cough, I fear I'll inhale even more of the rag. I doubt my captors would even notice if I convulsed.

Why has my uncle done this? Mercia isn't his. It's mine to rule as my mother intended. That uncle Edward isn't even honourable enough to attack Mercia in the daylight, with his Wessex warriors against my Mercian ones, assures me that my uncle is as weak as I've come to suspect.

He knows, oh yes, he knows it'd be impossible to overwhelm the Mercians in battle. And so, he's devised this plan to steal me away from Mercia, and then what? To rule in my place? How does he expect to explain what he's done and where I've gone to the Mercians?

If he means to explain it at all. Or perhaps he means to imply that I've run away from my responsibilities. Does he mean to argue that I'm too young to want to rule? If he does, I know no one will believe him.

I'm not some silly girl who thinks only of marrying and wearing pretty jewellery. I've fought and bled for Mercia, and I will again. If I only get the chance.

'Hurry up,' I can detect more people moving around now, their footsteps loud on the stone floor.

'I'm coming,' a voice puffs, rich with annoyance. 'I didn't see you knocking out thirty men and women, having drunk your fill and ensuring the rest were too insensible to act. Give a man a chance.'

This explains what's happened to my warriors. I note it with dismay.

How dare they do this? I hope my men and women all live. Although, they'll all be furious when they realise I've been taken on the night before my marriage. In fact, anger won't explain it. Not at all. I wince to think of Lord Athelstan's wrath. And then I shudder, considering cousin Athelstan's.

I want him to take on his father and also to keep Mercia safe in my absence. I hope he'll know the correct choice and make it when he's calm enough to face it.

'Stop moaning and just get on with it,' the more refined voice is filled with frustration. No doubt they need to get me across the border with Wessex before their actions are discovered with the advent of a new day.

I wish them luck with that.

I wriggle again, determined to test the strength of the ropes that bind me. If I can just delay them long enough then I'm sure someone will be awake, no doubt drunk still, but awake all the same. All I need is one person to see what's happening, and then they can raise the alarm.

My warriors, drunk or with a bad head, will overpower this small group of men easily. They've fought Viking raiders all of their lives. A few weak Wessex men, operating under cover of darkness, won't be a match for men and women who fight more easily than they breathe. They proudly wear the scars to show it.

I hear the jangle of harnesses as men mount their horses. I know my time is running out. Frustrated tears stream once more from my eyes, soaking my hair, not my cheeks. I try and scream, floundering on top of the horse, gasping for a full lungful of air, anything to attract the attention of someone.

The ropes dig into my back, cutting across me so that I'm puffing, and still I strive to win my freedom, even bound as I am.

'Shut her up,' the refined voice cuts through my struggles. I hear the heavy footsteps of my captor coming towards me. I thrash all the more. He already has a bloody nose. What else can I do to him?

Only, he seems to have gained some caution. Instead of approaching my feet, he shuffles his way to my head. The crack to the back of my head is enough to stun me. I almost miss the other voice's command.

'She needs to be upright, you damn fool. The king doesn't want his niece dead.' A pause, and I don't like it. 'Or at least he hasn't commanded me to kill her. I don't know how he'd feel if she did turn up dead.' There's a wistfulness in that voice that turns me cold.

A grunt of annoyance from the larger man. I'm being untied, but only to be thrust upright in the saddle, my leg bindings loosened so that he can tie my feet into the stirrups to either side of the horse.

All the time, I'm sightless, groggy and unable to take advantage of this brief moment of freedom. My head lolls, hanging low to my chest, and all I can think is that at least I can breathe more easily now I'm upright. But I don't wish to be in the debt of my abductors.

The ropes tightening on my left leg force a screech of pain. For a moment, I have clarity, my head snapping upwards. But someone must be helping my captor, for two large hands clamp around my right foot, tying me to the stirrups there. I'm helpless once more.

If only the animal were my own, but I can tell, from the width of the animal's back, that it's a horse bred for war. They can be fiercely loyal and not likely to respond to my frantic attempts to have it race away. No doubt, it's also tethered to another horse to prevent such an occurrence.

This assault has been meticulously planned. I don't think they'll have left anything to chance, which infuriates me.

'Are we finally ready?' The man, I assume is an ealdorman, is becoming increasingly frantic.

'Yes, my lord,' the honorific sounds like an insult to my ears. I'd have the man on his knees begging for forgiveness. But the man I've decided is one of my uncle's ealdormen merely grunts.

'Then let's leave this shit-hole. Why the king wants it, I'll never know. The Viking raiders are welcome to it for all I care.'

I lurch forward when the horse beneath me takes his first steps, and I'm almost grateful for the ropes that tie me so tightly to the saddle. I'm entirely without control. I hate it, hate it, hate it.

My chest heaves with anger and aggravation as the sound of horse hooves over the cobbles fill my ears. There's no cry of outrage, no sound of anyone coming to my assistance, and then we're through the entrance to the stronghold of Tamworth. I feel it as a shadow passing over my head, even though it's dark. The sound of night floods my senses, the stillness that only comes when everything sleeps.

Where are my gate wardens? Why is Tamworth entirely without protection?

Who the fuck has my uncle bribed to make this possible?

How haven't I realised how compromised my palace is?

CHAPTER 12

Time passes, but I've no idea how much.

The horse keeps up a steady gait beneath me, encouraged every so often by the gruff voice of the man who hauled me from my bed, trussed up like a piece of game.

My tears have stopped falling. Now all I can think about is revenge, on my uncle, on his son, and the rest of his children and wives.

Damn the bastard.

Every so often, my mind skips to what will happen in Tamworth when my absence is discovered. Who will take the blame? Whom will cousin Athelstan hold responsible? Who will Lord Athelstan berate? Will they come after me? Will they know that it's all uncle Edward? Or will they think I've escaped in the night, perhaps from a marriage I didn't want to make? Or will they believe Lord Rǫgnvaldr has abducted me to make me his wife?

I shake my head at the last thought. They'll suspect it was uncle Edward. Who else would attempt such a move? Not the Viking raiders. It's not their way to steal in under the cover of darkness. No, they're more likely to come with the rising sun, confident and cocky enough that they want everyone to witness what they do. Lord Rǫgn-valdr made his intentions clear when he attacked Derby.

At least I can respect a man who's prepared to bleed to achieve his greatest desires.

So, where am I being taken? I know it'll be somewhere in Wessex, or at least I hope it will be. The conversation between the suspected ealdorman and the ruffian has concerned me. Would my uncle coun-tenance having me murdered?

I'd have thought the suggestion ridiculous, but if he's consented to this abduction in the middle of the night from my palace and place of greatest protection, then I no longer know who my uncle is. Not at all.

No, I reconsider. I know exactly who he is. He's weak, feeble and greedy. It's not a good combination.

But would he have me murdered? My thoughts keep returning to that one possibility. Perhaps no, perhaps yes. Worse, I consider that he'll have me sold as a slave to some West Frankish count or noble family who'll never believe that I should rule Mercia.

None of the possibilities is enticing but provided I live, I'll be able to dream of getting vengeance and reclaiming my birth right as soon as the opportunity presents itself.

The thought of what's being done to me fills me with fury once more. I'm straining again, desperate to be free from the ropes that confine me. The horse beneath me rides on, but I twist my feet and rub my wrists together, knowing they'll be red and raw but not caring at all. I need to escape. I'll not allow this to happen to me.

'Keep still, you damn bitch,' the rough voice reaches my ears. The horse beneath me finally realises that its passenger is unwilling and grinds to a sudden and very abrupt stop. I only just keep in the saddle. I tense, expecting the strike around my head once more. I'm not disappointed.

'Sit still, or the damn horse will gallop off and throw you off in a river somewhere. He's a damn bastard as well.' The knowledge sobers me. I don't want to die. Of that, I'm sure. I want to live, to get my revenge. To get Mercia back.

I sit more quietly when the horse is encouraged to canter once more. The going is difficult. I can't hold on with my hands, and my legs are tied to the stirrups. Unable to see, I'm entirely at the mercy of the horse. Although his gait is steady, I can't find his rhythm. I bump around in the saddle. There'll be more than my legs and hands that are bruised and battered by the time I'm allowed free from the horse. I might not sit for a week.

I feel the night turning to day with the increasing calls of the winter birds and the rustling in the hedges that line the roadway. I hazard a guess as to where we are, hoping we're heading to Wessex. And then I hear something when the wind suddenly drops that makes my heart soar. I stay as still as possible, hoping I don't imagine it. I wish my horse would stop so that I could actually decide if I'm hearing what I think I'm hearing or whether my mind's allowing me to hear what I hope to hear.

But I'm not, and the confirmation comes too quickly, and from a source, I'd rather it didn't.

'Hurry up, you damn fools. We've been discovered.' It's the more refined voice that speaks, and fear thrums through it.

Good. I want the pleasure of taking his life myself. The thought of bathing in his blood is far from repellent.

I appreciate the importance of life and its sanctity. I've worked all these years to preserve the lives of all the Mercians, native or Viking raider born, I don't much care. But for this man, death will be slow and painful, and it'll come at my hand.

The horse beneath me is encouraged to greater and greater speed by the gruff voice. I try and stay as immobile as possible. I don't want to fall from the animal at this speed. If I did, it would be irrelevant if my uncle wanted me dead or alive. Such a landing would kill me easily, even if I were lucky enough for my feet to fall free from the stirrups.

But I'm praying, the words running through my mind, that my Lord God will see fit to rescue me from this outrageous attempt to claim Mercia without bloodshed.

Without right.

Without the support of the Mercian witan.

Damn it all.

As FAST AS my horse rides, I begin to make out the sound of the following force more and more clearly. Above the rush of the wind and the heavy breathing of the men who escort me, the sound of hooves becomes frequent.

I've decided that fifteen men make up this group and that the refined voice is in overall command. However, the ruffian keeps order amongst the other thirteen men.

I strain, desperate to make our voices, to know how close my allies are to saving me. My heart thrills, but I'm also aware that the early morning sunlight making itself known through the rough sack that covers my head means that we've travelled all night long. We must be getting closer and closer to the border with Wessex.

I'm assuming that my abductors have chosen to take the Foss Way from Tamworth to Wessex, which means that we'll cross the River Thames close to Cricklade, or so I think. Of course, they might also have chosen to take Watling Street, which means we'll cross the River Thames closer to London. Either way, there'll be a bridge involved.

What will happen when we reach the border, I simply can't say.

The border isn't fluid. The men and women who live close to it, as well as the kings of Mercia and Wessex, have long hammered it into shape. The only change in recent decades has been that Wessex has taken London. However, everyone within Mercia knows it rightfully belongs to it. My grandfather claimed London as his price for helping Mercia. The damn bastard.

Will they take me to my uncle, which seems more likely if we've ridden down the Foss Way, or will they take me somewhere else? Perhaps they'll hide me away in London or force me into the slavers market there to be sold and taken to West or East Frankia. I wish I knew.

Will there be a Wessex force waiting on the border? Will my warriors be unable to come into Wessex? Would they even risk it?

'The bridge is within sight,' the words are ripped from the mouth of the ruffian and cast back into the wind. I feel my horse tense, bunching his muscles for one final exertion to make it home. He must know that food and sleep await him over that bridge. The cold air that flows over me seems ever colder. I imagine it must be ice from the river the bridge crosses. It's been a bitter winter, and there's worse to come.

'Hurry, you fuckers,' the ruffian almost screeches the words, making him sound like a youth with barely a whisker on his cheeks, let alone a full beard.

Have my saviours come too late?

I wish I could see, but as much as I toss my head from side to side, I can't force the sack loose.

I almost despair.

'Have your weapons ready.' It's the one I assume is an ealdorman who gives the command.

'We didn't come here to die,' the ruffian announces, tension rippling through his voice.

'You were paid well enough. Do your damn duty,' the ealdorman instructs. I hear the sound of metal being pulled loose from scabbards and weapons belts.

Stealing my kingdom from me has all come down to money?

If I could hate them more than I already did, I would.

I hope they all fucking die.

'If they catch us, then kill her. Better she's dead than alive and back in their hands. I'll take full responsibility.'

This new instruction turns my already cold body even colder.

I can't feel my fingers or my toes. Only my face is warm, and that's because of the damn sack that covers it, warming it with my breath.

My warriors have caught us too late. Below the beating hooves, I can already hear the sound of sluggish water. If I can hear it, despite the clanking of harness and the drum of hooves, then I know we must be very close indeed.

Still, I offer a swift prayer that I'll be retrieved before we reach Wessex. Before I can finish muttering the words, my horse suddenly slows. We must be really close. I consider trying to force myself free from the saddle and think about thrashing again. But the sound of the running water makes me reconsider. I don't want to risk falling from the horse and being killed when I hit the ground. Neither do I want to chance falling into the River Thames. I'd never be found, and with a hood over my head and my arms and legs tied, I'd have no chance of escaping alive from the clutches of the river.

I'd sooner be alive than dead.

I don't want to make my uncle's usurpation of my rule any more straightforward than it already is. At least if I'm alive, there's always a chance that I can reclaim Mercia. That'll never happen if I'm dead.

The noise of my pursuers is as loud as the river now. Then I hear the sound I've been dreading, that of a hoof hitting the wooden walkway of the bridge.

I know where we are.

Below the rushing of the river and the thumping of my pursuers, I hear something else, and it turns my stomach.

There are more warriors here, many more warriors, and they're lining the bridge, laying claim to it. The intention is clear.

And then my horse walks over the bridge. I bite down on my frustration, listening, straining to hear. Despite everything that's occurring around me, I hear one voice above all others. I sit as straight as I can.

If I could turn toward him, I would, but I can hardly move my head from side to side, let alone swivel it like an owl.

I'll have to hope that Lord Athelstan knows that I sense him. There's nothing else I can do.

I don't want there to be a war between Mercia and Wessex. But I can tell, as the horse steps once more onto the hard surface of the road that meets the bridge as it joins Wessex, that there's a mass of warriors just waiting, no doubt, for the Wessex king to issue commands that send them into Mercia.

I hope my friends don't make a fight of it here.

They can't win a battle against the Wessex warriors. Not when there are so many of them and so few Mercians.

Well, no, that's not strictly true. The Wessex warriors will stand no chance against the Mercians if they came in force. The Wessex men are weak from a lack of fighting. They've grown fat on the riches of their kingdom.

But I don't want my friends and allies to lose their lives, not in my name.

Mercia will stand, no matter what my uncle believes.

I can only hope that everyone is still there by the time I manage to escape from whatever my uncle has planned for me.

The sound of my pursuers falls away as the horse once more picks up speed. My shoulders shake.

'Well done, men, you'll be well rewarded. I promise your second payment is waiting for you when we reach our destination.'

The talk of money forces my head backwards, my sightless eyes peering up at where I know the sky should be.

How could I have lost it all to greedy men?

CHAPTER 13

At some point, and despite it all, I fall asleep.

My eyes flutter open in shock when I'm unceremoniously lowered to my feet. My legs are untied, and even my hands at my back allowed their freedom. I grimace. My legs tingle painfully, and because the sack is still over my head, I've no idea where I am.

There's no sound, only hands on my back guiding me forward. I expect to hear the harsh rasp of the man who brought me here and the more refined voice of the suspected ealdorman, but instead, there's only silence. Feet seem to glide over the ground beneath me, but again, there's no sound.

Where am I?

The same hands escort me to a seat, pressing me down by my shoulders. I sit, even though I've only just stood, washing my hands one inside the other, as the feeling is slowly restored to them. I imagine, when I see them, that they'll be bloodied, bruised and red raw.

I feel the sack lifted from my head. I blink in the light from a hearth and a series of candles. Only then is the gag removed from my mouth.

I cough. Well, really, I choke. My tongue's drier than the summer-baked ground, and immediately a wooden beaker is pressed into my hand, filled with water. My eyes have been covered for so long that they stream in even the dim light. I blink, drink, and try to determine what's happened.

As soon as the beaker's empty, it's taken from me and hastily refilled. Only then do I feel able to speak.

'Where am I?' I ask, turning to see who tends to me.

In all honesty, I'm unsurprised when I meet the eyes of a woman. A simple gown of dark wool covers her stick-thin figure, a wimple over her hair. But it's the wooden cross around her neck that confirms my suspicions.

I'm in a nunnery.

'Where am I?' I ask again, but the nun shakes her head, a finger held to her lips in the age-old sign for silence, and my heart sinks.

It's a nunnery, and worse, it's an establishment that embraces silence for the holy women.

I make to stand, gathering myself up, thinking to walk away from the nun, but her hands rest on my shoulder. Their surprising strength forces me back to the stool. She lifts a hand clear from my shoulders and uses it to indicate that I should turn.

The smell of cooked meat reaches my nostrils. My stomach rumbles loudly. I've no idea how much time's passed or when I last ate. Surely no more than a day, and hopefully much less.

The instruction is easy enough to understand, but I don't want to eat. I want to find who abducted me and who brought me here, and I want to get back to Mercia.

Shrugging off the hand, I stand quickly, my legs unsteady, keen to make my way through the door and hopefully to where I can find a horse and get home.

My footsteps sound too loud over the wooden floorboards, but no one tries to intercept me, not even when I wrench open the door and stagger outside.

The sun's setting to the west. At least I know what time it is.

In the half-light of the deep winter's day, I turn and look at the building before me. It's impossible to tell that it's a nunnery from such a cursory glance. I take another step backwards and see the tall tower that marks the church. It must stand behind the hall.

There are walls all around the hall and the church, enclosing me in a space that feels too small for all I'm outside. I know this place to be a Benedictine nunnery. My heart sinks, but still, I stride toward the closed gates, hoping, trying to decide if there's a stable I can borrow a horse from amongst the small collection of buildings.

I shiver. It's bitterly cold, and I have no cloak. If I manage to escape, dressed as I still am in the clothes I was sleeping in when they took me, I might freeze to death before I make it back to Mercia.

I consider going back, but the door to the hall has swung open, and the nun watches me. Her eyes and posture tell me nothing, but I don't want to go back there. No, I stride toward the gates, where a solitary lantern burns. It's not much of a beacon, while the remnants of daylight remain, but it highlights the correct path.

The nun's spoken no words, given no signal, but as I step close to the gateway, two more nuns walk free from the small building. Beyond them, I can see a figure. I take it to be a man huddled around a fire. I know who he is, even from where I stand.

The two new nuns shake heads at me, indicating that I can't go that way, the one holding up both hands and crossing them to show the exit is barred to me.

I stamp my foot in frustration. I've never felt so powerless.

I'm all but a queen, well, really a king, but my power and influence have been taken from me. In this silent place, it's impossible to decipher where I am.

My stomach rumbles once more, and I shiver.

'Fuck it,' I mutter under my breath, turning to retrace my steps.

I'll eat and obtain some warmer clothes, I might even sleep, but in the morning, I'll demand answers. If none are forthcoming, I'll attempt to escape once more.

I can feel the eyes of the gate wardens on me as the other nun moves aside to allow me into the hall. I sweep past her, returning to the table and stool where my food steams in the air.

There's no one else around. I promptly realise why as a voice in prayer reaches my ears.

All the other nuns must be within the church.

I sit quickly and begin to spoon the meaty broth into my mouth. It's dull but good food. I appreciate the skill of whoever prepared it. The nun quickly refills my beaker of water and offers me a jug filled with it. I'd sooner drink wine or ale, but I doubt the nuns have it.

All the time, my mind is busy trying to think about what my uncle hopes to achieve.

As much as I'm relieved not to be dead, I don't want to be in a nunnery either. I know my uncle banished his second wife to a nunnery when she was deemed superfluous to requirements. He would have people believe she went willingly, but we all know the truth. She was too old, and he thought to take a younger bride.

His first wife was no one of importance. His second secured his hold on Wessex, and his third, a woman younger than I, gave him Kent. If she produces children at the same rate his second wife did, my uncle will soon have enough daughters to fill his own nunnery.

Does he plan to leave me here? Does he think I'll accept what he's done to me this easily?

When I finish eating, the room suddenly fills with other women, all wearing the same woollen dress as the nun who'd been tending to me. They look at me with only mild interest. It's evident that none of them knows who I am. Without my sword and weapons belt, I confess, I do look like any other woman. I don't even have my jewellery to show I'm a wealthy lady.

I've nothing but the clothes on my back. I'd hope that the red-raw skin around my wrists would give them pause for thought, but it seems not. Instead, they stream to their seats, and I count them.

There are thirty women, ranging from an old woman who walks with a crooked back and the aid of a stick to a girl who can't yet have had her first blood. She's far too young to be in a nunnery, and yet she looks angelic with her golden halo of hair.

They all wear the same rough dresses and the same wooden crosses around their necks, and not one of them speaks.

The routine they have is evidently well known. Quickly they fall to their allotted tasks. Some sit along the two tables, ready to eat, while three of the women at each table prepare to spoon the meaty broth into waiting wooden bowls. I watch them all while the woman beside me is offered her bowl, only half as full as my own.

Suddenly I feel ungrateful for my initial refusal of the broth. The portions others receive are far less generous. I wish I hadn't devoured it all. Wherever I am, the nunnery is clearly not wealthy. The food is good and filling, but there isn't enough of it. That's evident from the skinny frames all of the women have. Not one of them carries any spare flesh.

I feel ashamed, and yet it's not even my fault that I'm here.

Angrily, I turn from the impassive faces and stare into the heart of the fire.

For such a cold night, the hearth is well stacked, and yet the pile of wood waiting to join the flames is slight. I shiver.

In my hall at Tamworth, the hearth would be piled high with burning logs, and more baskets would be waiting to be added when the fire burnt through the wood. I shiver again.

In my hall in Tamworth, I'd have a thick cloak wrapped around me, and someone would be bringing me warmed wine and making sure I'd eaten enough and had all I needed.

A gust of wind rattles the roof above my head, and a small shower of water is dislodged and falls to the wooden floor with a wet thud. No one seems to notice. That fills me with unease. Evidently, this isn't a stray occurrence.

When everyone's finished eating, they disperse to assorted tasks. Some of them scrub bowls clean, and others take their sewing work close to a collection of candles. Yet more bow their heads in prayer or quiet contemplation while two of the nuns tend to the fire, eyeing up the logs that are burning and deciding where to place those that remain.

From my brief glimpse outside, the sun has only just set. Much of the evening remains, and there's little left to burn to think it'll be warm throughout that time.

No one speaks.

No one even makes eye contact with one another.

I tremble again. I'd like to be closer to the hearth, but I don't wish to draw attention to myself. For now, it seems they've all forgotten I'm here.

I wish there were a more comfortable chair to sit on. The stool has no back to it, and my back aches from being in the saddle all day. My thighs are chaffed as raw as my wrists from riding in such an uncomfortable position.

I fidget, stifle a yawn, and I wonder what's happening in Mercia in my absence.

And then those hands are once more on my shoulder. I'm encouraged to stand and walk away from the night-time activities of the nuns. I go where I'm directed, fully expecting to leave the hall, but instead, I'm taken to the far end of the hall, where wicker walls cleverly screen off an area. I'd thought it was the end of the building but clearly not.

I'm led to one of the spaces. My eyes alight on a dress the same as the ones the nuns wear. I'm supposed to wear it. There's also a bed, and I've never seen a narrower bed topped with a mattress of hay that seems to lack all hay. The nun bows her head and turns to leave, but I have a pressing need. I've no idea where I should relieve my aching bladder.

The nun looks at me, her brown eyes quickly alert with understanding as I mime what I want. The silence is oppressive, and it's infected me. I don't want to be the one to break it.

I'm led away then, through the main door and to a small building to the side of the hall. Inside, a single candle burns and the smell is enough to inform me that this is the latrine.

It's not what I'm used to, but nothing is, not at the moment.

I make use of it, and then I'm escorted back inside. I hazard a baleful glance at the lantern beside the gates, but I don't make any attempt to escape. I want to. But I'll not do anything that gives my uncle the excuse he needs to have me killed. Neither will I let the cold weather do it for him.

Inside, I shake as the warmth washes over me, even though I'd been cold before I went outside. I return to the small bed and turn to meet the eyes of the nun. There's nothing in her look to enable me to decipher what she thinks. I wish there were.

Instead, she beckons that I prepare for sleep, and so I do. Sitting on the side of the bed that rustles beneath my movements, I remove my boots, carefully untying the bindings and staring down at my naked feet when I've done so. They seem too pale in the dull light, but I can feel where they've been tied too tightly, first to each other and then to the stirrups.

I must have drunk too much before my capture and fallen asleep with my boots on. I'm grateful for that.

I bite down on the stab of pain and then pull back the covers to climb beneath the fur. It's a mean, thin thing compared to the luxurious furs I'm used to, and I shiver even as I settle beneath it.

The woman still studies me, and I resent her scrutiny. I've made it clear that I accept my fate for now. But still, she observes me, even as I settle and try and find some part of the mattress that isn't lumpy. A dry smell reaches my nose, confirming what I've begun to suspect. The bed is at least dry and free from dampness. I'm surprised, considering the leak in the roof.

I close my eyes, not prepared to gaze at the roof beams above my head, considering whether this part of the roof will leak or not. Behind my eyes, the day's events play out in dazzling clarity. I try to banish the images, try to think of something else, as my head begins to pound and my heart beats a little too fast.

I'm sure I'll not sleep, but then I must.

Waking is agony.

My mind feels foggy. When I blink open my eyes, I groan with physical pain and also one that cuts me to my soul. I'd forgotten where I was while I slept. Abruptly it all rushes back to me as I take in the blackened beams above my head and the very alert eyes of the nun who watches me.

I'd like to say that it's the same woman as when I fell asleep, but I'm not sure.

I saw little but eyes, a weak nose and a loose chin, and I'm sure the same greets me, other than for the eyes. I'm sure yesterday they were brown, and now they're blue. But they're no less stern. While I struggle to rise from my thin bed, my eyes alight on my raw wrists and the bruises on my feet that are stark in the early morning greyness.

I can hear the shuffle of others in the hall, but I don't know how long they've been awake for or how long I've slept. But the watchful eyes make me want to leap from my bed. Only my body has other ideas as I struggle to stand.

I think she'll chastise me, somehow considering she must remain silent, only she steps forward and offers me a small pot filled with some sort of lotion. The smell of it hits me first, and it makes my eyes water. I reach out to take the pot, unsure of what it is, but instead, she clamps my hand in one of hers, handing the container into my other hand.

With rough, if skilled hands, she scoops the gloopy texture into her hand and then begins to work it into my wrist. I wince, the movement reminding me of yesterday's pain, but the mixture immediately starts to numb and soothe. Happily, I allow her to swap hands and then bend to rub the lotion into my ankles. I decide it must be an ointment containing figwort. I know cousin Ecgwynn's mentioned it in the past.

I decide, although I can't honestly tell, that this isn't the same nun who watched me last night. She'd never have been so gentle.

When she's finished, I think I'm expected to rise, but instead, she presses me back into my bed. Another woman appears, as though summoned, and hands me a beaker of water, crisp and refreshing and a bowl of pottage.

I take both and then struggle, for I can't hold both and eat. Awkwardly, I look around, my eyes noticing a small table upon which I lay the beaker of water and then eagerly eat the pottage. It's flavoured with a thread of honey and eases my aching stomach. I try not to feel the scrutiny of the nun, but I know she watches everything I do.

The other nun leaves with my empty bowl. I realise I'm expected to rest all day long. I don't want to, but my skin prickles from the cold air, and as much as I thought the fur mean and thin, it's all I have to keep me warm.

I try and settle back, but I need to empty my bladder once more.

Without speaking, the nun seems to understand my intention. She follows meekly behind me after I've slipped my feet back into my boots, cursing their coldness and worrying that the ointment will transfer to the leather instead of my injuries.

If I thought it was cold in the hall, outside, the wind gusts, whipping my untidy hair into my eyes. I rush through the emptying of my bladder, desperate to be back inside. While I'm sure it's daytime, dark clouds obscure the sun, and I sense that rain, or even snow, is due to fall.

I can't see the gatehouse, and even if I could, I'm determined not to show too much interest in it. I need to lull the nuns into believing that I accept my fate. And I need more than the clothes I own to escape with. I also need to heal. My hobbling is painful, and my wrists ache when the wind touches them. I'm in no fit state to escape. Not yet.

Inside, I settle back into my bed with pleasure, the lingering heat making the experience pleasant.

I lie back, closing my eyes. I need to mend, and sleep is the best way of doing oo.

That it means I'll be unaware of the nun, who watches me, is a bonus.

Not that I think I'll sleep, but I do. This time, when I wake, the nun who guards me makes hurry-up motions with her hands. I rise, wincing as every injury makes itself known. She holds the dress out toward me, but I shake my head, looking down at my trews and tunic and indicating that I'll continue to wear them.

The nun, again, I believe a different one to earlier and yesterday, offers me the dress. I grimace. I don't want to wear a dress. I don't want to meekly give in to the demand that I become one of them against my will.

But I take it because there's no other option and slide it over my body, and then remove the trews and tunic. The wool's rough on my skin, catching on my sore wrists and ankles. I moan softly, hoping for some more of the ointment from earlier, but none is offered. Instead, I'm rushed from my bedside, with only time for a hasty swallow of the cold water that's been left for me.

The main hall is once more deserted, and I wonder why there was such a rush for me to dress. The nun walks in front of me, stopping only when she realises I've come to a halt before the hearth.

She shakes her head 'no,' and points where she wants me to go.

I sigh. I feel that I'm about to be forced to endure a long and tedious religious service, despite my hunger and need to once more empty my bladder.

I hesitate, unsure which complaint to voice first, but the sound of the priest beginning the service spurs the nun on. She marches to my side, grabs my arm and propels me with far more force than I would have thought possible toward the door.

I go, the curse ripe on my lips, wishing she would move her hands because they've caught on my wrists.

When I next encounter my uncle, he'll pay for every inconvenience I've been forced to endure. Damn the fucking bastard.

If I THOUGHT the nun's main living space was poorly maintained, the church is even more shocking.

The construction is half stone and half wood, but the door doesn't fit its space, and as the priest speaks his prayers and intonations, I shiver from my place at the rear of the church.

How the women endure this on the many occasions each day they must attend services, I've no idea.

The priest's voice battles against the creaks and groans of the building, but I hardly listen. I pray, but not to a God who would allow what's happened to me to go without punishment. I offer words for my mother and for the safety of Mercia but stop from calling for my uncle's punishment. My God might be vengeful, but I'll not call down fire and brimstone on my uncle. No, I intend to be that fire and brimstone once I'm free.

Not that the church is poor. Far from it. I eye the silver and golden crosses and chalices with distaste, the expensive altar clothes with their delicate stitches. Why do these women believe so much in showing wealth rather than repairing their buildings? Surely it'd be easier to do God's work if the surroundings were a little more pleasant.

And the priest? Well, he wears luxurious robes and, over them, a cloak that has to be three times thicker than my sleeping fur. What has he done to deserve such luxury other than garble the Latin he intones? He makes so many mistakes that it becomes impossible to ignore that he's not a worthy priest, even for such a poor nunnery.

My mother wouldn't approve of the arrangement.

Finally, the service ends. I'm encouraged to leave the church. I'd move quicker, but my entire body feels frozen in place. My feet are unresponsive, no matter how much the nun makes hurry-up motions with her hands, pushing her hands outwards time and time again.

When I eventually leave the church, I'm followed back to the main hall by the rest of the nuns. They're silent. I harbour the thought that their mouths are frozen shut, but I'm the only one to gasp in delight when I feel the heat from the fire. The rest go about their business, in a repeat of yesterday evening, only I think different women take responsibility for handing around the food.

Unsurprised, I accept the bowl offered to me, noticing the meal is the same as the day before and will probably be the same the day after as well. I see nothing but a life of unrelenting repetition before me.

My uncle decided not to kill me, but I might come to wish he had if I'm forced to stay here for much longer.

My foot taps under the table, and my eyes scour the faces of the other nuns, but my thought is on the priest. If anyone here can give me the answers that I seek, then it must be him. No one else will break an oath to speak to me. The priest hasn't taken such an oath.

But he's not joined the rest of the nuns in the hall. I consider that he might not live inside the nunnery. Perhaps he lives beyond the walled enclosure. It seems to make sense to me. After all, no man should be inside a house dedicated to women.

Perhaps he has a home just on the other side of the gates. Possibly, if he does, I could use that knowledge to plan my escape.

I eat the food. It tastes as good and plain as my other two meals, only this time, I genuinely appreciate the heat of the food. It floods my body after the icy cold of the church. How, I consider, do the other nuns tolerate it?

At the end of the meal, I remember that I still need to empty my bladder. I look for the nun who's watched me throughout the religious service, but I can't determine who she is. They all look the same in their simple dresses and wimples. Unwilling to wait any longer, I stand and make my way to the door. I'm aware of scrutiny, but no one leaps to forbid my action.

Is it really possible that they think I've become resolved to my new life so quickly?

I consider it as I empty my bladder, the cold keeping the worst of the smell of the latrine at bay. Do these women even know who I am? And if they don't, how many more of them have arrived at the nunnery beaten and bloodied, as I was? It's not a pleasant thought.

On the walk back to the hall, I peer into the darkness, tendrils of light peeking beneath the tightly sealed door of the small gatehouse.

Of all the rooms in the nunnery complex, I imagine it's the warmest because it's so small. Perhaps that's where the priest makes his home? It wouldn't surprise me to discover that his living arrangements provide such comfort. While I've met many men who've chosen to dedicate their lives to prayer and to serve their God, I've also met many who did so merely because of the better quality of life it promised them.

Not I admit that it promised them a longer life. The Viking raiders soon realised that churches hoarded a great deal of wealth inside them. Just as the church here does.

When I enter the hall, being careful to close the door firmly behind me, I'm aware that most of the women watch me from beneath their hoods. Making my way back to the table where I ate, some of those gazes flicker, whether, through boredom or surprise at my return, I'm not sure. Maybe they're not used to strangers amongst them, despite my earlier thoughts.

One of the women stands before me, something in her hand. She holds it out, and I realise I'm to take it from her, even though I don't know what it is.

Only then do I realise, and my heart simultaneously sinks and lifts.

In my hand, I'm holding the clothes I wore the day before. They've been cleaned of all the mud that clung to them, but they require repair. Another nun presses thread and needle into my hands, and I smile in thanks.

It seems I'm allowed my warmer clothes back, but only if I can mend them myself.

I'm not known for my needlecraft. I can kill and maim with a sharpened edge, but forcing two pieces of fabric to adhere to each other has never been my skill.

I eye up the rips and tears with dismay, trying to decide where to start. The other nuns have fallen to their tasks. Some sew, and some merely sit in quiet contemplation. At the same time, others have wooden pieces before them, playing the familiar games that occupy many people on a winter's night, only without the aid of ale or conversation.

I'd much sooner be playing than sewing, but then, the other nuns aren't blue with cold and must have coverings over their legs. I'm not so lucky, and if I'm to heal and grow strong, I must do all I can to assist myself.

Resigned, I thread my needle, drag together the largest of the ripped pieces of fabric, and begin my work. I foresee a long and frustrating evening before me, and I only hope I won't be forced outside into the church again.

CHAPTER 14

I choose my time carefully but know I can't wait indefinitely to escape my prison. The worry of what is happening in Mercia without me presses dully against every activity I do as I'm forced to follow the same daily activities as the other nuns. And that includes attending all the Offices that must be heard in the cold church.

Not even the young girl or the ancient woman is excused from the nightly service of Matins. I take to only removing my nun's dress and wimple between the longest spell of the night, between Compline and Matins, that I'm allowed to sleep continually through.

I realise quickly that it's the only time I can even attempt to make my escape. It's when everyone sleeps, or so I notice when forced to visit the latrine at that time, during my fifth night of imprisonment.

The brands that mark the gateway are extinguished. Only feeble light from the banked hearth illuminates the main hall. A single candle burns in the latrine, placed strategically away from the door so it doesn't gutter in the wind.

My injuries have been slow to heal, despite the silent ministrations of the nun with her pot of ointment.

I'm slowly learning to tell the nuns apart and not just from eye colour. But also from the shape of their mouths and chins, age and the way they silently communicate. The majority use their hands, but one or two merely use their eyes, somehow expecting me to work out what they're thinking.

Initially, I thought to defy the ban on speaking but quickly changed my mind. Aside from the ring on my finger, which I try and keep hidden, I don't think anyone knows or suspects who I am. That can only aid me. If they suspected I was nobly born, they'd remain more attentive as I slowly seem to accept my fate.

I blame the deep cold for my general lethargy, that and the lack of sleep and good food. There's enough food, but there's not an excess of food. Already, I feel my mended trews growing loose around my waist.

And the boredom is intense.

Until I find my chance to escape, and then my thoughts are consumed with how I actually bring it about.

I've no blade, and there's nothing in the nunnery that could be used as a weapon. Neither are there horses beside a few donkeys and a stubborn mule. When I leave, it will be on my two feet and under my own power.

Each day blurs into another, but then there's a feast day, and I feel a glimmer of hope. The food that day is slightly more elaborate, not just pottage, but roast meat, and the sisters, although still demur, seem more excitable than usual. The Abbess, I notice, even drinks some wine and allows the Sisters to sip either ale or wine, whatever they choose.

I have none keen to keep my senses alert.

After Compline, I retire to my bed and undress, as I normally would, but I don't allow myself to sleep, despite the demands from my body that I do so. Instead, I lie still, listening to the sounds of the other women, the creaking of the wooden roof beams, the slight creaking of the church door, and the noises from outside. It's a windy night, making it difficult to isolate any sound as usual and, equally, as unusual.

I doze, waking with a start and a curse for my fallibility.

From either side of me comes the snoring or gentle breathing of those who sleep. I've no idea how late or early it is, but I slide from my bed, all the same, stepping into my nun's robes as I do so. The floor is bitterly cold, and I'm pleased I've managed to retain my sturdy boots.

I know I must move quickly, as though visiting the latrine, and so I do, making for the main door and slipping through it. A sudden rattling noise from outside masks the usual creak. In the deep darkness of a winter's night, I gaze toward where I know the gateway is.

I want to reach it, try the door, maybe even the gate itself, and see if my actions are noticed. I'm hoping that everyone is sleeping soundly, the effects of the rare treat of ale or wine making the nuns even sleepier.

I argue with myself for precious moments and then dash to the gatehouse. I can see nothing, and I can only hope that my memory of where it is in the complex is correct. I dare not risk looking behind me. I don't want to know if my actions are being watched.

As the wind buffets my dress, plastering it against my legs, I hold my hands out in front of me, hoping to prevent walking into something. I take fifteen or so steps in the strange position and then another fifteen. I really should have taken the time to count how many paces I'd need to take before trying this.

When I reach fifty, I fear that I'm going the wrong way, and it almost stops me, only for my hands to brush against something substantial and wooden.

Almost crying with relief, I run my hands over the barred gate that stops me from leaving, trying to see how it's closed. Does it have a lock that I'll need to steal the key for, or is it more straightforward than that? Again, I wish I'd found this out sooner. I'm aware that I've been gone too long already. Yet, apart from the wind, it truly does feel as though I'm alone. The nuns sleep like the dead.

Beneath my hands, I feel cold metal and realise I've found what I was looking for. Running my hands over the mechanism, I decide there's no key, only a sliding bolt. Carefully, I try and ease it backwards, a grin on my face as the well-oiled mechanism slides easily.

But I stop there. I don't want to risk opening the gate. I know that

I'd just walk away then. I wouldn't have the will to wait until I'd gathered some supplies to last me through my walk back to Mercia.

I turn away from the gate, catching sight of the candle through the wooden walls of the latrine, and quickly make my way toward it. I'm cold and in desperate need of it.

By the time I make it back to my bed, I'm shivering and feeling sick with exhaustion. My eyes close immediately, and when the bell rings for Lauds, they open heavily. I struggle to drag myself upright and only just make it through the church's door before the priest's drone begins. I feel the Abbess' eyes on me and demurely bow my head as though listening.

But I'm not. My mind is alive with possibilities. I vow to take advantage of the next such occasion. It's close to Christmas. I'm sure there will be more, and soon at that.

In the end, I'm surprised when the next such event occurs only three days later. It catches me by surprise. I'm not used to marking the day of every saint's life. A tremble of panic almost has me reconsidering my decision.

But no. It's been over two weeks. I need to get back to Mercia because it appears that my uncle won't face me. I refuse to allow his cowardly actions to win him Mercia.

Once more, at the evening meal, I'm alert to those who drink wine or ale and even make it look as though I partake as well. Although no one is precisely merry with drink, I do notice some less stern faces and a few additional logs on the hearth.

Beyond the closed doors, the day has been clear, if cold, even the wind barely rustling the remaining brown leaves where they lay on the floor. When we retire for the night, I hear the rush of rain falling against the roof and think it is a good thing. I need something to mask my furtive endeavours. Last time, the wind covered any stray noises I made.

I've not really managed to gather any supplies to aid me, although I have two pieces of bread and a beaker to drink from, although no water carrier. I leave them wrapped in my nun's robe as I pretend to sleep.

I've not yet fully recovered from my last broken night's sleep, and I come perilously close to sleeping. I jerk awake more than once. The final time, I deem it time for me to leave. I've too few clothes and so slip my nun's dress over me and wrap my bread and beaker in the fur that covers my bed before wrapping it tightly.

I suddenly realise how those attacked by the Viking raiders must have felt, with nothing to their name but what few possessions remain to them when they flee for their lives. Did they feel fearful or relieved to have their lives? Or were they as determined as I am to reclaim all that was taken from them?

I pause then, straining to hear anything above the heavily falling rain. But I detect nothing other than the odd heavy snore from someone who's undoubtedly enjoyed more than just a taste of ale or wine. I consider that it's probably the Abbess. She might have watched how closely everyone else made their choice, but no one watches her and how much she had. Apart from me.

I walk to the door, trying to mirror my actions when forced to visit the latrine. I stumble a little, and at the door, I make a small amount of noise, hoping it merely alerts the other nuns, who might have stirred, of someone's need to visit the latrine. If any are awake, although I doubt it, they'll enjoy my discomfort on a wet night.

Outside, I turn and gaze longingly at the gatehouse, visible through the slanting rain and in the shadow of a sickle moon. The courtyard has become a morass of mud. Should I venture to the gate. There'll be no masking my footsteps, and I'll also be drenched.

Do I go, or do I stay?

I want to go desperately, but do I have the courage?

The fact I even think it discourages me, and I seek my resolve in thinking of Mercia and Lord Athelstan. They've both been stolen from me.

Without delay, I take my first steps, the mud squelching beneath my boots and the rain covering my face.

With more speed than caution, I dash across the muddy court-yard and take shelter against the gate, my back to it, peering back the way I've come as I catch my breath. So far, I'm unobserved.

Hastily, I reach for the gate bolt and manipulate it with my free hand. Once more, it slides easily, and I pull the gate toward me, allowing just enough room to slip through it. Then, of course, I realise my oversight. There's no means of closing the bolt behind me. I can only pull the gate against the wall. Suddenly, the lack of wind is a blessing because the gate will stay closed, even if it's not locked. Or so I hope.

I peer into the darkness, trying to see beyond the streaming rain and reorientate myself so that I know the correct path to take.

What I don't expect to see before me is a small collection of canvasses constructed in the lee of the nunnery walls. A fire, located at the centre of the canvas houses, struggles to survive against the beating rain. I can smell the tang of wet horses and men.

Fear engulfs me, and I half turn, thinking to make it back inside the nunnery and to my bed before my absence is noted.

But I don't. Instead, I peer into the darkness, trying to make sense of what I'm seeing. Why are these men here? Only before I can truly consider that, I hear the shuffle of large animals. I realise I've found a way to speed my escape if I can just find where the horses are being kept.

A loud snore suddenly rips through the air, and a grimace touches my cold cheeks. Whatever these men are doing here, they're asleep now. I finally slink away from the gate.

In the dim light, I'm careful where I place my feet, desperate not to fall over one of the ropes that helps hold the canvasses upright. I reach out with my free hand, not wanting to encounter any unexpected obstacles. And then I'm close to the first shelter, with the door closed and the rumble of sleep coming from inside.

Closer to the fire now, I squint, trying to see where the horses are. Slowly, I turn. I'm at the heart of five canvasses. All have closed doors for the night. During the day, they open onto a fire. Behind the one furthest from the nunnery gates is another shelter, seemingly missing one side, and it's from there that the sound of animals sleeping comes.

I shiver, licking water from the end of my nose, my heart beating loudly in my ears. I fear a hundred warriors could be behind me, and I wouldn't hear them over the sound of my heartbeat and laboured breathing.

Moving as carefully as possible, I slide between two of the canvasses and arrive at the one the horses shelter under.

White eyes seek mine. I hold my hand out and whisper to the first animal I see that's awake. There's a snuffling along my hand, and no complaints when I run my hand along the horse's nose and then move to rub its back.

The animal has no harness, and although I can see the equipment, I know it'll be too noisy to move. Instead, I reach for what I can see, a blanket, thinking it'll keep me warm during my escape. The horse is tied up by a piece of rope running from the halter, and with fingers grown numb by the rain, I try to undo the simple knot. But my hair's in my eyes, the light poor, and I only have one spare hand.

My heart continues to thud, and in frustration, I lower my precious bundle, resting it on my wet boots, and renew my attempts to undo the knot.

I feel as though it takes forever, but finally, the rope comes loose, and hastily, I gather my bundle and then turn to jump onto the animal's back. The horse is tall, and without the aid of stirrups, I consider how I'll make the leap. Only then a new worry presents itself.

I've not realised that the continued snoring has ended and that I can hear movement from one of the canvasses. I freeze or at least try to, but my body trembles because I'm bitterly cold. I hide behind the horse's shoulder, the animal unperturbed by the night time activity, and I hope I won't be seen.

The sound of water hitting the floor is loud, even above the rain. Whoever is awake should only be for a moment or two. I stand as still as possible, wishing I'd put the rug around my shoulders, biting my lips to stop them from trembling.

Damn, I'm cold and miserable. No one who saw me now would suspect me of being the Lady of Mercia.

The fumbling seems to go on for a long time. Eventually, I hear the sound of a substantial body settling on a camp bed, with the attendant creaks and groans of protesting wood and rope. I breathe out slowly, and it plumes before me, mingling with the horse's breath.

And then my eye rests on something I know I can't leave without.

In the feeble glow of the fire, I can see that a weapon's belt has been hung over the ropes of one of the canvas dwellings, the glint of iron calling to me. I'd feel much better protected if I had a weapon.

I bite my lip again. I already have a horse, which I never imagined possible. Do I really need a weapon as well? Shouldn't I just go now?

The thought of being alone, in the dark, without the ability to protect myself feels more terrifying than escaping from the nunnery.

'I'll be a moment,' I whisper to the horse, and still clutching my retrieved bundle, I turn to reach for the weapon's belt. There's a myriad collection of weapons on there, but I determine to take the seax. I'll struggle to carry anything else without the aid of my weapon's belt, and I don't want to take the whole thing.

The risk of iron hitting iron is too high.

From the canvas, I hear an expulsion of wind, and grimace. Bloody men.

I grip the seax and pull it toward me, holding my breath. The weapon is heavy, and my fingers are unresponsive due to the cold. I fear I'll drop it until the moment I hold it firmly in one hand, resting my bundle in the other.

I exhale and turn to make my way back to the horse. Only there's an obstacle that wasn't there before.

'Where do you think you're going?' the voice is rough, but I recognise it all the same.

The man who captured me.

'What you doing out of your warm bed?' he menaces. I peer into his face. It's as wet as mine. His beard and moustache are threaded with water, and his eyes alight with a threat.

I clutch the weapon tightly, cursing my stupidity. I could be gone from here, but now I face a man I detest while my body is all but numb with cold. I know I won't be able to beat him in combat.

My eyes flicker behind his bulk, but he blocks the path back to my placid mount, and his voice is raised. I'm sure whoever accompanies him will soon be awake, and potentially, the Abbess as well.

Fuck.

I have to think quickly, despite my sluggish state. I've come this far. I just need to get to my horse.

'How did you get out?' my abductor muses, looking beyond me to where the gate must still show as being shut.

I take the small chance and dart to his side, seax in my hand, ready to strike if he should go after me. I don't think he wears more than a tunic and cloak above his trews. And I saw no weapons. If he lunges for me, I'll slice him.

'Hey,' he's startled by my move as I try to rush beyond him, but not startled enough. His hand grabs my arm, and I cry out, turning to kick and punch in an effort to get his massive hand off my arm.

He grunts, and his other arm connects with my chin. I taste blood, and it turns me wild.

I'm stabbing viciously with my seax. I can feel it penetrating his skin, the stench of hot blood filling the air. I think I'll get away when I feel his attack weaken. Only then he reaches down to grab my foot. I tumble into the mud, my mouth filling with dirty water, as a shriek rips from my mouth.

I'll not allow him to do this to me. Not again.

I push my hand down, feeling them slide in the mud, the seax still gripped tight as I push myself upwards. His hand still holds my leg, but that's the only area where he grips me, and I can get away from him.

I just need to get to the horse. Then, I'm sure I'll be able to escape.

My left foot connects with something substantial, his face, I hope. I stagger upright. I'm drenched, dirty, shivering and extremely angry.

Really, I think, did my uncle need to leave his thug outside the nunnery walls to ensure I remained inside? Did he know me so well?

'Get back here,' the words are muffled and yet loud enough that I hear others rousing from their sleep.

I slip in the mud, trying to propel myself forward but going nowhere fast.

From my left, something hits me. I'm thrust back into the mud, a heavy weight on half of my body. I'm kicking and punching, the seax stabbing in my other hand. And I'm howling in rage and hurt.

While I battle the man half on top of me, my foot is once more grabbed, and I have two enemies to overpower.

A fist connects with my stomach, driving all air from it, and I struggle to breathe. Another punch and then another, and one that lands on my muddy face, and tears cloud my vision.

I can't breathe, I can't move. I feel a rope around my caught leg and know I'm almost out of options.

I stab upwards once more, meeting the eyes of my attacker, enjoying the surprise on his face as my seax connects with his punching arm. Blood warms my hand. I'm hacking at the man as he wilts at my attack. His weight leaves my body. I only have the rope to contend with.

I'm sure a slice of my seax would sever the link.

I'm deaf to the noise in the camp, focused only on escaping, as I sit upright, not even peering at the groaning body to the side of me. I feel down my leg, fondling for the piece of rope, only for my eyesight to suddenly go dark.

I scream, but my outrage is cut off mid-shriek by a blow to my back that makes the sound leaving my body more of a gargle than a scream.

I find the end of the rope, my seax ready in my hand, only for all of my strength to desert me as the world goes entirely black.

I don't even have time to think, 'fucking bollocks,' as I crumble into the quagmire.

I STIR.

Rain's pouring onto my face, and I'm cold. That's an understatement. I feel as though I've died, been buried, and abruptly come awake.

My teeth are clenched so tightly together that my jaw aches. All of my body hurts.

My eyes flutter open, peering upwards into heavy grey clouds, only to close again from the force of the rainwater hitting me.

I groan and try and turn, hoping against hope that somehow I'm still outside the nunnery gates, but knowing that I won't be.

The ground beneath me squelches. I realise I've been abandoned in the courtyard. Opening my eyes again as I turn onto my left side only confirms it.

A moan comes from deep inside me.

I've failed.

I'm trapped.

And worse, there are men beyond the gate being paid to ensure I remain trapped. I'll never have another chance to make my escape. From now on, I'll always be suspected, and the nuns, and especially the Abbess, will see deceit before they think to trust me.

But I'm still alive. Just.

I roll entirely over, thinking to stand upright, but my stomach aches so much it's an effort to breathe.

Only then do I realise that I'm being watched from beneath the shelter of the roof of the main hall.

The Abbess is there, her face etched into a grim line. I groan again.

Not only do they know that I tried to escape, but they don't plan on helping me. Not this time.

For a brief moment, I consider just staying where I am, rolling over in the sticky mud and allowing the wind and the rain to drive all heat from my body.

I'll never have Mercia again. It'll never be returned to me. And I'll never marry, have children and continue my mother's dynasty.

My uncle's won.

He has everything he could have possibly ever wanted, and I've nothing.

I'd cry, but I'm beyond self-pity as I finally accept my fate.

The only way I'll manage to escape is with my uncle's agreement or with the aid of my Mercian warriors, who would be able to overwhelm the feeble guard if they only knew where I was.

But is that enough to make me get up, force me to bathe and see to my wounds? Can I live with such a slim hope?

I don't want to, but neither do I seek my death. Not for many years to come. Somehow, I must have my revenge on those who did this to me, even if I'm an old crone with no teeth left to her, I'll still be able to raise my sword arm and take their heads from their bodies.

The thought cheers me. I appreciate that heat is starting to work its way along my frigid limbs.

This, then, is when I must decide. Life in the nunnery, or death, here, in the muck and filth of the nunnery courtyard.

My uncle's smug face flickers into being before me, his mouth opens in laughter, and his hands seem to reach for the ring of Mercia that still makes its home on my finger.

No, I decide. No. I'll accept this for now.

I'll live to fight another battle, and I'll enjoy it when it comes.

With my teeth clamped shut to stop my inadvertent groans from erupting, I force myself to my knees and then onto my feet, and slowly I push myself upright.

My hair's plastered to my face, my body shaking uncontrollably, and my clothes are almost tattered, but it'll take more than a beating to make me give up.

I take a step, feeling the world sway around me. I swallow and take another two. The Abbess continues to observe me.

And then I'm almost running so desperate to get inside. I need to remove all my clothes, clean myself from head to toe, and then see what can be done about my injuries.

The Abbess stands to bar me from entering. I make to move around her, but she's surprisingly quick to block me once more. She's shaking her head, and her hands reach out to keep me from getting any closer to her.

I furrow my forehead, unsure why she's watched me for all this time if she means to prevent me from entering.

Her cold eyes peer at me. I find myself mesmerised by their indifference in them.

Abruptly she mimes taking her clothes off, and I appreciate that

I'm not allowed inside in the state I'm in. This flummoxes me. Am I just supposed to strip off out here? Her refusal to move away from the door indicates that I must.

I bite my tongue to hold back my frustration and then pull my tunic over my head. The fabric's soggy and unmanageable so it gets stuck over my head. I pull, and I tug, and eventually, I'm free, although my pale flesh is puckered and blue with the cold. A downward glance reveals my chest is a shade of deepest purple, perhaps even black. No wonder it's painful to breathe.

My boots are next, and my unresponsive fingers fumble to undo the ties. But finally, I stand on the wooden floor and begin the task of pulling my trews down. This is as hard as removing my tunic, but only when I'm naked before her does the Abbess allow me admittance.

I open the door with a hiss of pain, trying not to notice that I'm entirely naked and that every nun is watching me.

I know better than to be embarrassed by it. I stride to the hearth, the heat of the flames painful over my marbled flesh. Aware I might burn myself, I haul the cauldron of water to the side, reaching for the rags to hold the handle by. There's a wooden half-cask close to the hearth. I slosh the water into it, mindful of my cold flesh.

It barely covers the bottom of the cask, and I stomp outside to draw water from the well. By the time I've done so, I'm almost clean from the rain that still falls, but painstakingly, I return to the hearth and hook the cauldron over the hottest part of the flames once more.

Most of the nuns have returned to their tasks, but some still watch me. I glower at them, pleased that my nakedness affronts them.

By the time that water has boiled once more, I can feel my eyes growing heavy, but know I need to clean myself before I sleep.

With the cask barely half full, I lower myself into it, shivering in the heat, my face suddenly flushed, my stomach aching from my shivering. The sting of the water on my hands alerts me to injuries I hadn't even realised I'd obtained.

I reach for a rag to clean myself with, and only then do I realise I have no means of drying myself. I hardly care anymore. What will I even wear when I'm clean?

Slowly, I realise that the nuns have all left, the ringing of the bell calling them to the church. Well, all apart from one. The Abbess watches me with her cold eyes. In her hand, she holds out linen for me to dry myself with and my hated nun's robes. I take the linen and stand as quickly as possible but not silently. Once more, I gasp, but the Abbess is shaking her head at me, thrusting the robe at me, and belatedly I realise that she means I'm to go and listen to the service.

I shake my head in denial. I need to sleep, but she's adamant, her arm shaking the robe at me yet again. I step from the bath on shaky legs.

Does this woman have no compassion?

The priest's voice reaches me, and the Abbess's arm shakes more and more violently. When I don't move to take the robe, she reaches across with her free hand and slaps me sharply across my bruised stomach.

I double over, nausea engulfing me, but when she threatens to slap me again, I take the robe and slip it on. The fabric catches on my cuts and bruises, but it's nothing to the pain from the slap.

Without time to empty the water, I'm marched to the church. I'm forced to sit beside the Abbess at the front of the church. When my head nods in sleep, I feel an elbow against my bruises, and with tears streaming down my face, I resolve to listen to the service.

While the nuns pray and the priest drones on in his terrible Latin, I think of all I'll do when I'm free from the nunnery. I vow to leave no one alive, not my uncle, not the warrior, not the Abbess, and if the nuns aren't careful, none of them either.

It's the only thing that gets me through the service, which drags on far longer than average, and then back to the main hall. I slink to my bed and settle on it, aware that I've lost my fur covering and that I'm not likely to get another one anytime soon.

CHAPTER 15

I'm awoken in the night by a commotion. I roll from my bed, groaning softly, the creak of the wood grown too familiar to me, my wounds only just beginning to heal. The Benedictine way of life doesn't agree with me and wouldn't agree with me even if I weren't recovering from my escape attempt.

I need to sleep all night long, but I'm not allowed to because of the daily routine of prayers and services, all supposed to be for God's glory, but really more so that the women are kept fully occupied.

This new problem frustrates me.

I stagger from my chamber, and I'm not alone. The other nuns are also peering from behind their wicker screenings, and I follow their gaze.

The main door is open, a bitter wind blowing around my naked feet, but what's happening in the courtyard holds my attention.

There are voices filled with anger and complaint, and a figure lies on the ground. The more I peer at it, the more I think I know who it is, and the more I listen, the more I know who the man is as well, and I hate him.

I can certainly make out the angry gesticulation of the nun as the man shouts at her. Of course, the nun's replies are non-verbal, and it's that which makes me realise how angry she is.

Without thought, I rush outside, keen to know if my deductions are correct. I only realise my stupidity in not putting on my boots when my feet immediately burn with the cold.

But by then, it's too late. I know who's outside, and I have to go to her.

More, I wish I had my sword to batter the bastard who's brought her here.

Eoforhild's slumped on the cold ground. In the light from the gate warden's brands, always lit since my escape attempt, I can see where blood pools on the floor. Immediately I tumble to my knees, desperate to know if Eoforhild still lives.

'It wasn't part of the agreement,' I've not heard the Abbess speak before. Her voice is far from the raspy tone I thought it would be.

'Well, it is now,' the man offers, his voice gruff. I'm reminded of that night, only a handful of weeks before, when he took me from my bed and trussed me up. I'm reminded of when I tried to escape six nights ago.

His face is bloodied and bruised. I notice with delight that his front tooth's missing. I don't know whether he has Eoforhild or me to thank for the injury.

Without hesitation, I reach down to where I know Eoforhild has always kept a spare knife. I'll cut him here and now. I'll have my revenge, and then I'll cut the Abbess as well.

But before I can turn, with my fingers clutching the blade, a meaty hand encircles mine, and a leering face, stinking of sweat and ale, is beside mine.

'Put it down, you damn bitch,' he states, shaking my hand to dislodge the knife, and even though I grit my teeth and try and hold on, the clatter of metal on the floor reaches my ears far too quickly. I'm still weak.

'I see she lives,' the man complains. 'I suggest you see to your warrior before she succumbs to her wounds. She didn't go down easily.'

'Bastard,' I manage to squeeze through furious lips, shocked by the sound of my voice after weeks of not using it. He slaps me around the face with his other hand. Damn the man. When I escape from here, he'll be the first I take my revenge on. Well, the second, the Abbess, will be first.

Laughter greets my words, punctuated by a grunt, and I think that Eoforhild gave almost as good as she got. And then the odious man is beside the Abbess once more.

'Take her, or you'll lose all the endowments. He was most adamant about that.'

Without a backwards glance, the man stamps his way to the gate, where he waits impatiently for it to be opened before marching outside. I think of making a run for freedom, but simultaneously, Eoforhild emits a groan of pain. I'm reminded of the encampment beyond the gate. Somehow, the nunnery has become the safest place for me.

When I turn back to Eoforhild, I notice the Abbess is gone. Before I can look at the gate once more, it's shut, and I'm alone with a bleeding Eoforhild in the middle of the freezing night.

With gritted teeth, I manage to grab Eoforhild beneath her arms and begin to haul her inside. The Abbess might be happy to leave her to die, but I'm not.

By the time I reach the door, now closed against the night air, I'm not even shivering anymore, but rather too hot, with sweat pouring down my face and back. My injuries ache. But no one has come to help me, and I'll not leave Eoforhild to die from her wounds, or the cold, whichever takes her first. She can't help herself.

She lands with a dead weight on the cold ground as I reach to swing the door wide. A blast of heat, which I'd earlier thought measly, covers me, and still, I stagger, aware I'm making a great deal of noise in the dead of night. All of the other nuns have returned to their beds. I'm as little regarded, even now, as I have been ever since my arrival and thwarted attempt to escape.

Eoforhild moans once more as I heave her inside and then turn to shut the door tightly. Now I pause. Where should I take her? Even in the pale glow from the low fire, I can tell that she's almost as white as death.

The fireside, I decide, even though it's almost at the furthest point from where I stand.

Uncaring of how much noise I'm making, I persist, crumbling to the floor, breathing too fast, when I'm finally content that she's where I want her. Only then do my eyes settle on Eoforhild's face, and I gasp, tears forming in my eyes.

How dare the bastard do this to her?

Blood seeps from her damaged mouth, and her eye has already darkened to almost black. But that's not the worst of her injuries. No, that comes from her chest, where I can see blood pooling in the glow of the flames.

She's been stabbed.

Frantically, I rush back to my small bed, grabbing everything I can think of as quickly as possible. I have a new fur, but it's thinner than the old one.

Returning to her, I throw the fur around the lower part of her body while grasping a piece of linen to use as a bandage to stem the blood flow. Not that there's much anymore. I whimper and then take the time to calm myself.

I can help her. I know what to do. I've seen this before. I just need to forget that it's Eoforhild that I minister.

Hastily, I turn to stab at the fire, unheeding of the careful division of the logs. I need it to be hot. I need boiling water and for the temperature in the room to increase rapidly.

I turn to Eoforhild, touching her face and assuring myself that she still breathes. Carefully, I move to remove the tunic that covers her upper body. It's torn and ripped, and yet it's still almost impossible to pull over her head.

While I grunt and heave, trying not to knock the linen from her wound, a hand lands heavily on my shoulder. My head swivels determined to berate whoever tries to stop me, but I meet the concerned face of one of the older nuns, a knowing look in her eye. She doesn't speak, but quickly she makes it clear that she'll assist me.

I almost start to cry again, the relief is so intense, but I simply take the knife from her hand and cut through the sturdy linen of the tunic.

She nods, turning to the fire, an unseen selection of pots being taken from the deep bag she carries at her side.

I swivel to watch her, amazed to find someone willing to help me. As if aware of my gaze, she turns back to me, gesturing with her eyes that I should be attending to Eoforhild. And so I do.

More gently now, I remove her tunic, laying bare the full extent of her bloody injury and the welter of bruises that covers her chest. Her skin's white, almost tinged with blue, and when my fingers brush it, I shiver at the intense cold.

I shake my head. I don't see how she can recover from this, but the nun is at my side, peering at the wound. She tuts, the most sound ever allowed in this place of complete silence, and turns back to the fire. I bend to try and cover more of Eoforhild's body with the fur, only to find a thicker fur handed to me by another of the nuns.

Sharp blue eyes meet mine. I nod my thanks, dipping low to cover Eoforhild's feet, thrusting her arms beneath the feeble warmth.

I glance up, finally realising that I'm not alone in the hall. Another two nuns are more carefully arranging logs on the fire. The first nun seems to wait impatiently for a small pot of water to boil in the ashes. She has a selection of items laid out on the table closest to the hearth. I recognise the dry smell of herbs.

Feeling helpless again, I simply settle beside Eoforhild, unsure where it would be safe to lay my hand on her. In the end, I don't, not until the first nun joins me, her eyes once more focused on the wound, as she indicates I should take the linen away from the puncture site.

When I do, I inhale all over again. The flesh around the side of the wound is jagged and gleams whiter than marble. I grimace, for there's little blood, and I can't think that's a good sign.

With careful hands, the nun wipes the site clean with a piece of rag, the movements almost a caress, before she packs the wound with her careful preparation of herbs. The smell is calming, and the knowledge that I don't have to do this alone is even more reassuring.

The fire at my back blazes into life with a sudden roar. I spare it a glance, noting how quickly the blue heat of the centre has formed. The nuns are far more skilled than I am in such a simple task.

When the wound's packed, the nun turns back to the fire, indicating I should pull the thicker fur tight around Eoforhild's still form. I watch my friend, finally thinking to voice all the questions that haven't yet occurred to me.

Why is she here? How did my enemy find her? I stay away from thinking about her chances of survival. Eoforhild is a fighter, but I'm beginning to suspect the wound is older than I believe. The blood in the courtyard looked fresh, but I think it might only have been the wound being ripped open once more.

I feel helpless but not alone. Through what remains of that long winter night, I stay by her side, the three nuns keeping me company. Their efficient movements reveal to me that while I might have thought I hated all these women and their constant silence and failure to assist me, they're all highly skilled. And more, they're prepared to save my friend.

Not only that, but they stay with me even when the other nuns wake and trudge to the church for the early morning service. I note as we hear the voice of the priest that some of the nuns do close their eyes and pray, but not all of them. Perhaps I'm not the only one who believes there's more to worshipping than just silently mouthing prayers.

I wake with an ache in my side and down my back, surprised to find myself curled around Eoforhild. The main room of the nunnery is slowly coming to life, the rim of a grey morning beginning to lighten the gloom of the room. The nun with the herbs inspects Eoforhild, and I sit upright, the room suddenly spinning.

Her face remains severe, but the look she shares with me makes me feel hopeful. I touch Eoforhild, pleased to feel warmth coming from her body and that her flesh has lost the blue pallor.

Scrambling upright, I look around, fearful of seeing the Abbess, but instead, I hear only the murmur of prayer coming from the church. The nun meets my eyes, understanding flashing in them. One of the other nuns comes to Eoforhild's side, a bowl in her hand. The smell of a meaty broth reaches my nostrils. I almost wretch. It's too early for such food, but it seems Eoforhild must have it.

The nun indicates that I'm to support Eoforhild's head. I shuffle, on stiff legs, to sit beside her head. With only a grimace of distaste, I watch the nun expertly spoon the mixture into Eoforhild's slack mouth, watching her manipulate her jaw so that it's swallowed. When more than twenty spoonful's have been served, the nun nods her head, satisfaction streaming from her blue eyes. She indicates that I should carefully restore Eoforhild's head to the floor.

I do so and then turn as the main door opens, and the nuns all flow back inside. I expect to see surprise on their faces. Instead, they merely stride to their place along the benches to wait expectantly for the first meal of the day.

When the Abbess follows them inside, I expect her to react angrily, but all she does is join her fellow nuns. Those who were assisting me stand as well, with one of them turning to swing the cooking pot to the side of the fire. They work together to spoon the pottage into the waiting bowls, and soon everyone is eating, apart from me.

Once more, a hand touches my shoulder, and the concerned eyes of the nun with the pots of herbs indicate I should join those eating. I think to shake my head, but my stomach rumbles loudly in the silence. I know better now than to turn my nose up at the food I'm offered.

There's never enough of it, and I'd do well to eat now.

I stand on stubborn legs and make my way to the waiting bowl at the far end of the table, as far as possible to get from the raging hearth.

I shiver and clench my teeth tightly closed.

I have so many questions, but I'll not get any answers.

Not in this closed community, and not until Eoforhild wakes.

I can only hope it'll be soon and she'll have more reassuring news than her current state suggests.

. . .

THE DAY PASSES SLOWLY. I'm forced to attend to the duties assigned to me outside, even though the wind is bitter, and I'm sleep deprived. There's no sympathy on the faces of the nuns who work alongside me in the gardens. Neither are they as severe as they have been. When I make mistakes and drop things because my fingers are cold and clumsy, the usual critical looks don't shoot my way. I'm grateful for that, even though I wish I could be excused from the task of tending to the winter-bare herb garden.

When I'm finally allowed back inside the building, the heat assaults me. I shudder as it washes over me.

Instantly, I rush to find Eoforhild, but she's not by the hearth, and I turn, my stomach suddenly filled with dread. Surely someone would have told me if she'd died?

I spin, trying to find where she might be if she still lives, and then I remember. This main hall is not the usual place where the sick are tended. I rush from the warmth, back into the bitter cold and to the other building, smaller and closer to the church, where the sick are treated. The hope, I assume, is that being closer to God will make them heal more quickly.

My footsteps sound loud as I thrust open the door, my eyes wild, hoping that Eoforhild is there.

Four sets of startled eyes glance up at me, a rebuke on the face of one that I should shut the door quickly to stop the heat from escaping. I do so, my glance having found the reason for my search.

In the infirmary, there's a large hearth and a selection of six beds, which are currently all empty, apart from one. It's the warmest and most inviting part of the entire nunnery.

I dash to the side of the occupied bed, my eyes alighting on Eoforhild with a soft sigh, and a gentle chuckle reaches my ears. I turn, surprised to hear such a sound, but the nun who tended to my friend throughout the night has eyes filled with an apology, perhaps realising why I was so worried.

She greets me with a respectful bob of her head and pulls back the fur to show me the puncture site. I grimace at the welter of bruises, bad enough in the early morning light but now revealed to me in all their glory of purple and red. There's even a hint of black at the core of some of them. The nun pulls back the poultice over the site of the stab wound. I gape, amazed to see the white skin already turning red, the surrounding area looking far healthier.

As I pull my eyes away from her healing work, she nods, a happy movement. I believe she's telling me that the chances of recovery are good. I nod, tears falling from my eyes, and into my hand slips a beaker filled with warm fluid. She indicates that I should drink it, and although I've no idea what effect it will have on me, I do so all the same. She's helped my friend. I can't imagine that she means me any harm. Why Eoforhild got such treatment when I didn't is beyond my understanding or ability to ask without the aid of speech.

The mixture is sharp on my tongue, although I can also taste honey, no doubt used to alleviate the acrid taste of the mix. But the after-effect makes me shiver, not with cold, but with the delight of suddenly being warm.

I swig all of the drink, the warmth seeming to bloom from my stomach to the far reaches of my body. When I offer it back, I grip the nun's hand in both of my mine, trying to convey my thanks.

She nods, and I hope she understands, but I can feel my eyes drooping. In a heartbeat, she has the furs thrown back on one of the other beds, and I crawl between them.

For the first time in many weeks, I actually feel as though someone here cares for me.

CHAPTER 16

W hen I next wake, there's a querulous voice at my side. I turn to gaze at Eoforhild. She's trying to sit upright, but the nun keeps pushing her down again, a look of concern on her face as she shakes her head.

I leap from the bed and add my entreaties to the nun's. Only I surprise myself by speaking. I've become used to not exercising my voice, and it sounds strange, even to my ears.

'You need to lie down, or you'll dislodge the poultice.'

Eoforhild looks at me, her surprise evident in her rapidly blinking eyes.

'You're alive?' she gasps. I chuckle, ignoring the annoyed tut from one of the other infirmary nuns because we speak.

'I could say the same about you.' A tear's sneaking its way from her eye, and I note it with shock. I never thought Eoforhild was capable of emotion.

'We all thought you dead. But I came looking, all the same, when I heard a rumour of your survival from Osgod until that damn bastard caught me. Sneaky git. Snared me while I slept.'

'And stabbed you and then brought you here?' I'm hoping she might know where 'here' is, for I certainly don't.

'So it seems. Why are you staying here? Mercia's in an uproar. You need to get back there.' The sudden urgency in her voice has me reaching for a seax that's no longer around my waist.

'I can't leave. They won't let me. I've tried. I'm trapped here.'

'Of course you can leave,' Eoforhild scoffs and then winces as she once more tries to sit upright.

'Your uncle's claiming Mercia, saying you're dead. Your cousin Athelstan has been searching for you everywhere, as has Lord Athelstan. They think King Edward lies, and they're right! You need to escape.' Outrage colours her voice.

I sigh then, wishing I could say something else but knowing I can't.

'I have to stay here. It's either this or death. There are at least ten guards outside the gates. If I go within a few steps of them, they threaten me. They want to kill me. All that keeps me alive is the fact that they aren't allowed to enter the nunnery grounds. No men can, other than the priest.'

'Ten men, is that all? I'm sure we can take them on ourselves.' Eoforhild's tone shows her disdain for fearing to take on ten men. After all, we've faced higher odds in the past.

I shake my head, suddenly weary. It was a shock to come across those men when I tried to escape. I'd not realised such precautions had been taken to ensure I stayed a prisoner. My injuries are taking too long to heal.

'Tell me of Mercia?' I demand to know, and something in my voice makes Eoforhild close her mouth tightly, her lips a harsh line of disapproval. I think she'll say nothing else out of her unease with my ready acceptance of my capture. Only then she begins to speak, to try and force me to leave the nunnery.

'We were roused, on that terrible night, to find your bed empty and signs of struggle. Fifteen horses were gone from the stables, and it was deduced that Lord Rǫgnvaldr or King Edward had taken you. Lord Athelstan rushed south. Your cousin Athelstan went north. Both men were convinced that their assumption was correct.'

'Lord Athelstan suspected your uncle's involvement and cursed everyone for being so damn foolish the night before your marriage.

He was foul-tempered with everyone. Your cousin Athelstan was no less scathing. They left Lady Ecgwynn to keep Tamworth safe with the aid of Ealdorman Æthelfrith.'

'I was with Lord Athelstan, as were Ymma and Mildryth, when we found the group of men whom we deduced had abducted you. I'd never seen a horse rush so fast over the ground. I thought he'd killed the horse with his haste. The fact that he'd been right to suspect King Edward gave him no delight.'

Here she pauses, refusing to meet my eyes.

'You should have seen him. He was in such a state. His face was white, his hands trembling, and yet he refused to give up. Our horses rushed closer and closer. And then we saw you, of course, we saw you, trussed up on that horse, your hands bound and your head covered by a sack, just before they stole you into Wessex.'

'Lord Athelstan was determined to follow you and win your release. But there was a force of two hundred Wessex men waiting for us by the bridge over the River Thames near London. As much as we tried to get across the Thames, it was impossible.'

'We had our weapons with us, but our collection of twenty or so warriors was nothing against so many Wessex warriors. But we fought all the same. Those men were useless against us. They only prevailed because they outnumbered us so heavily.'

'And then, when we thought it couldn't get any worse, the force streamed into Mercia itself, moving beyond the banks of the River Thames, reinforced by more and more men who seemed to spill from Wessex. I'd never seen so many Wessex warriors in one place. Honestly, I didn't think King Edward could lay claim to so many warriors. They menaced us and threatened to attack Mercia.' She shook her head, clearly not seeing the room in the nunnery but rather the events of that morning on the riverbank.

'We had no choice but to return to Tamworth to prevent further bloodshed and to see what would happen in your absence. Your cousin had returned from the north by then, empty-handed and seething when we told him the truth of what had happened.'

'He threatened to ride into Wessex himself, and only the intervention of his sister stopped him from doing so. I heard all that was said between the brother and sister, Ealdorman Æthelfrith and his two sons. They blamed one another, and I thought it would descend into all-out war there and then.'

'Lady Ecgwynn berated them all, told them they were making King Edward's job easier by arguing amongst themselves. She forced them to consider the implications of what had happened and to try and think rationally.'

'The only solace we could take was that the Wessex forces stayed close to the border. Although Ætheling Athelstan had seen Lord Rognvaldr and his men, they, too, stayed away from Mercia. For the time being.'

'But then King Edward rode into Mercia as though he were a conquering king. He waited all of seven days before calling a witan and trying to force Ætheling Athelstan to swear allegiance to him and having Mercia proclaim him as their king. Lady Ecgwynn realised what would happen and took sanctuary in a nunnery in Mercia. Your uncle didn't appreciate her use of his favourite ploy for getting rid of unwanted women.'

'Ætheling Athelstan had ridden to Gloucester to escape your uncle and to see if he could gain assistance from the Welsh kings. That's where we were when news reached me of where you were, and of course, I came to find you.'

'Where do you think I am?' I ask eagerly.

'Wilton Nunnery,' Eoforhild states the destination with certainty, but I'm not convinced. If I were at Wilton, surely it wouldn't be a place of silence? After all, Uncle Edward's second wife is at Wilton. I can't see her taking a vow of silence or even of holding her silence. She'd want to laud her triumph over me. I don't share this with Eoforhild, and she's keen to continue talking.

'But I tell you, there'll be an uprising. There are few in Mercia keen to have a Wessex king ruling over them. I know the witan won't declare King Edward as ruler, despite his two hundred warriors. Now that I know you're here, I can return to Mercia, inform Ætheling Athelstan, and bring a force to extract you.'

Eoforhild suddenly looks around in confusion, unsure what to make of our surroundings. I don't want to say it, but I know she'll not be allowed to leave here. Like me, she's become a prisoner.

'Ætheling Athelstan is determined to find out who betrayed you to King Edward. Your uncle is already planning to have a coronation in Mercia, even though he's not yet been accepted as ruler. He has his men everywhere. Derby and Nottingham have pledged themselves to him, and Lord Rǫgnvaldr has been promised Lincoln. It's a disaster.'

'But it's only been a few weeks,' I complain, and she nods and winces, all at the same time as the movement jars her wound.

'This has been planned for some months, I'm sure of it, long before Lord Rǫgnvaldr attacked Derby. Ætheling Athelstan fears that Mercia might be assaulted by Dublin when Lord Rǫgnvaldr realises how weak your uncle really is.'

I nod. The news horrifies me, and yet it's only what I've managed to work out for myself in the last few weeks. Well, the part about my uncle is. That Lord Rǫgnvaldr was also embroiled is somehow to be expected.

I know I was betrayed. Perhaps, I berate myself, I should have been less keen to humiliate my uncle and Archbishop Plegmund, and to fight Lord Rǫgnvaldr. They've taken their ultimate revenge on me, and I'm helpless to do anything. And now Eoforhild is as well.

'You must rest and heal,' I state, my voice flat and lifeless. 'Only then can we plan our escape,' I say the words, but I don't mean them. Not even with Eoforhild here can I be assured that I'll be able to defeat the men who hem in the nunnery. They closely guard the gate, forcing the Abbess to keep me a captive for whichever ealdorman brought me here.

Whatever the arrangement is between the Abbess and the ealdorman, she's keen to adhere to it. The cruelty is all her own.

'We must escape, get back to Mercia,' Eoforhild's voice is rich with resolve.

'In good time, yes, but you must fully recover.'

She glances at me, something in my voice alerting her to how defeated I am. Only then the Abbess enters the infirmary, her gaze razor-sharp, and I shut my mouth. She terrifies me now that I've witnessed her malice.

I'm surprised Eoforhild, and I've been allowed to speak as much as we have.

She snaps her fingers at me. I rise, conditioned to her demands on me, and fearing another slap.

Eoforhild gasps in horror. I turn back, trying to reassure her, but I see shock and disgust before I follow the Abbess outside.

I don't even have time to thank the nun who saved Eoforhild's life.

I'm led to the church across the courtyard, a brisk wind blowing as I avoid the frozen puddles formed on the muddy surface.

Inside, the Abbess gestures that I should take to my knees at the front of the church. I do so, shivering despite the cloak I wore outside. I swear it's colder in the church than it is in the herb garden.

I clearly determine her intention.

I've missed at least two of the services that I must attend each day, and it seems I'm to make my amends to my God. I bow my head, pleased to offer prayers of thanks for the survival of my friend. But the God in this church is unfeeling and heartless, and when, hours and hours later, I'm finally allowed to rise from my cramped position, no part of my body doesn't cry out in pain.

I can no longer feel my feet or my hands. I stagger, made ungainly by the passage of time, to my feet. The Abbess, who's spent all of her time beside me, ensuring I pray as I must, shows no such signs of any distress.

I think her as cold and heartless as the church.

This place doesn't serve the God my mother worshipped.

This God seems only to serve the Wessex king and his ambitions, and I'd do anything to return to Mercia.

But I know it's impossible while my uncle lives. No matter what Eoforhild might believe or what my cousin might hope. I think of Lord Athelstan, the man I should have been married to weeks ago. Will he continue to look for me, or will he realise that with Eoforhild's disappearance, I'll never be found?

The thought's far from reassuring, but I also know I don't want to see anyone else injured fighting for me.

Mercia must survive, no matter who rules her. I hope my Mercians can realise that.

EOFORHILD HEALS SLOWLY, but her resolve never leaves her. And despite the vow of silence that the nuns have all taken, those in the infirmary allow quiet speech.

I think this a blessing until I realise that Eoforhild can only speak of one thing. My escape.

'I can't leave. It doesn't mean I don't want to.' The words fall from my lips with too higher frequency, and Eoforhild isn't the only one who grows frustrated. She might well still be confined to her bed, but I'm condemned to the nunnery when I should be running my kingdom.

'When I'm healed, I'll return to Mercia and bring back an army.'

'You'd bring a Mercian army into Wessex?' I demand to know. I can't bring myself to tell her that she'll never depart from here. It seems she's not yet realised the true nature of her captivity.

I'd tell her, but I want her to be healthy and well before she learns the truth.

'Wessex has taken an army to Mercia. It's no great thing to do the reverse,' her argument doesn't persuade me. Rather than squabbling about absconding from the nunnery, I try and reason with her.

'But if the Mercian warriors are in Wessex, who'll protect Mercia?'

'The Wessex army will. Not that it'll need protection. King Edward has an alliance with Lord Rǫgnvaldr.'

That doesn't make Mercia safe, far from it, but I can hear the vexation drumming in Eoforhild's voice, so I hold my silence.

'As soon as Ætheling Athelstan knows where you are, he'll come for you.' I don't doubt that he would, but I do suspect his father will never reveal my location to him.

'He's made a vow at your mother's gravesite that he'll find you and restore Mercia to you. I imagine it made his father furious, but I left before news of that reached King Edward.'

The news thrills me, and yet at the same time, I know my cousin can't help me. No matter what, my cousin must remain on near-equitable terms with his father. As much as it pains me to think about it, it's the only way forward. For now.

'What of cousin Ælfweard?' I ask the question that I've been dreading. I don't want him to have my kingdom. He's too young, foolish, and too damn stupid.

'I heard nothing about him. I think he remains in Wessex.'

'Good, cousin Ælfweard would be cruel to the Mercians. My uncle will merely be determined.'

'I don't understand the distinction?'

I'm not surprised.

'King Edward wishes to live up to the reputation of his father. Cousin Ælfweard wishes to show cousin Athelstan that he's more fitted to be king after his father's death. But Ælfweard has no military expertise. He'd soon turn his frustration at trying to handle so many men who live by the sword into petulant cruelty aimed at the Mercian people.'

'But it won't matter when Ætheling Athelstan frees you from here, from Wilton. We are in Wilton, aren't we?

Finally, I think she's thought herself around to this.

'I've no idea. I've seen nothing beyond these walls since I was brought here.'

'Are we even in England?' she abruptly asks, the thought clearly just coming to her.

'I must assume so, but an England where no one speaks other than us, and I'm sure they'll soon tire of allowing us even that.'

'We'll flee before that happens,' Eoforhild announces staunchly, but I know we won't, as she settles to sleep again.

The wound Eoforhild took was deep and infected. It's a miracle that she's healing, but for someone as fit and healthy as her, it's taking a long, long time. Outside, the weather is starting to change, with the days slowly growing in length. The need to always wear as many clothes as possible is no longer as imperative as it once was.

Soon Eoforhild will be on her feet and keen to be gone. I don't know what the Abbess will do then. I take hope in the knowledge that Eoforhild has been healed. Why I think to myself, would that have been allowed to happen if the Abbess were only to order her killed later?

Equally, Eoforhild won't be allowed to leave the nunnery. And I know, with absolute certainty, that she'll never stop trying to leave and that she won't accept her incarceration. As much as I'm pleased not to be alone in the nunnery, I begin to dread the day she understands that almost as much as I fear to think of my uncle's triumph in Mercia.

CHAPTER 17

I no longer recognise the man before me. He was once my uncle, my mother's favourite brother. Now he's none of those things. I no longer wish to claim any kin to him, and I haven't since our last meeting when I was the victor, and he was forced to slink from the hall at Tamworth, defeated and aged.

He looks even older to me now, his age showing in the lines on his face and slashes of grey streaking his hair.

He appears before me in clothes fit for the king he believes he is, even going so far as to wear his kingly-helm and royal cloak, even in the small nunnery that's my prison. His cloak is so heavy with jewels and furs that I'd struggle to walk upright if the thing were swirled around my slim shoulders instead of his broader ones.

Uncle Edward's eyes pierce me with the malice he must feel toward me. I always thought he should have cousin Athelstan's kindly eyes, but instead, they swirl with daggers and desire. He's different from the man I last encountered when I broke him and thought Mercia was secured as mine to rule. Now he comes in triumph, and he exudes it as though it were a pleasant fragrance and not the foul stench of deceit and treachery.

This. This thing that stands before me is no longer my uncle, no longer the son of King Alfred. No, this thing, for I refuse to think of him as a man, is riven with desire and want and need. I'm shocked to discover that my lowest expectations of him have come true.

How could he do this to me?

And yet I think I've always known him capable of such vulgar ambition. I think my mother knew it as well.

For all the years Lady Æthelflæd held Mercia, uncle Edward was like a dog nipping at her heels. Or rather, a fox watching the hens, just waiting for an opportunity to tear through the defences and take its first bite of the juicy flesh on the other side. But prepared to wait and plot and scheme for the most likely time to find success.

I wish I'd been able to guard against his hovering malice. I wish I'd appreciated it for what it was.

I'd blame myself for the current predicament; see the fault as mine, but I don't. This isn't my doing. I'm the victim. I'm a victim of circumstance and the ambitions of men who believe they can win whatever they want. Either with their sword, their cock or the might of the corrupt Church officials at their beck and call. I've tried to play their game. I even beat them at their game for a short while, but no more.

And certainly not from my current place of imprisonment.

I wonder then why my uncle has come here.

'Niece,' as he sits before the hearth in the main hall of the nunnery, he addresses me with insolence. I feel my rage boil. Three years have passed since I was first brought here. Three years, and only now does he deign to make an appearance, perhaps make an accounting of what's been done.

Eoforhild hisses beside me, and I'd caution her, but she knows her mind, and I'm not about to chastise my friend and only ally in the silent world I now inhabit. Even hearing my uncle's words shatters the silence I live within, broken only by the voice of the priest and those people who seek medical aid from the nuns.

'Uncle,' the word's barely audible, my chest too tight with fury to truly allow me to breathe life into the word. And it's been too long since I last spoke, anyway.

All the same, my response must exhibit my real emotions because his eyes flicker to mine, meeting them for the first time.

'Now, niece,' and he smiles, a sickly thing that makes me wish I had a blade to hand to slice it from his face. 'There's no need for anger to characterise our meeting. You were outwitted. Be pleased you still breathe.'

Eoforhild tenses as though she'll strike, and I reach out and touch her arm. A caution, and thanks. She's never put aside her compulsion to guard me, despite being kept a prisoner, the same as me.

I try to think of a suitable response. All the times I've imagined this conversation in my head haven't prepared me for actually facing him. I wish I had more to taunt him with, but he has won, and I can't deny that.

'Why are you here?' It's far from what I thought would be my primary consideration, but the words seem to have more than the desired effect. My uncle's mouth slams shut. I watch him attempt to control his emotions.

I hear nothing about Mercia from my place of imprisonment. Perhaps, I think, all isn't as my uncle hoped it would be. Probably, my cousin rules Mercia in my place. That would suffice.

Only then does my gaze flicker to the man standing beside him. Archbishop Plegmund looks far from the assured archbishop he is. What, I wonder, has upset them both so much?

'You'll be unaware that I was proclaimed king of Mercia, as well as Wessex, when you disappeared.' Uncle Edward's hand rests on the arm of a wooden chair I've never seen before in the nunnery. Has he genuinely taken to travelling with his favourite chair?

'I imagined you would be. And, of course, I didn't disappear. I was abducted. Against my will.' Uncle Edward makes no response to my complaint. This I find interesting.

'The people of Mercia believe many things about what happened that night. Some say you're dead, some say you were sold as a slave, others, and this is the most prevalent rumour, that you're alive and well but a prisoner in Wessex.'

'So, most people believe the truth then?' I'm pleased that my uncle's ruthless scheming is exposed and well-known, and that Eoforhild didn't take the truth with her when she was caught trying to find me.

'Perhaps they know their version of the truth.' I squint at my uncle, wondering what he means by that.

'And what does this have to do with me? Have you come to release me? To give Mercia back to me?'

'No, but I've come to resolve the issue.'

The finality in my uncle's voice is perhaps intended to drive fear into my heart, but as he says, I'm lucky to breathe still. I'd almost wish he'd killed me three years ago rather than send me to this exile amongst the silent nuns where my every action is looked upon with dismay.

'They rebel against you, don't they?' I delight in asking the question and ignoring his threat.

Uncle Edward refuses to meet my eyes. The knowledge that the Mercians haven't forsaken me strengthens my resolve to show no weakness.

'You should have known they'd never accept you as their king. You're a stranger to them, and worse, you're the son of the man who refused to assist them when the Great Heathen Army threatened them.'

'They accepted my sister, who was that man's daughter.'

His retort is immediate but also confused. How can he still not understand Mercia and her people?

Before I reply, I move closer to the hearth, the chill of the floor making my feet ache, as so often happens. My old leather boots have long since disintegrated. Now I must make do with the soft shoes the nuns wear.

If I must speak with my uncle, then I'll do it in comfort and take advantage of the fact that the nuns are too in awe of their king to complain.

I settle on the bench closest to the hearth. The tendrils of heat warm my face. I almost shiver in delight.

'Your sister wasn't going to rule Wessex anytime soon. Anyway, she claimed the kingdom through her Mercian husband, and Mercian mother, not through her Wessex-born father.' My voice is filled with the disdain I feel for my uncle. How dare he not even understand that most simple of facts?

I expect my uncle to argue with me, to state that his father didn't abandon Mercia, but while the truth may have been subverted, those closest to the royal family know what truly happened all those years ago.

'Then, the Mercians will never accept me?' My uncle demands to know.

'Never,' I confirm, confused by the question. I thought he'd come to arrange my murder. Perhaps I've not understood his intent correctly.

'Then it little matters what I do to the Mercians?' The words are spoken in a rush, as though to hide what he means. I understand all too quickly.

'If you attack the Mercians, they'll repel you. No matter what the people of Wessex might think, the Mercian beat the Viking raiders just as much as Wessex did. The survivors of those bloody battles yet live, and if they don't, their descendants, skilled in the same battle techniques, do. Whatever you think of doing to Mercia, I suggest you reconsider immediately. You'll not win against them. They don't want Wessex to rule them.' My voice has grown firm with determination. I hold my uncle's gaze.

I note the flicker of unease and also the resignation in the downward curve of his lips.

'You speak so fiercely of your 'Mercians', and yet you're still trapped here, no one can find you. It seems you hold them in higher regard than they do you.'

I laugh, the sound strange to my ears and far from what my uncle expected with his weak insult.

'Even I don't know where I am, although I do have a good idea. The Mercians aren't welcome in Wessex. You've ensured that it's almost impossible for anyone to discover where I am.' There's no malice in my voice. I could be talking about the weather. Again, my uncle looks far from pleased.

'Tell me why you're here?' I've had enough of speaking to him. It's evident that he doesn't come to release me. In that case, I'd sooner not be forced to talk to him. If he means to see me dead, I'd have it happen as soon as possible. I've been his winning piece in the political machinations that have allowed Wessex to attempt to take control of Mercia for long enough.

'I need something from you. And you won't like to give it to me,' Uncle Edward states, staring into the heart of the fire and not at me at all.

'What do you need?' My heartbeat's steady, and yet there's urgency in my voice.

'I need you to abdicate your right to rule Mercia.'

'Why would I ever do that?'

'While these rumours persist, the population remains restive. If they know that you no longer wish to rule, then they'll have to accept my overlordship.'

'Didn't you listen to what I said to you?'

'If they can't have you, then there's no choice for them but to accept me. It's logical.'

'Not to the Mercians. And others could lead them, good Mercians, not the king of Wessex.'

'Who? To whom would they turn? Whom have they turned to?'

In all honesty, I'm not sure that there's anyone the Mercians would accept, not unanimously. It would need to be to end the persistent defiance uncle Edward must be facing. Neither do I wish to make someone else my uncle's next target.

'It's not my place to tell you. You say you're king there, and you have been for the last three years. You should know who's respected and who isn't.'

My uncle's anxiety is evident in the swift glance he sweeps around the room and in the tapping of his foot against the wooden floor.

Does Mercia still stand aloof from Wessex? In my absence, have they maintained their staunch independence? I wish I knew more than what my uncle is prepared to tell me.

'You must either abdicate your right to rule or give up your life. Those are the only options available to you now,' uncle Edward's words seem to gloss over what he means. But I understand all too well.

'I'll do neither. You'll need to find another way.'

'So, you'll not die for Mercia then? That does surprise me?'

'I won't willingly give my life to a venture that's doomed to failure. My death won't magically make the Mercians want you as their king. Why would it? And why now? I've been missing for three years. Yet you say that the rumour is that I live, and I'm your captive. And somewhere in Mercia, men and women rise against you in protest. What will they do if you truly kill me and present my cold, lifeless body to them? They certainly won't immediately see the error of their ways. And what will cousin Athelstan do? I assume that you and he aren't reconciled either.'

The remark brings a sneer to uncle Edward's face. I wish I could slap it away.

'Your dear cousin is assisting the rebels. He refuses to be named as their king, saying he can't be because you live and, in the meantime, seeks out allies wherever he can find them.'

'And I imagine that, unlike yourself, he's good at making allies. He shares my mother's ability to beguile and demand complete obedience.'

'Then why doesn't he claim Mercia as his own?' My uncle's words are spoken in confusion.

'Because you'd use it as a further means of taking control. Cousin Athelstan, it seems, understands both you and the Mercians far more than you do.' My voice is rich with condescension. I'm at a loss to explain how my uncle has ruled all these years without facing more threats to his kingship.

'You think you're very clever with your insights and snappy retorts, don't you? But, you imperil Mercia by refusing to assist me. If Wessex must take an army into Mercia again, then I will.'

I smirk. I can't stop the delight from showing on my face.

'You expect Wessex men to potentially lose their lives over an argument about who wears a shiny bauble on their head? How have you ruled Wessex for so long without some rudimentary understanding of their deep-seated hatred for Mercia? Honestly, uncle, I'm speechless that my grandfather ever thought you were capable of ruling in Wessex and of ruling the Anglo-Saxons, as he called everyone. You lack even the most basic understanding. Wessex won't attack Mercia, even if the king commands it. It won't happen. You're lucky to have had what success you have.'

'It will. The warriors of Wessex are sworn to serve my royal household. They've fought Viking raiders before when they threatened Wessex. This is no different. Mercia now threatens Wessex.'

'How does Mercia threaten Wessex? Have the Mercians gathered the warriors and the fyrd and threatened to march to Winchester? Have they endangered your family? Have they done anything other than asked for their ruler back?'

'You don't know what Mercia has done in your absence.'

'I might not, no. But I don't think I'm wrong when I speak as I have. Tell me, where was the battle between Mercia and Wessex?'

'They've threatened their king,' indignation thrums through his statement.

'They don't acknowledge you as their king, so how can they have threatened 'their' king.'

Uncle Edward's mouth opens as though he'll speak, but it snaps shut again

'How do you know they've not accepted me as their king?' here, he casts an accusing glance toward Eoforhild, and my previously restrained fury breaks through.

'How would she know? She's been a prisoner almost as long as I have. But I'm right, aren't I? You called a witan as soon as my disappea. ːnce was discovered, probably at Tamworth. But no one came, did they? No one voted for you as king. You didn't take an army, despite all your threats and the men you had waiting on the border when you abducted me, and so couldn't claim it through military might either. Could you?'

Here my uncle's expression fluctuates, and I consider that I've said too much and given away too many of the summations I've been keeping to myself.

Yet my uncle doesn't answer my accusations directly. What, I think, does he wish to keep so secret?

'If you'll not relinquish your claim to Mercia, then I must show the Mercians that you're truly dead.'

It's not what I want to hear, and yet, despite Eoforhild at my side, I'm caught unaware.

The hot breath against my cheek is the first I know that uncle Edward brought more people with him than just Archbishop Plegmund.

Eoforhild leaps to her feet more quickly than I do, and yet she's too slow to stop a giant of a man from clamping his arms around her body and pulling her tight against him.

All of her screams and grunts are effortless. I can't help, for a man menaces me with a glinting blade in his fist. For a moment, I consider it might be the man who abducted me in the first place, and while I try to avoid him, I back myself into the waiting arms of another.

As the captor's arms tighten around me, in the same way, that Eoforhild has been restrained, I suck in a deep breath. I'm determined to screech so that all the nuns, in their fortress of quiet contemplation, are aware of the king's intentions towards me.

Whether they try and assist me or not is irrelevant. I want someone to know that my uncle threatened me.

I kick out, but the warrior's too skilled. He merely squeezes me tighter and tighter until I'm forced to stop screaming because the air has been crushed from my body, leaving me gasping.

In the initial attack, I turned as though to escape, so even as I gasp for my life, I can't gaze vengefully at my uncle. No, as always, he's the sort of man who gives instructions rather than carrying them out. It disgusts me that he's so like my grandfather. My mother might have revered her father, but I worked out his personality for myself long ago.

And then, my world turns black, the breath stolen from me altogether, and I think, if this must be my death, then at least I'll see my mother again.

WHEN MY EYES FLICKER OPEN, confusion floods my mind. If I'm dead, why can I see candles burning and hear the priest's voice inside the small church?

Abruptly, I sit upright, gazing around me. I'm trying to determine what my uncle's had done to me, to prove my death while leaving me alive again.

I imagine he thinks he's a benevolent uncle.

I think he's too weak to kill his niece, even though he's stolen her kingdom.

'You're awake then?' the sound of Eoforhild's voice further confuses me. Why, then, did my uncle come to my prison?

'What happened? Is my uncle still here?'

'No, he's gone,' her failure to answer my first question worries me, as does her refusal to meet my eyes.

'Tell me what he did?' I ask, aware that I feel intact. No part of my body has been touched. I have no injury, and neither do I feel injured.

'He took it.'

'Took what?'

Her soft sign of resignation stills my heart, and I realise what she won't say. With my hand in front of my face, my fury returns. Damn the bastard.

'My ring?'

'Your ring,' she confirms. I gaze down, noting the part of my skin that reflects more whitely than the rest of me.

The signet ring of Mercia, mine since my mother's death. For some reason, my abductor failed to take it from me. I can't count the number of times I've sought solace in knowing I still possessed it.

The fact that my uncle has had it taken from me now confirms that it shouldn't have been left with me on that terrible night all those years ago.

'When the Mercians see it, they'll believe you dead. They know you'd never have given it up while you lived.'

'Or tricked,' I say the words sourly, rubbing the space with my other hand.

I've been deprived of my luxurious clothing and my weapons, but at least I had my silver signet ring. But no more, and I feel its loss as though I've just realised how permanent my imprisonment was all over again.

'Damn the bastard,' I say the words too loudly, expecting a hiss of condemnation from the nuns, but of course, they're all in the church. I'm sitting on my bed, facing Eoforhild.

Yet, as much as I want to rant and rave, pull my hair and plan my revenge against my uncle, something stops me.

'Come, we'll sit by the hearth. It's bloody cold.' If Eoforhild is surprised by my calm acceptance, she follows me without speaking. Perhaps she's realised what I've worked out.

In the great hall, the fire glows more warmly than I think I've ever seen it, logs glowing with the heat of the forge. Has Archbishop Plegmund rewarded the Abbess for her excellent work once more? Has he finally seen that the nuns have enough food and fuel to see them through each year without enduring the dearth that has, more often than not, categorised the three winters I've endured here?

I would hope so, if only for the sake of the nuns.

As much as I might hate them for being involved in the king's great subterfuge, I pity them for the little good it's done them. Perhaps my final humiliation has brought that to an end?

I shiver as the heat covers me. I can't recall feeling so warm for a long time, not even during the summer heat, when all the nuns, myself included, work in the herb gardens.

'My uncle must be desperate,' I start, looking around for any sign that he's still here before I open my mouth. But all traces of his presence are gone, even the wooden chair. Not even the scent of the warriors hangs in the air, and it was heady.

'Yes, he must be. All this time, I would have thought Mercia was reconciled to his rule.'

'Truly? I'm not really sure what I expected, but I can't imagine the Mercian nobility being keen to take the knee before the Wessex king. Not after everything they've done to secure Mercia against the Viking raiders. But, I was unsure how vocal their opposition would be. I was sure they'd think me murdered. Or perhaps,' and my mouth pulls down as I speak. 'Married to Lord Rognvaldr in secret and too ashamed to show my face in public.'

Eoforhild's eyes open wide at my words, and then she laughs, realising they were spoken in jest.

'Yes, I expected the Mercians to have accepted King Edward. What choice do they have?'

I nod, but I'm still thinking.

'It seems I have many more allies in Mercia than I might have thought. It appears to me that uncle Edward has found out just how limited his reach truly is. I imagine Mercia rises against Wessex, and he takes my ring to prove my death. But it will only prove that I'm still alive. Why else wouldn't he have revealed it before?'

'I should like to see that,' Eoforhild muses, perching on the bench opposite mine. We're none the worse for our encounters with my uncle, and yet I feel violated. I think Eoforhild does as well. Our eyes are busy, even as we speak, seeking out the shadows that dominate the room, ensuring that we're truly alone.

'Perhaps there's still the potential to see it,' I offer excitement beginning to thrum in my voice. 'My uncle, he seemed old and tired, worn down by ruling and by his failures, despite his treachery. My grandfather was the same. I remember him being an old man, but he can't have been more than fifty or so. Uncle Edward must almost be the same age by now.'

Eoforhild nods vigorously at my words.

'I agree. Despite uncle Edward's crown and his rich robes, he looked far from a warrior king that the Mercians would accept as their ruler.'

I nod, fearing to get swept up in the potential future. I've just envisioned, and yet doing so all the same.

'Imagine what would happen if my uncle were to die?'

But Eoforhild's thoughts have run counter to my own.

'We would never know, even if he had died, and of course, Lord Ælfweard would be king in his place. You and he have no love for each other. And that's if he knows you still live. He might believe you dead as well. It certainly seems to be a well-kept secret.'

'But Archbishop Plegmund knows.'

'Yes, but why would he reveal that to anyone? No, the only chance you'd have would be if the Abbess thought to tell you and then opened the gates so that we could rush back to Mercia. But I can't see that happening.'

I grunt, my dream of the future dispelling before it's even fully formed before my eyes.

'I suppose so.'

A silence falls between us, only the crackle and spit of the fire audible. The occasional 'Amen' comes from the church where the sisters hear one of their tedious offices of the day. I've lost too much of my life in that church already.

I so want to make more of my uncle's visit than I can. I dream of escaping, of evading the ragged collection of warriors who guard the main gateway, alert to every coming and going in the nunnery, as few as there are.

Has, I wonder, the king paid them handsomely for their service to him? Even now, do they drink good wine and ale, eat heartily of whatever foodstuffs the king has brought them, aware that while they guard me, they can grow fat and useless.

I should like to escape just to watch them try and catch me. I'm sure that the swelling bellies of the ten men would make it impossible for them to mount their horses and chase after me.

But which way would I go? How would I know, for sure, that I'm heading in the correct direction? And surely, there must be more than the ten lazy men tasked with guarding my uncle's greatest secret?

'But it changes nothing,' Eoforhild eventually states, her flat voice cold and sobering.

'It changes everything for Mercia but nothing for me and you. I'm sorry you've been stuck here with me.'

Eoforhild nods. This isn't a new sentiment.

'You saved my life, and it's my honour to guard you, even if it is only against the pinching of the Abbess and her mean little minions. I'd have expected holy women to be more gracious and less foul.' Eoforhild's face twists at her words. I chuckle, despite my self-pity.

'Some of the nuns in this nunnery are far from the holy and committed women I always thought devoted their lives to serving their God. I'm sure it would have shocked my mother.'

'Well, this is Wessex. They've always taken their God seriously but only used him to serve their ends.'

If uncle Edward could have done me a favour while visiting, it would have been to take the priest away. The Abbess as well.

As though thinking conjures her, I hear the priest's final faltering prayers and then the sedate pace of the women as they make their way back to the great hall.

My sigh is heartfelt.

The day has been filled with revelations, but none of them has altered the fact that I'm a prisoner. And one who has no chance of escaping. Not while my uncle lives.

CHAPTER 18

SUMMER 924

The clash of my sword against the side of the offered black shield rings through the still, blistering air.

It's hotter than hell in Wessex. I would have thought I'd be used to it after all my years in landlocked Mercia, but here it seems even warmer, too hot, too sticky, too everything.

I'm dressed for training in my much-repaired old tunic and trews, with Eoforhild in front of me, a lazy grin on her face as she thwarts my attack. She told me it was too scorching for training, and I told her it wasn't, but blatantly, she was right, and I was wrong. Now sweat beads my face, my hair, tied back and out of the way, will be tacky with salt, and my clothes in need of washing yet again. Will this boiling summer never end?

Only my stubbornness keeps me hammering on her shield. That and a need to stifle the lethargy that's affected me of late, which makes everything too much effort, even just dressing.

My prison, for that's what it is, has been my home for too many years now. I came here a younger woman than I currently am, with only twenty-eight years to my name. Now I'm well into my thirties. Any chance I might once have had of marrying and having children is receding quicker than the tide on the turn.

I think of the man who was supposed to become my husband and realise that he must have married long ago. He had his dynasty to protect, and I'm sure he must think I'm dead. He might even, and this horrifies me, be reconciled to my uncle. It might have been a matter of political expediency. It could have been necessary to hold onto his position.

I didn't think this place would be my prison for the length of time that it's proven to be. I was convinced that my bloody uncle would face punishment for his crimes with a quick death and that I'd be released as soon as that happened. But my uncle didn't die when I expected him to. That much is evident from my continued imprisonment.

I always thought cousin Athelstan would come for me or that Lord Athelstan would. I can't decide if I'm disappointed in them or proud of their pragmatism.

Two years have passed since my uncle stole my signet ring from my hand.

I've been forgotten about, passed over. It's strange to be alive when everyone thinks I'm dead.

The nunnery garden where we train is alive with the sound of insects, busy with their tasks in the heat of the day. Everywhere I look something is getting on with its life. All apart from me.

I sigh heavily, allowing my sword to drop to the rapidly browning grass with a clatter that temporarily overrides the buzzing of the insects. At least they don't forget that I'm here, as they still and then pause their tasks, worry stopping them, before resuming their busyness, convinced there's no danger after all.

I consider why I persist with my training. Too much time has passed since my abduction for me to be useful to anyone. I imagine that all my allies are dead, just as that bastard Lord Rǫgnvaldr is, or that they've profited from my removal from power.

I was a warrior once, a proud and talented fighter with skills that most men would have envied. My uncle made me nothing, through his treachery and deceit, through his cunning and his deviousness.

Only the ten warriors who guard the entrance are a reminder that

I'm even inside the nunnery. To the outside world, they just appear to be men protecting the women secluded within the cloister. No one would guess that their role serves two purposes, to keep me inside and to ensure no one learns that I am inside.

I'm allowed to see no one who enters the nunnery for any purpose. Should even the blacksmith come to see to the horses the nunnery now owns, I'm escorted to my mean living space within the hall. There are no windows to be able to see out of or for them to be able to see inside.

I hate my uncle, and every day, when the nuns pray for their king's health and well-being under the guidance of the priest, I refuse to join them, thinking instead of what I'll do to him if I ever have the chance. I don't pray for his death, but I pray that when it does come, it's a long, lingering, painful death. I pray he repents of all he's done and knows, with dazzling certainty, that the only place he'll be going after his last breath is to the hottest reaches of Hell. Not the Heaven he hopes will be his afterlife.

I hear nothing of events outside the four walls of my prison. I have no visitors, and other than the Abbess, I think the other nuns are as ignorant as I am. I no longer try and make the priest speak to me. He's as frightened of the Abbess as the rest of the nuns. The other nuns have sworn never to talk to me about anything they know of the outside world.

Despite everyone's best efforts, I do know two important facts that please me.

I know the treasonous Viking raider bastard Lord Rǫgnvaldr is dead, and welcome to his death. The news came to me via the priest in the church. I doubt he even realised that he misspoke when he asked for prayers to be said for the dead man who'd become King Edward's ally.

More importantly, and from uncle Edward's lips, I know that Mercia rebels against him. The country he took from me has never acquiesced to his command. He's a small man in a vast kingdom that wants him gone. The Mercians fight for me, for Mercian independence, even though they don't know I yet live. They fight for what my mother gave them and for what I would restore to them if I only had the chance.

Perhaps, if they knew I yet lived, they might come for me. Have me as their figurehead. Allow me to rule as I should have done. But uncle Edward stole the signet ring of Mercia from me, and since then, I know that the Mercians believe me dead.

In my prison, even my uncle forgets about me. This half-life is no life at all, not for me. I was a woman of action and political importance. This is the cruellest punishment that could have been inflicted upon me.

Despite the fact I'm sure she hates me, the Abbess has allowed me to train and have a sword and shield ever since my uncle's visit. I imagine she knows who I once was. I believe she takes pity on me. I try to think more kindly toward her, but I don't welcome her compassion. I do embrace my blunt weapons and the feeling of power they give me, even as pathetic as it might appear.

And I'm thankful for Eoforhild's constant company. It's not the life that either of us thought we'd be living.

I bend to retrieve my sword, and my back twinges as I do so. I simply can't maintain my high fitness standards here, not with all the restrictions upon me.

I may not run. I may not walk too fast. I may not practice on holy days and feast days and when someone might be visiting. I may not wear what I wish, but always the terrible dresses the other nuns wear, made from the coarsest material available and itchy as Hell. I must wear a wimple, shield my hair, pray when commanded and eat when allowed and what I'm given.

Ah, they plan to kill me through boredom.

When I stand, Eoforhild has a strange expression on her red face. I think, 'do I look as out of breath as her,' before I turn to follow her gaze, perplexed by what could have so shocked a woman I know incapable of showing any great emotion.

No matter what the nuns did to us, Eoforhild showed no hatred. I've long envied her bland face.

Lifelessly my just-retrieved sword tumbles to the ground, shattering the silence of the nunnery, and I know my mouth has dropped open.

'Well, I can see you need to do a bit more practice with that,' cousin Athelstan comments laconically. He bends to retrieve the temporarily forgotten sword. 'I think it could do with being a touch sharper as well,' he offers, running his finger along the long-blunted sword before he offers it back to me, his hand around the blade, the hilt extended to fit into my hand.

I grip the sword, my knuckles white with pressure.

Cousin Athelstan is older and perhaps wiser as his eyes sparkle at me, the glory of the summer's day shimmering from his sun-reddened face. He has much to tell me, but I take my time examining him. Over five years is a long time to miss out on seeing a friend, an ally, and someone I counted as my brother.

Cousin Athelstan has broader shoulders than ever before, his face dusted with the stubble of his blond hair. Above his mouth sits a moustache that makes me want to giggle. It looks so out of place on the face of my childhood ally.

He also has more scars than I remember. Others have joined the slash on his chin, the most worrying the nick he wears below his left eye. Someone nearly blinded my cousin. I hope they died for the affront.

He's dressed very smartly, in military garb that's clean and service-able, even if it lacks the embroidery I'd expect to proclaim his royal birth. Cousin Athelstan has been a man of Mercia for far longer than he's had any loyalty to Wessex. Wessex is the land of his birth and the kingdom over which his father and grandfather ruled.

His tunic is a tight fit, and yet I can see that there's ample room for his warrior's muscles. His boots shimmer like the clearest of the night skies when clouds are banished as temperatures plummet in the depths of winter.

He stands alone, and yet his confidence is absolute. He's the young man I remember but become a man confident in his abilities and prowess. I'm overjoyed to see him, regardless of my earlier disgruntlement at the lack of contact throughout our time apart. Why has he come now?

'Do you have anything else to wear?' cousin Athelstan asks abruptly, his rich voice brusque, his hand indicating my torn clothes.

'Why? What?' I stammer and then remember who I am. 'It's good to see you too, cousin,' I tease. A lightness is returning to my entire body that I've not felt since I was forcibly removed from Mercia, ridden away under cover of darkness by my uncle's most trusted ealdorman.

Cousin Athelstan's presence here must mean something monumental has happened, and I guess at what that might be.

'Well, of course, it's good to see you as well,' he stutters, for a moment, his confidence gone in the wake of the awkwardness of our meeting. 'I didn't think I'd need to say that,' he grumbles, the hint of a smile returning to his lips. 'But anyway, do you have something else to wear? I didn't think to bring you new clothes because, well, I just didn't.' He shrugs as he finishes speaking, the ripple of muscle showing that I was correct about his warrior's build and the limits of his tunic. I cock my head to one side, assessing him.

Is cousin Athelstan still the person he used to be? What's happened to him during our time apart?

'Why would I need new clothes?' I grill, remembering his words. It seems like a strange request to make until I remember my hideous tunic and trews. Cousin Athelstan's face brightens even more, his curved mouth forcing his moustaches upwards. I really must make him shave it off.

'It's true then? They've managed to keep all news from you in the last five years? I can hardly believe it, not with your tenacity.' There's shock in his voice but also warmth that I've not heard from anyone throughout my captivity. Such simple things: the laughter of a friend and the delight at knowing that I've not been forgotten.

'If I could hear our God, I'm sure he'd have told me everything I needed to know, but here, with this stubborn lot of bitches, I've learned next to nothing. They enjoyed it. They've enjoyed keeping secrets from me.' I raise my hand to indicate the main hall of the nunnery as I speak. I'd not realised how furious I was. At everything, and especially at the holy bitches. They forced the priest to preach of forgiveness and loving enemies and then assembled to thwart all of my attempts to learn of what happened beyond the walls of the nunnery.

'Well, that's as it might be, but no more. I'll tell you everything you need to know and more besides.' His tone is friendly, his gaze filled with understanding. I remember then that Athelstan, while maintaining his freedom, has been excluded from almost everything his father has ever planned. Cousin Athelstan was banished to Mercia from Wessex, just as I was exiled from Mercia to Wessex.

'Yes, do tell me why you're here,' I demand, the heat leaving me slowly, and once more, he smiles, real joy and delight transforming his face from the grave one of his youth to one a little more carefree.

'I've come to take you home, to Mercia,' he announces, clearly enjoying the way that sounds on his lips. I wonder how many times he's considered saying those words in the last few days.

'Home to Mercia? Why?' I command. I almost can't believe what I'm hearing, what I'm hoping he'll say next.

'I always promised I'd come for you, and Mercia needs you much more than this place does. There are more than enough Wessex women to pray for my father's soul. You have a duty to Mercia.'

There, he's said it without saying it. His father is dead; he must be.

'Cousin Ælfweard is king?' I pry. He shakes his head, no trace of remorse on his face. None at all.

'Cousin Ælfweard was king for a whole six weeks, but now he's dead as well. I'm going to Winchester to claim Wessex for myself.' I know my mouth hangs open in shock at his words. I close it, aware that cousin Athelstan doesn't wish to see the pink of my tongue, as he meets my gaze fiercely. There's no hint of grief or sorrow for the death of his father or his step-brother.

'How?' I say slowly, imagining all sorts of family deceits and betrayals, but cousin Athelstan shakes his head.

'The king,' we both notice he doesn't say, 'my father,' 'was killed after trying to put down a rebellion in Mercia. I was accepted as king of Mercia on his death, and the resistance dissipated. Cousin Ælfweard was proclaimed king of Wessex just two months ago. But he's dead as well, from some form of contagion that spread throughout the Wessex warriors encamped in Mercia and which he brought with him to Wessex.'

'So, you're the king of Mercia, and Wessex has no king?' I seek clarification.

'I'm the king of Mercia, and I plan on becoming king of Wessex with your help,' he confirms. I rush into his arms to embrace my brave, calm cousin who endured so many years of hardship under his father. If I can't have Mercia, I'd want no one else but him to have it.

Only when I pull away from the embrace do I realise my mistake.

'Apologies,' I cry, immediately taking to my knee, aware that behind me, Eoforhild has been on her knee all along.

'Oh, stand up,' cousin Athelstan complains, bending to grip my hands and ensure I position myself beside him.

'Never do that to me again. Unless you must because it's incredibly formal, and you have no choice but to do it. Promise me.' But he leaves me no time to answer before he continues speaking.

'I've a job for you and a husband if you still want him.'

'A husband?' I question, my heart thudding. Cousin Athelstan still smiles, pure delight on his face, and my immediate worry dissolves.

'The people of Mercia have never forgotten you, you won't know that, but they haven't. One of those who have never stopped thinking about you is Lord Athelstan. He's been waiting for you, and I confess he's a little impatient. I've had to have him restrained so that I could tell you the news.'

I stare at cousin Athelstan as though he's lost his senses. I can't quite decipher all he's telling me as he stands before me, almost hopping from foot to foot with excitement.

'So, I'm free to return to Mercia?' I finally stumble. He laughs at my hesitation and sweeps me into his arms.

'You're free to return to Mercia, and you will, if you want, of course, marry Lord Athelstan. Between us, we'll do all we can to unite Mercia and Wessex and rule together. You'll birth sons who'll rule in

Mercia, and I'll not become a father. I've no desire for my own children, not after the mess my father made of it. But first, you'll help me win Wessex from cousin Edwin. But even before all that, I must return this to you.'

I can feel tears falling down my face even though I'm not crying. Finally, slowly but surely, I begin to believe what my cousin is telling me as he places the signet ring of Mercia's eagle back on my finger. I'd forgotten its weight, and abruptly, I feel more whole than I have since it was taken from me.

'I think I'll just go as I am,' I mutter, looking down at my much-repaired trews and tunic. Eoforhild nods at me, her sobs of joy making it almost impossible for her to stand from where she kneels. I grab her hands and pull her upright, just as cousin Athelstan did for me. I link my arm through hers, and we sway as though a winter storm thrums through the tranquil garden of the nunnery, buffeting it.

We must both look a sight, tears pouring down sweating faces, but I don't care.

Unheeding cousin Athelstan's royal status, I link my other arm through his, and together, the three of us stroll to the waiting open doorway. For the first time in over five years, the gateway's flung wide open, and no one blocks the path. The warriors on guard duty are bowing to my cousin, the sight of the road beyond the gateway causing my pulse to rise ever faster and my breath becoming ragged.

I don't even return to my small sleeping area. There's nothing there that I wish to keep, but I'm aware that the nuns have spilt from the hall and watch me, as silently as ever. Their dull interest lacks the usual maliciousness.

The Abbess stands proudly in front of her nuns, her head titled backwards, her eyes and weak chin little changed from when I first met her. Time doesn't seem to touch her. She's lucky.

I want to walk away, to think nothing more of this place, but I can't.

Instead, I turn to face them all. I hold my head as haughtily as the Abbess does and then think better of it.

I walk to face her, meeting her eyes evenly, aware that despite it all, she did me many great kindnesses, even if I've only just seen them for what they are.

'I'd thank all of you for caring for my friend and me. Our time here together has shown me that you're all mindful of your devotion to your God and to the house you serve.' My voice rings deeply, and some of them flinch. A world of near-constant silence makes the simplest of sounds seem terrifying.

'The nunnery hasn't profited greatly from having me as a prisoner, and I'd see that rectified. I'd also see that you have a priest more able to conduct the offices you hear daily.'

I keep my eyes firmly away from where I know the priest hovers, to the side of the ten guards. All the same, I notice him startle when I involve him. It seems he hasn't realised that his lack of education is noted.

I meet a few surprised eyes and smile, ensuring they know that I feel no anger toward them. They could be forgiven for thinking that I do. It isn't lost on me that I did until my cousin arrived.

And then I pause and turn to look at cousin Athelstan.

'Where am I?' I ask a question that's long plagued me. His shock is clear to see in his tranquil blue eyes, but he recovers quickly enough.

'Thanet, my lady. Close to Canterbury.'

Ah, so much suddenly makes sense. Canterbury is in Kent, on land held by King Edward's third wife and, of course, home to Archbishop Plegmund.

'How did you find me?' I then think to ask.

Again, cousin Athelstan looks confused.

'The Abbess sent word of where you were once she heard of King Ælfweard's death.'

I meet the woman's eyes, for the first time appreciating the intelligence there and seeing her for what she is. Her spite and malice were out of necessity. Or so it seems.

I walk to her side, curtsey, and then stand to plant a kiss on each of her cheeks.

'Thank you,' I breathe, and she smiles. I swear, I've never seen a more joyous transformation.

Impatient now, I turn aside from the Abbess and her nuns and gaze out beyond the open gateway.

True to cousin Athelstan's words, Lord Athelstan is tied to his horse, an embarrassed expression on his sweating face. I grin at him, one eyebrow high as I take in the extreme action cousin Athelstan has taken to be the first to tell me the news.

Launching myself away from my cousin, my king now, I run toward Lord Athelstan. He slides from his horse, wrenching his arms from the coils of rope that held him tight and which one of his brothers has finally released. We embrace, both trying to speak simultaneously, to savour the moment and to counter the five years of silence in a matter of moments.

'I promised myself,' Lord Athelstan mutters into my bound hair as I finally quiet my laughing and crying all at the same time. 'I promised myself that I'd find you.'

'Come, Lady Ælfwynn,' cousin Athelstan comments from behind me. 'There's time for that. There'll always be time for that now, but we must attend the witan at Winchester. Then you must be returned to Mercia and given back your hall in Tamworth. Your warriors are waiting for you there.'

I can scarcely believe what's happened, but then, my disloyal uncle couldn't live forever. No man ever does. I can only hope that throughout the ages to come, his name will fall into disuse, eclipsed by his son, my cousin, Athelstan, king of Mercia, and soon-to-be Wessex as well. I don't doubt that cousin Athelstan will secure the kingship of Wessex. Cousin Edwin has never been a man worthy of a royal helm.

What else my cousin might achieve remains to be seen, but I know he'll do nothing alone. I'll be by his side. I might not rule Mercia as my mother did, but the name of Lady Æthelflæd will never be forgotten. And I'll be just as respected and just as revered, and I need never fear that my king will turn against me.

Not now that cousin Athelstan is king, and King Athelstan is, and always has been, my staunchest ally and my greatest friend.

CHAPTER 19

R evenge. The thought of it has filled my nights for many years. Yet, faced with the objects of those I wish to seek vengeance against, I'm reminded that it's a hollow victory. Cousin Athelstan has been proclaimed king by the Wessex witan. I had to set aside my claim to Mercia to ensure it formally, but I've no regrets. And I'm pleased by my cousin's cleverness in making my father's third wife his ally as well. I understand now why my cousin's refusing to marry. He doesn't need to, for my uncle left two small sons, and they, I realise, are where cousin Athelstan believes the future lies.

In the lull after the witan, I've made my way to the New Minster at Winchester, Eoforhild as my only companion. I'm not yet used to the noise of people conversing or even being around people who actually look at me. In the nunnery, I was, more often than not, met by downcast eyes. Even those who saved Eoforhild's life came to resent me. In the end.

It's quiet in the New Minster, and I appreciate that as I take in the vast wealth on display, the massive tower that stands above the entrance. It makes my plans at St Oswald's Priory, for the continued remembrance of my mother and father, look mean and cheap. Cousin

Athelstan assures me that the stonemason finished his work. I plan on seeing for myself soon enough.

What great wealth my uncle had at his fingertips. How could he have had so much already and yet demanded Mercia as well?

Cousin Athelstan has told me of what happened in Mercia during my absence. Only now have the rebels finally been won around, and only because he was elected king and promise to find me.

During his life, my uncle was beset by problems in Mercia, and his death came as he fought the rebels near Farndon, close to Chester, and so in the northwest of Mercia. It was only one in a long line of disputes he was forced to contend with. He wanted to press on with claiming back the lost lands of Mercia and was successful only in Thelwall, Manchester and Bakewell.

Lincoln remains outside Mercian rule.

If he'd allowed me my freedom, I know Lincoln would be Mercian now. I also know that the work of reclaiming Mercia for the Mercians would be almost at an end.

Neither was my uncle's alliance with Lord Rǫgnvaldr long-lived. Lord Rǫgnvaldr died three years ago, and his successor, Lord Sihtric, was no ally of King Edward. Even cousin Athelstan is wary of him. Lord Sihtric has many sons and a great deal of experience in ruling, having been the king of Dublin before claiming York. It seems he neither needs nor wants an ally to rule York well.

Bamburgh remains aloof, and in the north, King Constantin of the Scots bides his time. King Constantin says all the right things to keep potential enemies and allies content while waiting to exploit whatever situations arise. My uncle would have done well to learn from such an example.

Apart from my uncle's usurpation of my title, little seems to have changed in my years of absence. That begs the question of just what my uncle hoped to achieve. After all, on his death, he unexpectedly arranged for cousin Athelstan to rule there while Ælfweard had Wessex. My uncle sought to unify Mercia and Wessex but drove them apart when he died.

Why?

The question won't stop revolving in my head. And that's why I've made my way to the New Minster.

Beneath my feet lie the rotting corpses of my grandfather, my uncle, in fact, two of my uncles, and cousin Ælfweard. My grandmother keeps them company. I pity her such poor companions in the afterlife.

To begin with, I walk over the spot where I know the stone floor can be removed to allow access to the crypt below. Time and time again, I step backwards and forwards over it.

I don't wish to face my uncle's corpse. I'd find no comfort in doing that, unlike when I visited my mother's shrine, but I seek something.

What it is, I'm not yet sure.

I hope the silence will bring it to me.

Eoforhild remains silent and alert behind me. She'll allow no one to interrupt me. I look forward to allowing her to relinquish her attendance on me when I'm reunited with my other warriors at Tamworth. For now, she's all I have. I hope she'll stay with me when I return to Mercia, but I can't deny that she's served me exceptionally well. It might be that she seeks a different life now.

I stop pacing abruptly, my thoughts streaming back to my final meeting with my uncle.

He came to me as a king, in all of his finery and with his high ideals. But he stole from me, all the same.

Uncle Edward thought himself a mighty king, made from the same mould as his father and in the same forge. But he wasn't.

My grandfather nearly lost all, and he abandoned Mercia to her fate. Only my mother was prepared to vouch for Mercia and ensure it stayed intact. My grandfather cared only for Wessex and London. He stole London from the Mercian people and never considered giving it back. For this, he was lauded as the saviour of the Saxon people.

But really, he was the saviour of Wessex.

If my grandfather wanted anything for Mercia, it was to use it to protect Wessex. My mother refused to allow that to happen.

But my uncle's motivations are impossible to determine. I'm forced to conclude that he simply wanted control of Mercia because he thought he should have it. What sort of king does that make him? What kind of man?

Not one I wish to lay claim to. That's a certainty.

Carefully, I sit on the stone floor. I have something I need to say to my uncle. I consider what he said to me when we last met.

'You must either abdicate your right to rule or give up your life. Those are the only options available to you now.' Those words have rung in my head multiple times over the last few years.

A smile touches my lips.

'It seems, dear uncle, that you've given up your life so that I might rule. I didn't need to abdicate anything, not in the end.' I say the words softly. I don't want anyone else to hear what I must say.

'It seems, dear uncle, that in the space of two months, your least favourite son has overshadowed all that you ever accomplished.'

I'm warming to my subject.

'It seems, dear uncle, that you've failed.' I chuckle now. The image of my uncle being forced to listen to my words as I was forced to listen to his amuses me. And then I stand and walk away.

I won't be able to take my revenge against my uncle personally. But I don't need to. Not anymore. King Edward's reputation will suffer for the decisions he made about his wives, his children, his sister and his niece. I couldn't ask for more.

I PREPARE to return to Tamworth with Eoforhild and Lord Athelstan. Cousin Athelstan is forced to remain in Winchester. There's still a great deal for him to organise, but I'm desperate to return to Mercia and Lady Ecgwynn. But, before I leave, I seek out my uncle's third wife. Lady Eadgifu is, as I've always known, younger than I am.

I find it strange to speak with her, but her sons beguiled me when I spoke for Cousin Athelstan before the witan. I wish to know those boys now that my cousin has clarified that one of them will rule after him.

She's not the woman I've imagined her to be.

'My lady,' Lady Eadgifu speaks first, and I admire her poise. 'I would apologise for your incarceration. I'm outraged that my husband used one of the Kent nunneries to keep you locked up. Had I known, I'd have argued for your release.'

I don't know how to respond to her statement, and all of my carefully phrased words are suddenly beyond me.

She presses on.

'King Edward assured everyone that you were dead many years ago. He was quite convincing,' Lady Eadgifu's words have the ring of sincerity. Still, I don't know how to respond.

Only then, young Edmund rushes to his mother's side. His eyes are wide with excitement as he stops before her.

'The king says I'm to have a pony. He says he'll teach me to ride himself.'

I look at the small boy, so reminiscent of cousin Athelstan when he was a child, and I know my gut reaction to meeting him was right.

'Do you know who taught King Athelstan to ride?' I ask Edmund, the second youngest of my uncle's sons.

'No?' he asks in surprise. But then his forehead wrinkles. 'Was it you?' he asks, and I nod and laugh.

'It was, yes. You remind him of that when he teaches you.' I won't mention all the times my cousin fell from his horse or the curses he spoke when he did so. Instead, I remember the innocence of that time before his father tried to drive a wedge between us.

'I will, my lady,' Edmund's voice is young and filled with high spirits.

'When you're older, I'll send you a mount from Mercia. We breed excellent horses there.' Edmund grins and reaches for my hand and grips it.

'I should like that,' he whispers when he forces my ear close to his lips. 'King Athelstan has a Mercian horse, and it's the best horse I've ever seen.' It's as though he imparts a great secret to me before rushing away, his footsteps loud on the wooden floor.

'It seems you've made my son your ally,' Lady Eadgifu comments, with no complaint in her voice. 'King Athelstan has done the same. I'd be pleased to be your friend, as well in time. It seems we both have wounds that need healing and that we must be grateful for more than just the death of King Edward, but also Ælfweard. He made my life hell. I'm sure his other brother and sisters will continue to do so.' There's ruefulness to her tone, but I'm curious.

'How did King Athelstan make you his ally?' It seems strange to me, given the fact that she was his stepmother.

'He and Lady Ecgwynn offered my sanctuary in Mercia after Ælfweard was declared as king. I didn't wish to marry again. One husband is enough for me, and Ælfweard was far from subtle with his intentions. I travelled to Mercia. I returned to attend the witan. I've been to Tamworth. It's beautiful. I can see why you fought so hard for it.'

I'm still absorbing what Lady Eadgifu says to me. By rights, I should call her queen, but she doesn't insist on the title, just as cousin Athelstan doesn't insist on his.

'I hadn't truly considered the passage of time. I'm suddenly fearful that Mercia has changed in my absence.'

She considers my words.

'I can't reassure you. I only know what I saw. Lady Ecgwynn will welcome you.'

'The last I heard, she was in a nunnery, evading her father.'

Lady Eadgifu nods sagely. 'A nunnery provides a haven when women need it most. All you can take from your experience is that you were kept alive. Small consolation, I know.'

I grin then, just as Edmund did only moments ago. Words seem beyond me, but Lady Eadgifu reaches for my hand and grips it tightly.

'King Edward is gone,' she states confidently, shaking my hand to reinforce her belief. 'Life can only be better without him.'

THEY'RE WAITING FOR ME. I somehow knew they would be. Just across the bridge that takes me to Mercia, they wait. It'll be the first time I've touched Mercian soil in many years.

Lord Athelstan hasn't mentioned this to me, but I'm sure it's by his hand. Riding in front, desperate to be home, my eyes alight on the small back of warriors, the Mercian eagle banner fluttering gently in the breeze stirred up by the river.

It's a warm summer's day, almost too hot to truly be enjoyable, and the slight breeze is welcome to cool the sweat that's formed on my face. Mercia beckons to me, ripe fields bobbing in the slight breeze. Even the smell of dust and heat makes me realise that I'm genuinely nearly home.

Behind me, Eoforhild lets out a cry of delight, finding the means to voice her surprise and delight as she encourages her horse to canter over the wooden bridge. Words fail me, and at the same time, my heart feels constricted.

What if they're changed?

What if Mercia's changed?

I'd not genuinely considered that both might have happened.

My horse crosses the bridge behind Eoforhild. I don't know what to look at first.

Ealdorman Æthelfrith stands smartly to the side, his warriors attentive. However, some of them have discarded their byrnies in the heat. I've not seen the ealdorman since my release. His sons all supported cousin Athelstan at the witan in Winchester, but he chose to protect Mercia in her king's absence.

My eyes rake in his appearance. He's older, of course, but his eyes sparkle with delight. I know then that he hasn't changed. I'd embrace him, but my gaze is drawn to my women. Eoforhild has already flung herself amongst them, her horse milling about uncertainly, but I feel strangely reticent as I hear the rowdy reunion.

I've had many years to think about the night of my abduction. I don't believe that I blame my warriors. But they probably blame themselves. How, then, do I rebuild our bonds of trust and respect?

'My lady,' Eoforhild calls to me from amongst the mass of laughing and crying. 'Come, join me.'

I want to, but something holds me back, and time stretches until total silence has fallen amongst the waiting warriors.

It falls to Ealdorman Æthelfrith to break the silence.

'My lady. I'd welcome you back to Mercia. Be assured, it's entirely as you left it.' I appreciate the implication that I left and wasn't abducted, but I still don't know what to say or do.

None of the many ways I once envisioned this reunion is correct, and it's been so damn long.

Lord Athelstan is attentive beside me. I can hear his soft breath. I almost think he'll reach out and take my hand, but he doesn't. Instead, he speaks softly.

'It's a lot to take in, I know, but better you greet them here than in Tamworth. It's here that they last saw you.'

I nod, still mute but mindful of Eoforhild's impatient glance, I dismount, handing the reins to Lord Athelstan. Resolved, I turn to meet my women. I'm aware that someone is missing, but only as I focus on every face do I realise it is Erna. I imagine she's grown up and married. I feel a pang of remorse for her absence.

'My lady,' as one, my warriors take to their knees, even Eoforhild joining them. I look down on bowed heads, noticing the lines of grey that thread some of the hair. A tight smile touches my lips.

'Stand up, you bunch of fools,' I command, aware that my voice catches. They do as I order, and still, we stand and face each other, silly grins on all our faces.

'You look older,' I say, the first thing that comes to mind.

'So do you,' Ymma comments, the smile never leaving her face, which has more lines in the corner of her eyes than I'd like to see.

And then I'm flinging myself amongst them, as Eoforhild did moments ago. Lioba, Firamodor, Mildryth and Leofgyth. We're laughing and talking and hugging, and there are no recriminations, only pleasure and surprise at seeing our maturity reflected in the eyes of one another. I hope there'll never be any blame between us. Not now we're reunited.

CHAPTER 20

Cousin Athelstan sends me to Mercia with explicit instructions to discover the truth of my betrayal. I don't know why I'll have more success in finding the truth than he has. But somehow, I do. Six months after being released from the nunnery, I face the man who kidnapped me and nearly murdered my friend, Eoforhild, when he found her tracking down rumours of my survival. Now, as I gaze at him, I'm not sure that I need to take my revenge on him at all.

In my mind, he's always been a huge man with bulging muscles, and thick slabs for thighs and arms. And that's what he looks like, but now he's beaten as well. Not by force of blows or anything like that, but rather by the knowledge that five years ago, he made a decision that's brought him here.

Beside me, in Tamworth, my new husband watches the man with barely concealed hatred. This man, I've learned his name is Wulfheard, kept us apart for many, many years. Added to that, he's eluded capture since my release, even though so many were seeking him out.

Beneath my skirts, the swell of the child I carry can be felt, if not seen, and I almost wish it were not so, for Wulfheard deserves to feel the edge of my blade against his neck, and yet I can't risk it. Neither do I want to risk it.

'Tell me everything,' I say to him. He's been beaten and bruised, my husband and his brothers assiduously tracking him down, but before me, he's been cleaned up and given fresh clothes.

'My lady?' his voice is the one I remember, and yet tempered with the swelling down one side of his face where he's fallen from his horse. Not the fault of my husband but rather the fault of the man's clumsiness.

'Tell me everything. I would know the truth of what happened to me. I've only been able to piece together certain events. I would know all of it before I pass judgment on you.'

The hall in Tamworth remains mine, although cousin Athelstan is the king of Mercia. His gift of Tamworth is a sign that I'm high in his favour.

Cousin Athelstan is nothing like his father, which will ensure that Mercia ceases to be used as a means to an end by the Wessex king. When Athelstan is crowned as king of the English, I'll watch it and smile, and I'll be pleased for my cousin and the Mercians, both.

But I must find out what lost me Mercia, in the first place.

My enemy sighs, and then resignation covers his thrashed face. I imagine he believes being captured will mean his death, and so he's nothing to lose by telling me the truth.

'Lord Rǫgnvaldr Sigfrodrsson,' tumbles from his lips without further maltreatment.

It helps that Rǫgnvaldr Sigfrodrsson is dead, as is King Edward, but I listen all the same. I need to know, finally, what brought about my failure.

'It's well known that Rǫgnvaldr Sigfrodrsson was my enemy,' I assert.

'Yes, he was. But neither did he want King Edward as a neighbour. Not until he was offered something to make it worth his while.'

'And what did my uncle promise Rǫgnvaldr Sigfrodrsson?'

Now my enemy smiles, a rare thing, seemingly, that doesn't sit well on his face, despite the bruises.

'Something he never gave him. King Edward wasn't a man of his word.'

I consider that Wulfheard taunts me, but then I reconsider. No doubt King Edward broke promises to him as well. And certainly, Rǫgnvaldr will have done.

'So Rǫgnvaldr Sigfrodrsson had you kidnap me?'

'Yes, and also no. Rǫgnvaldr wanted me to take you to York, to become his wife.'

'Was that what King Edward promised him?' I hiss the words. I'd never have married Rǫgnvaldr, despite his relentless rumour-making.

'My lady,' Wulfheard bows his head, refusing to meet my eyes. I allow silence to fall to consider the truth of those words.

Would my uncle truly have allowed me to marry the Viking raider ruler of York and Dublin? It seems too risky to me. And yet, if I was the prize, why didn't it happen? And how did Rǫgnvaldr fool himself into thinking it would in the first place?

Why would the king, whose father gained his fame for driving back the Viking raiders, suddenly allow his niece to marry one?

I shake my head, disappointed in both men but less than surprised.

'Then how did I end up in a Benedictine nunnery in Kent?' The words snap from my mouth.

Wulfheard has the good grace to look remorseful.

'King Edward bid me take you there. He didn't want you in any of the royal nunneries. And, of course, there are few nunneries dedicated to a rule of silence.'

I nod my head, determined to keep my building fury under control.

My uncle stopped at marrying me to his enemy and at ordering my death. I'm not grateful to him, not at all.

'And what was your prize in all this?'

Wulfheard again looks remorseful.

'Gold and silver, and forgiveness for my lawless ways.'

'And did you at least receive that?' I should like to know that six years of my life is worth more than a few coins.

'Some, my lady.'

'So why did you keep silent after the death of Lord Rǫgnvaldr? I could have been freed three years before I was?'

'It wasn't Lord Rǫgnvaldr who terrified me the most.'

I've never been scared of my uncle, even when he locked me up. Why I consider, would he have such a hold over this man?

'King Edward held my family as hostage to his wishes. You, my lady, weren't the only one to lose years of your life.' I gasp at the words, unable to help myself. I want to hate this man, but perhaps he's as deserving of my pity as I am of his.

'And your family? Have you been reunited with them?'

A twist of Wulfheard's face, and I know the answer even before he shakes his head, tears glistening in his eyes.

I nod. I should feel some satisfaction, but I don't.

I've never believed in cruelty. Violence, yes, and possessing the ability to defend against those who mean you ill. But not cruelty.

I despise my uncle all over again.

'Yet you ran from my warriors who tried to hunt you down?' It's my husband who speaks into the heavy silence.

'I'm without my family, and yet I don't welcome death. Not yet.'

My husband grunts.

'How did you gain access to Tamworth?' I might know the overall plan now, but what happened that night still disturbs me. Whoever sought to capture me must have had the aid of someone within Mercia, specifically someone close enough to me to know the layout of the building complex.

'Rǫgnvaldr Sigfrodrsson wasn't your only enemy,' Wulfheard admits, his eyes flickering into the far reaches of my hall. I startle. Does my enemy still reside in Mercia? Is my life threatened to this day?

'And who would they be?'

'Members of your household troops. Those with leanings in favour of the Viking raiders, and of course, those who spied for the Wessex king.' Wulfheard all but spits the final two words.

'I need names, not random suggestions,' My husband barks, but I nod along. I, too, require names. That night will haunt all of us for many years. We must do more to ensure our safety. While cousin Athelstan seeks to rule Mercia and Wessex under one crown, some will never welcome it.

Wulfheard sighs heavily as though he must still consider his loyalty to people who might yet live.

'And don't give me a list of people who are already dead. Someone must still live.' Again, it's my husband who speaks. Behind him, his father watches on. He supervises the proceedings as an ealdorman of Mercia.

'I can only do so much,' Wulfheard states, shrugging his massive shoulders. 'Many of them are dead. None of your enemies were easy men. When King Edward thwarted Lord Rǫgnvaldr, the traitors amongst the household troop paid with their lives. There were five of them, and while we rode south, they went north to meet with Lord Rǫgnvaldr. He slaughtered them when they arrived without you.'

'I'd know their names?' I notice my voice quivers. This is it. The moment I've been waiting for all these years.

'Morcar, Wulfstan, Harald, Beornstan and Bjorn.' I listen, my mouth falling open a little, trying to conjure an image of these men just from their names.

'Five of them?' my husband gasps, the knowledge shocking him, and indeed, I turn to gaze at my father by marriage. Fury clouds his ordinarily placid face. It seems that he recalls these men.

'They were all sworn to Ætheling Athelstan,' Ealdorman Æthelfrith provides the connection. 'Why would they have turned against him?'

Here Wulfheard turns almost amused eyes to gaze at the older ealdorman.

'Not all men believe women should rule. They were five men who were pleased when Lady Æthelflæd died. They weren't pleased when Lady Ælfwynn was given the rule of Mercia. They believed King Athelstan should rule after Lady Æthelflæd.'

'Was that your motivation as well?'

'No, my lady. I did it for the money. Disappointingly.' His nervous laughter is filled with regret.

'And who else?' The revelation of these names has caught my father by marriage's attention. He leans forward from his chair and fixes his steely eyes on Wulfheard.

'They bribed one of the gate wardens to ensure that he got everyone drunk. I forget his name. He was poorly paid for his treason. I killed him when he wasn't quite drunk enough. Stupid fool.'

A thread of silence falls between us all.

'And, of course, Erna gave all the information in the first place.' My back stiffens at this. I'd thought Erna dead in the attack. Now it seems that might not be right.

'She'd do no such thing,' I leap to defend her.

'The stupid girl didn't know she did it. She was bragging about her position with Lady Ælfwynn. She didn't know that the young man she sought to impress was one of the enemies.'

'What happened to Erna?' I turn to meet the eyes of Ymma. She remained in Mercia throughout my captivity. I know we discussed Erna went I first returned, but I can't recall what was said.

Her face registers her shock and also resignation.

'She left. We never truly knew why. One day she was here, and the next, gone. We searched for her, but she was never found. I confess I'd almost forgotten about her in the intervening years.' Confusion haunts her voice. She, like I, can hardly believe what we're hearing.

Did Erna realise what she'd done? Or was she also killed by someone who worried she'd reveal their identity? I wish I knew, but I doubt I'll ever know the truth of what happened to my young squire. I've missed her since my return to Mercia. I should have asked the question much sooner.

'And any other?' I suddenly wish I didn't ask the questions. I suddenly wish that Wulfheard had been captured dead. I always knew my uncle was the bastard behind the attack. To realise that others helped him willingly and without due consideration will haunt me for many more years than my dead uncle will.

'Yes, there were more. Archbishop Plegmund spared no expense when he arranged for you to be kidnapped and held in Kent.'

'Archbishop Plegmund?' Again, I'm not surprised to hear the archbishop's name mentioned. I was kept in Kent, in one of the nunneries he had control over. It makes sense that he was involved. Plegmund would have been able to enforce his will over the abbess of the nunnery. It was no less a man than the archbishop himself, lauded for his accomplishments and wisdom, who terrified the abbess so much that she never once, in five years, spoke to me or told me where I was.

'Yes, he was here that night. You must have heard him?' Suddenly, much of my memories of that night make more sense.

How dare someone as holy as a damn archbishop meddle in secular affairs?

If he weren't dead already, I know full well that King Athelstan would have had him removed from Canterbury. Perhaps even excommunicated for his sins.

'Was Archbishop Lodeward involved?'

It was Archbishop Lodeward who was involved in the battle in Northumbria all those years ago when Lord Rǫgnvaldr and I reached our initial agreement.

'I can tell you that Reeve Sigehelm showed us where to go. He met the force at the border with Wessex and rode with us to Tamworth.'

'Reeve Sigehelm did?' the incredulity in my voice is impossible to mask. 'Are you sure it was he?' I ask the question even though I've believed every other name that Wulfheard's shared with me.

'Yes, my lady. He was instrumental in what happened.'

Reeve Sigehelm still holds his position in Derby. I feel my hand shaking. What should I do? He's always professed to be fiercely loyal, and I know that King Athelstan has no argument with him, none at all. But I'm reminded of my suspicions regarding Lord Rǫgnvaldr's easy infiltration of Derby just before my abduction.

'Of them all, he provided the most information. He knew where you'd be sleeping, and how many guards there'd be, and when you'd be at Tamworth. He approached King Edward with the suggestion, as I understand it.'

I gasp. Already I know that Ealdorman Æthelfrith is issuing instructions for Reeve Sigehelm's arrest. At the same time, I try to find my composure.

'He must be tried for treason,' my husband speaks. I nod, but the movement feels strained. My thoughts are a confused riot, and I don't know what to think.

As I said, I long suspected my uncle's involvement, but Wulfheard has named so many others that I realise it wasn't all my uncle's fault. Yes, he wanted me captured, and yes, he paid the men well to capture me, but none of it would have been possible without the assistance of those close to me. Those I trusted implicitly.

I feel let down. Somehow, in my years of captivity, I've created a narrative where I was a helpless victim. My family betrayed me, while those who should have protected me were powerless to act. They were too drunk at the feast that heralded my marriage. Never have I considered that my allies might have played a role in my capture.

I imagined that men might have been bribed, perhaps in fear for their families, as happened to Wulfheard. To realise it was a justifiable decision for someone such as Reeve Sigehelm has me questioning those achievements that I claimed before I was abducted.

I feel betrayed all over again. For a time, I see nothing, my eyes staring into the distance as though I can sear through the intervening years, see events as they must have played out that night.

I remember the laughter, the drinking, the excellent singing, and the even better storytelling. I recall feeling as though I had all I'd ever wanted and had accomplished all my mother might have desired of me.

I recollect feeling strong and powerful and dismissive of all who tried to threaten Mercia. I can almost taste the meat served to me and the scent of the heady wine, the heat from the hearth, piled high with enough wood and charcoal to last the Kentish nuns over a month.

My future husband had been at my side, and I'd been filled with joy and longing for what the next day would bring.

I recall watching my cousins dancing and laughing; Lady Ecgwynn finally restored to me, having forgiven me for deceiving her in the wake of the attack on Derby.

I remember all that and suddenly realise I was as much to blame as everyone else.

I let down my shields. I allowed everyone within Tamworth to feast and celebrate my impending marriage. I didn't fear an attack when Lord Rǫgnvaldr had been so easily swept aside at Derby, my blade drinking his blood. I'd felt safe and comfortable and powerful. So, so powerful.

I'd known, that night, that my destiny had been to rule the Mercians.

I'd believed entirely in myself, and that arrogance had ultimately cost me my kingdom.

'Lady Ælfwynn,' the voice that recalls me to the here and now is that of my father by marriage. His eyes are hard, his face resolved.

'I'll ride to Derby myself and bring back the reeve. Then we'll hold a trial for both Wulfheard and Reeve Sigehelm. I'll have King Athelstan informed of my decision.'

I nod, the words seeming to tumble in the wrong order so that it takes me too long to understand what Ealdorman Æthelfrith's telling me.

'Yes, yes, a trial.' I eventually confirm when silence builds between us.

'And I'll send warriors to hunt for this Erna as well.'

'Excellent,' I agree, but my eyes are back on Wulfheard. He seems to taunt me with his knowledge. I see pity on his hard face, and my sympathy for him has dissipated.

The damn bastard.

I stand, smoothing my dress over my belly, highlighting the child who grows there.

I'll have to protect him or her when they're born. I can't allow such revelations of treachery amongst my closest allies to derail my calmness and growing confidence.

'When they're all found guilty, I'll wield the killing stroke.'

So spoken, I turn away, concentrating on walking sedately away from Wulfheard and his amused eyes.

I honestly had no intention of having Wulfheard executed for his crimes, but I must. While he lauds it over me that potential traitors surround me, I must act. I must ensure that men and women realise I'll never allow a repeat of such profound betrayal.

I know my mother would approve of my decisions.

She never refused to undertake such tasks, even when they pained her.

I might not be the Lady of Mercia, but I must guarantee my future safety. A powerful husband, and a close connection to the new king, won't be enough to do that. I must do this. Not because revenge is the only way to feel safe but because I must do what I can to prevent the same from ever happening again.

I don't do this for my cousin or for Mercia.

I do this for myself.

I should have been the Lady of Mercia, and I was for six months. But I'll not be again.

I'll be something else entirely, and that will have to suffice. The decision seems to lift the anxiety that's been crushing me since my return to Mercia.

Nothing has been as I remember it, not even Cousin Ecgwynn. She greeted me warmly and assured me that she'd arranged everything the way I used to like it. And she had.

I realise abruptly that while Mercia may have remained the same, I have not.

I'll assist my kingly cousin and my husband, who dreams of an ealdordom in the future. But more than anything, I'll keep my child safe, even if I have to adorn myself in the blood of my enemy to do so.

Even if I have to adorn myself in the blood of my allies to do so.

I'll not lay down my sword and seax. I'll keep them closer than ever before.

This betrayal has been a family affair, but more, it's been a betrayal by those I trusted far more than I did my family.

I'll never be so blind again.

CHAPTER 21

King Athelstan's arrival is unexpected, and yet, as I hold the sword high above my enemy's necks, I feel his strength thrum through my body. I stand taller. I plant my legs that little bit wider. I know, with every ounce of my being, that I'm doing the right thing.

Whatever qualms I might have had since I reached my decision, they vanish as though puffs of smoke merging with grey clouds overhead.

I didn't expect King Athelstan to come. Neither did I demand that he attend, and yet he's here all the same.

I don't turn to meet his eyes or even acknowledge his presence in any way other than to calm my rapid breathing and to refocus on what must be done.

These men will die, but they'll die well, even if not in the heat of battle.

I've never been a cruel woman, and I won't be now.

Not even the sobbing of Wulfheard forces me to pity him. He knew what he was doing. They all knew what they were doing when they kidnapped and deprived me of Mercia and Mercia of me.

I can feel the eyes of many on me, not just King Athelstan's, but I still take a moment to find the core I've only ever found in battle. The part of me that has always enabled me to kill with an appreciation for the life taken, but the firmness of my resolve.

Only then do I open my eyes, gaze down at Wulfheard's exposed neck one more time, and finally begin the action that will end his life.

I feel my child in my belly, as though he or she watches my actions. It's early to learn a life lesson, but I consider that he or she does all the same.

The sound as the sword slices cleanly through Wulfheard's neck is nothing but what I expect to hear. The resistance on my blade is no greater than when I killed any other, despite Wulfheard's size and strength.

There's no applause for my actions. Neither when I lift my head is there any form of disgust on the faces of the audience, merely respect and acceptance that it is true justice.

I nod to Eoforhild and Firamodor, who've brought Wulfheard to his place of execution on the training ground to the rear of Tamworth's palace. They haul his headless body up by his shoulders and neatly drag him away.

The parched earth quickly absorbs a swirl of blood on the ground, and I turn to gaze at my next victim.

Reeve Sigehelm doesn't carry himself with the same grace and resignation as Wulfheard. Even now, his eyes plead with me. I know he wants nothing more than to cry for mercy, beg at my feet, his trews showing his fear, and the sharp stench a too vivid reminder that this is the work of the battlefield, not the training ground.

Luckily, Ymma and Mildryth have such a firm hold on him that he can do none of those things. Although I'd have preferred to gag him, I've shown some mercy by allowing his mouth to remain free. I'd expected protestations of innocence to fall from his mouth without ceasing. But his mouth merely falls open and closed, with no sound issuing forth.

Still, I refuse to pity him.

It's been shown that it was Reeve Sigehelm who took advantage of Erna's innocence and extracted secrets from her. While I've chosen to try and contain my fury at Wulfheard it's more complicated with Reeve Sigehelm.

Wulfheard did it for the money and because his family was taken from him. Sigehelm had entirely different reasons, and worse, he was someone I thought was my ally but clearly wasn't.

And more cruelly, he knew my warriors well enough to appreciate that Erna could be exploited.

Firamodor and Mildryth wait for him to take to his knees. When he fails to, although his entire body trembles, Firamodor hooks her leg around his, unbalancing him so that he crashes to the ground. His head almost impacts the dark piece of wood that acted as a rest for Wulfheard's neck, which will do the same for Reeve Sigehelm.

I hear the air expelled from his lungs, and deciding this spectacle has gone on long enough, I hurry Firamodor and Mildryth along. The priest, seeing my intent, crashes through his prayers, my arm high in the air even before he manages to gabble 'amen'.

I don't know if Reeve Sigehelm is sensible enough to detect my actions, and I've no intention of finding out.

This time, the cut is just as clean. A slither of blood arches through the air, landing across my face. I taste Reeve Sigehelm's salt, and it seems to ignite my body, so much so that I turn, sword raised once more, facing whomever my next enemy might be on this battlefield.

I'm a life taker, an oath keeper, a woman of iron and salt. I'm my mother's daughter.

I'm a woman forging her path and reputation.

All will fear me.

Eoforhild hisses softly to me, but the thud of my heartbeat is too loud in my ears. I can see nothing before me but all the men who tried to stand in my way, who thought I should conform to what they believed a woman should be.

First, my father. I know what he was, and I thank him only for my birth. If I could have come into being without his aid, then I'd have thought nothing at all of him. I didn't mourn him, but I ensured people thought I did.

Secondly, my uncle, a man who should have cared for me and

exulted in my triumphs. Instead, he tried to steal it from me, and when that failed, he had me stolen away from it.

My mother always warned me to be wary of King Edward and his ambitions. No man should have a father like King Alfred, but he did, and he was always in his shadow. So much so that he stole from his family. I'll never forgive him, but I'll take delight in pitying him, as I believe my mother did, although she never told me her true feelings. She was a woman who could hide her emotions. Her brother would have done well to learn that lesson.

Then there was Lord Rǫgnvaldr Sigfrodrsson, a man who said he was my ally but who was really the wolf in sheep's clothing. He's welcome to his death. I could only wish it had come at my instigation.

I feel a little cheated, although I've been told that Rǫgnvaldr died from a wound that turned bad. I harbour a hope that it might be the one I dealt him. Rumour tells me it was one on his neck and that it seemed to heal only to become infected eighteen months later. His throat swelled so much that it was difficult to swallow and breathe, and he all but choked to death.

It was a slow and painful death. I hope it all began on that fateful day in Derby when I wanted to face him in fair combat, and he escaped, too terrified to face me.

And then Lord Ælfweard. Another of my cousins. He was a small man with big ambitions and absolutely no skill. I would wish death on no one younger than I, and yet, I can't mourn him either.

Few truly believed in me, and all of those who did were Mercians, apart from King Athelstan, who by rights is a Mercian anyway.

If these men still lived, I'd cut them down now and think nothing of doing so. Revenge might not be a Christian construct, but I'd have taken it all the same.

It's cousin Athelstan's voice that restores me to myself.

'Lady Ælfwynn, cousin, Ælf,' cousin Athelstan's voice reaches me and drags me back from my battlefield and my quest for vengeance.

'Lady Ælfwynn, this was done well.' Respect fills his voice as he stands beside me, with no hint of fear on his face, which still carries his stupid moustache. My blade remains upright, and blood drips down its scabbard onto my naked fingers.

'Lady Ælfwynn,' his words are firm, the words of my king, but more importantly, my cousin.

'It's done,' he confirms, his blue eyes blazing into mine, refusing to flinch in light of my transition from dutiful lady to warrior.

'It's done,' he whispers as though calming a foal. Only now do my muscles slacken, my hands relaxing around the scabbard, only now sensible of the blood on my new gown, sprayed across my straining belly, the red a reminder of the war I must yet wage to bring my first child into this world.

'It's done,' I confirm, offering my blade to Eoforhild. She takes it with a soft whisper. I detect a slump in her shoulders, as though she didn't know if I'd hand it back to her or not.

I can see where my husband waits for me, his expression neutral, his eyes purposefully focusing on my face and not on my clothes. I nod toward him, an indication that I accept, as King Athelstan says, that this matter is, indeed, done.

'The king's justice has been served.' There's almost the hint of a question in King Athelstan's voice, and I reach out and grip his hand, my mouth turning upwards.

I nod. 'It has, yes.' He clutches my hand within his. Even in such a movement, I feel his strength and his steadying force. 'But I'd ask a boon of you,' I've thought about this. I've spoken to my husband about my wishes.

King Athelstan turns and peers into my eyes, mildly curious.

'I would give you anything. You know that. You've only to ask.'

'I know,' I confirm, stealing myself to say the words I've been turning over in my mind since my conversation with Wulfheard.

'I'll not rule Mercia for you. Not now. I'd raise my children outside Mercia and not in Wessex.'

Confusion swamps my cousin's intelligent eyes. I watch his mouth open and close as he tries to decipher my meaning. Perhaps more, he tries to understand why I've made the request.

'Then I'll find you somewhere else to rule for me, somewhere you'll be adored and respected as you should be.'

I swallow the sudden lump in my throat at his easy acceptance of my request. King Athelstan has always been pragmatic about rule and ruling. His hold tightens on my arm as we leave the training field, ambling toward the great hall in Tamworth. The place has been my home for much of my life but has filled me with nothing but sorrow since my release.

Before we step over the threshold, I turn once more to King Athelstan.

'I rescind my right to be known as the Lady of Mercia. From now on, I wish only to be Lady Ælfwynn, cousin to the king, wife of my husband, and mother to my children.' As I speak, I rub my hand protectively over my expanding stomach. King Athelstan notices the movement, a strange look in his piercing blue eyes.

I consider that he takes in the sight of me, wearing my mother's priceless golden torque, a gift from her Mercian husband. Does King Athelstan see it as meaning I'm a Mercian and should remain one, as my father and mother intended? Or does he see it for what it is, a family heirloom and nothing more?

'Then that, dear cousin, is exactly what you'll be.' King Athelstan pauses, and I wait, unsure what he'll say next but aware that he wishes to say something, not prepared to relax my tight stance just yet.

'And in time, my young step-brother will greatly love your children when he becomes king on my death.'

I nod. Our parents have shaped both of us in ways they could never have imagined. I wish my cousin would consent to marry, but no doubt, I imagine he desires that I'd rule Mercia for him.

I appreciate the fact that he's supportive of my decision, and that means that I must be supportive of his.

I take his hand and place it on my stomach, where my first child kicks against me. I grin as King Athelstan jumps at the unexpected movement.

And then he laughs, gripping my hand tightly.

'Come on Ælf, enough of this. The future is ours to do with as we want.'

CAST OF CHARACTERS

Mercian Court

Lady Æthelflæd (c.870-918), sister to King Edward of Wessex

m. **Lord Æthelred** of Mercia who dies in 911

Lady Ælfwynn, their daughter and only surviving child born c.888

Archbishop Plegmund, Archbishop of Canterbury from 890

Ealdorman Æthelfrith of part of Mercia,

His sons – Lord Athelstan, Ælfstan, Eadric and Æthelwald

Wessex Royal Family

King Edward, official title is King of the Anglo-Saxons in all but two of the surviving charters

m. 1 **Lady Ecgwynn** – (little is known about her)

Athelstan

Ecgwynn also known as Edith

m. 2 **Lady Ælfflæd** – (she was 'divorced' in the late 910s and spent the remainder of her life in Wilton Abbey, where she was later joined by two of her daughters)

Ælfweard

Edwin

Æthelhild
Eadgifu
Eadflæd
Eadhild
Eadgyth
Ælfgifu
m. 3 **Lady Eadgifu** – (the daughter of ealdorman Sigehelm who died in AD902/3 fighting for King Edward against his cousin, Lord Æthelwold, she would substantially outlive her husband)
Eadburh
Edmund
Eadred

Lord Rǫgnvaldr Sigfrodrsson of Dublin/York/grandson of Ivarr of Dublin/Ivarr Ragnarsson

Lady Ælfwynn's warriors
Eoforhild
Ymma
Lioba
Firamodor
Leofgyth
Erna (her squire)
Mildryth

Archbishop Lodeward, of York
Wilferth, Bishop of Worcester
Hywel, Clydog, Idwal, kings of the Welsh kingdoms
Sigehelm, Reeve of Derby (fictional)
Ealdred, Portreeve of Gloucester (fictional)
Wulfheard, enemy (fictional)
Sigurd, son of Ivarr (fictional)
Ælfhere, one of the traitors (fictional)

Places Mentioned

Tamworth, the ancient capital of Mercia

Derby, one of the Five Boroughs – in the Danelaw until reunited with Mercia, the others are Nottingham, Stamford, Leicester and Lincoln

Lincoln, one of the Five Boroughs – in the Danelaw, not yet reunited with Mercia

Gloucester, in Mercia

St Oswald's Priory, in Gloucester

Worcester, in Mercia

Thanet, in Kent – part of Wessex after the marriage of King Edward to his 3rd wife, Eadgifu

River Thames, river in England

Winchester, the royal mausoleum of the House of Wessex

New Minster, religious building in Winchester where King Alfred, his wife and his son, King Edward, were buried.

HISTORICAL NOTES

The idea that Lady Ælfwynn was Athelstan Half-King's wife stems from the knowledge that his wife was called Ælfwynn, that this woman became foster mother to the orphaned future king, Edgar, and that Lord Athelstan earned the nickname 'Half-King' which may have been on account of his royal wife. The argument is suggested by S Jayakumar in the paper, 'Eadwig and Edgar' in *Edgar, King of the English, 959-975* ed. D Scragg.

As to why I've had Lady Ælfwynn give up Mercia, this is because it wasn't Lord Athelstan who became ealdorman of Mercia after his father's death, but rather Ælfstan, who I assume is the older brother of the four brothers – Eadric and Æthelwald also went on to hold ealdordoms under later kings. Ælfstan held the ealdordom of Mercia (not all of it – perhaps the area to the west and south) for several years, and only in AD932 was Lord Athelstan made the ealdorman of East Anglia, a position he held for two decades, and under several kings.

Lady Ælfwynn perhaps fared better in her marriage, if it did take place, than all of her female cousins (no spoilers here because their stories are told in The King's Daughters).

If she was Lord Athelstan's wife, Lady Ælfwynn was accorded far greater status under her cousins than under her uncle. This may have been because 'England' was more united under her cousin kings, or rather, the job of uniting Mercia with Wessex was already complete. The first 'Viking period' was ending, and the hope of peace was on the horizon.

I've made much of King Athelstan's Mercian upbringing. For those who've read on in the series, or read the Brunanburh series, it should be clear why. However, it must be noted that Athelstan's Mercian upbringing stems from the later writings of William of Malmesbury, and so is not contemporary.

King Edward wore the warrior helm of Wessex or of the Anglo-Saxons. I've chosen to make more of the separation of Wessex and Mercia than others might if they follow the line of reasoning that King Alfred's intention was always to form 'England' by uniting all of the old kingdoms. This interpretation should be more critically considered than it has previously been.

The Anglo-Saxon Chronicle A – The Winchester Manuscript – does not mention Ælfwynn at all but instead has King Edward of Wessex/the Anglo-Saxons taking control of Tamworth as soon as his sister dies.

The Anglo-Saxon Chronicle E – The Peterborough Manuscript - only mentions Lady Æthelflæd's death in 918 and not what happens immediately after in Mercia. The Winchester entry was written in the heartland of Wessex, where Edward ruled. The Peterborough entry was written in an area of land traditionally known as the Danelaw – it perhaps had no loyalty to either King Edward or Lady Ælfwynn. The bias of the sources should be carefully considered.

Lady Ælfwynn's fate is recorded in the Anglo-Saxon Chronicle C with its Mercian bias. We are told that she was deprived of all power and 'led into Wessex three weeks before Christmas.' This entry is dated 919, although it's normally taken to mean 918 due to a disparity between the dating in this part of the ASC – known as the Mercian Register – where a new year is taken to start in December as opposed to in the Winchester ASC where the new year starts in September.

Apart from the potential, later charter (S535 in the Online Sawyer resource 948. 'King Eadred to Ælfwyn, a religious woman; grant of 6 hides equated with 6 sulungs, at Wickhambreux, Kent, in return for 2 pounds of purest gold') that names a 'Lady Ælfwynn' nothing else is known of her life, unless she is indeed, the Lady Ælfwynn that Ealdorman Athelstan marries.

This dearth of information has allowed me to envisage all sorts of events within Mercia following the immediate death of Lady Æthelflæd.

What can be said with confidence is that this was a time of shifting alliances and in which I genuinely think anything could have been possible. Any alliance between Lady Ælfwynn and Lord Rǫgnvaldr is pure conjecture, but York feared the pretensions of King Edward of Wessex, and it seems highly likely that Mercia might as well. King Edward's death, putting down a revolt in Farndon, Chester (northwest Mercia), does beg the question of just who was in revolt against him.

Perhaps, for the kingdoms of Mercia, York and Northumbria, they would have preferred it if the Viking attacks had continued to plague Wessex, as this might have distracted Edward from looking northwards.

The events of much of the rest of the tenth century in England can be found in Kingmaker, The King's Daughters, The Brunanburh series, and the six books about Lady Elfrida, which begins with The First Queen of England. And, of course, the Earls of Mercia will take readers to AD1066 (when it's completed).

Thank you for reading and letting me dally over a thousand years ago!

In writing this novel I've made use of many readily available resources online. For information on charters, please visit the Electronic Sawyer https://esawyer.lib.cam.ac.uk/about/index.html. My preferred edition of The Anglo-Saxon Chronicle is the one by Michael Swanson, but there's also an easily available one on the internet. For a description of Gloucester at this time, and the priory, in particular, I've accessed an article by C Heighway, '*Gloucester and the*

New Minster of St Oswald' in 'Edward the Elder' ed. N Higham and D Hill. For a description of Worcester at this time, I've accessed an article by N Baker and R Holt *'The City of Worcester in the tenth century'* in St Oswald of Worcester ed. N Brooks and C Cubitt. I grew up near Tamworth and Derby, and my descriptions are based on my recollections. I can also advise readers that the A38 that runs between Lichfield (Tamworth) and Derby is often shrouded in mist!

There's no single history of this time period that I can recommend to my readers – there are books on Mercia and books on Wessex, and books on the Vikings. I can recommend C Downham's book, 'Viking Kings of Britain and Ireland', which attempts to amalgamate as much information as possible into one volume regarding the Viking leaders active during the period. I would also recommend books on 'Athelstan' by Sarah Foote and the very readable 'Ælfred's Britain' by Max Adams, which doesn't stop with Alfred's death, despite the implication in the title. Sometimes, I forget how long I've been studying the time period and its intricacies. But be assured there are journal articles that are entirely incomprehensible to me, even now! And be assured that I'm trying to remedy the situation. My first work of non-fiction will be published in late 2023/early 2024, and will piece together the lives of the royal women of the House of Wessex.

ABOUT THE AUTHOR

I'm an author of historical fiction (Early English, Vikings and the British Isles as a whole before the Norman Conquest) and fantasy (Viking age/dragon-themed), born in the old Mercian kingdom at some point since AD1066. I like to write. You've been warned! Find me at mjporterauthor.com. mjporterauthor.blog and @coloursofunison on twitter. I have a monthly newsletter, which can be joined via my website. Once signed up, readers can opt into a weekly email reminder containing special offers.

facebook.com/mjporterauthor
twitter.com/coloursofunison

BOOKS BY M J PORTER (IN CHRONOLOGICAL ORDER)

Gods and Kings Series (seventh century Britain)

Pagan Warrior (audio available now)

Pagan King (audio available now)

Warrior King

The Eagle of Mercia Chronicles (from Boldwood Books)

Son of Mercia (ebook, paperback, hardback, large print and audio)

Wolf of Mercia (ebook, paperback, hardback, large print and audio)

Warrior of Mercia (ebook, paperback, hardback, large print and audio)

Eagle of Mercia (May 2023)

The Ninth Century

Coelwulf's Company, stories from before The Last King

The Last King (audiobook now available)

The Last Warrior (audiobook coming soon)

The Last Horse

The Last Enemy

The Last Sword

The Last Shield

The Last Seven

The Tenth Century

The Lady of Mercia's Daughter

A Conspiracy of Kings (the sequel to The Lady of Mercia's Daughter)

Kingmaker

The King's Daughter

The Brunanburh Series

King of Kings (Feb 2023)

The Mercian Brexit (Can be read as a prequel to The First Queen of England)

The First Queen of England (The story of Lady Elfrida) (tenth century England)

The First Queen of England Part 2

The First Queen of England Part 3

The King's Mother (The continuing story of Lady Elfrida)

The Queen Dowager

Once A Queen

The Earls of Mercia

The Earl of Mercia's Father

The Danish King's Enemy

Swein: The Danish King (side story)

Northman Part 1

Northman Part 2

Cnut: The Conqueror (full-length side story)

Wulfstan: An Anglo-Saxon Thegn (side story)

The King's Earl

The Earl of Mercia

The English Earl

The Earl's King

Viking King

The English King

Lady Estrid (a novel of eleventh-century Denmark)

Fantasy

The Dragon of Unison

Hidden Dragon

Dragon Gone

Dragon Alone

Dragon Ally

Dragon Lost

Dragon Bond

As JE Porter

The Innkeeper (standalone)

20th Century Mystery

The Custard Corpses – a delicious 1940s mystery (audio book now available)

The Automobile Assassination (sequel to The Custard Corpses)

Cragside – a 1930s murder mystery (standalone)

Printed in Great Britain
by Amazon

28306090R00128